MAIA DYLAN

EVERNIGHT PUBLISHING ®

www.evernightpublishing.com

SNIPER TEAM BRAVO: VOLUME ONE

Copyright© 2017

Maia Dylan

Editor Book One: Carlene Flores

Editor Book Two: Karyn White

Cover Artist: Jay Aheer

ISBN: 978-1-77339-369-8

ALL RIGHTS RESERVED

MAIA DYLAN

DEDICATION

A year ago I lost my dad to cancer and a stroke. He was the greatest man I ever knew and made sure we lived a life filled with love and laughter. He was a returned service man, and someone who risked his life to save many and protected those who couldn't protect themselves. This is for my dad.

And for my hubby, who is so very much like my dad. Love you, baby.

MAIA DYLAN

THEIR LINE OF DRIFT

Sniper Team Bravo, 1

Maia Dylan

Copyright © 2016

Prologue

"Come on you slack-jawed, sitting on your hands, total waste of space assholes!" Second Lieutenant Devon Roberts muttered as he stared at the screen of his radio, willing it to respond. He and his team had been holed up in this bombed out derelict building for over thirty-two hours and he was about to flip the fuck out if they didn't get the go ahead. He had advised them of their target's visual confirmation more than ten minutes ago.

Devon and the four men who reported to him made up Sniper Team Bravo—a team of specialists whose job it was to deliver highly accurate rifle fire against specific enemy targets that cannot be engaged successfully by the regular infantry because of range, sensitive nature of the target, size, location, or visibility. At least, that was what the team's description was on paper. In reality, when the powers that be had a target they needed eliminated, and it had to be done quickly and with the least amount of collateral damage as possible, they sent in a team like Bravo.

Today's mission was to be their last, and Dev would be damned if they left this godforsaken desert without taking this bastard out. As soon as the job was done they were gone, back to base, and then states side in less than a week. Dev had heard from the lawyer looking after his grandmother's estate and the house was his. Bravo team had a plan, and they couldn't wait to get started.

"LT, these fuckers don't look like they're going to hang around for much longer. I can see trucks moving in from the south. Do we have a go, or not?" Marcel asked from the window where he knelt behind his Remington PSR.

"I can see trucks inbound from the south," Maddox warned from his prone position on the floor, his scope set up through the broken window of the room.

"Trucks inbound from the east," Sam called from the other room.

"LT," Glenn "Reaper" Webster said from his kneeling position in front of Maddox. "If we don't get a mission go on this then all this fucking intel is wasted, and al-Hassad is in the wind." His voice remained calm and steady as the man himself, despite the fact he stared down his scope at a man whose life he could end with less than three pounds of pressure on the trigger.

Devon understood his anger, he felt the same way, but if this was going to be a righteous kill shot, then they needed confirmation from base that they were—

Just then the radio clicked. "*Sniper Team Bravo, you have a go for target.*"

Hell yeah!

"Reaper, you have a go. Egress, east stairwell down to the main level, out the back and then three clicks north to the extraction point," Dev said calmly as he packed his equipment into his pack. His team then moved into what he called action mode, and the tension seemed to fade from the room. They were never more calm than when they had a mission to complete and a target to take out. Reaper and Maddox then went through their targeting sequence dialogue that oddly, Dev found comforting.

Reaper exhaled once and then seemed to slow his breathing to an impossible rate. "Sniper ready."

Maddox put his eye to the scope he held in front of him and seemed to match his breathing to Glenn's. "Target, confirmed, 11 o'clock."

"On target. Range it."

"Range is 952 yards."

"952 yards."

"Wind, three-quarter value, push left by 2."

Reaper made the appropriate adjustments to his rifle without taking his eye from the scope mounted to the top of it. "On target."

"Fire when ready."

The report of Reaper's Remington RPS sounded through the room. "Hit."

Maddox held his position for a moment as he stared down his scope. "Target down, confirmed kill." Devon was about to move toward the door that led to their egress point when he saw Maddox tense. "Shit! RPGs! They've got fucking RPGs. Incoming!" Maddox leaped up in a single swift movement, grabbed Reaper by the back of his BDUs, and threw them both against the south wall just as the whistle of an inbound RPG could be heard.

Devon threw himself against the floor, up against the far wall, sending up a quick prayer that all five of them made it out of this alive. Then the world exploded around him.

Chapter One

"You know, when I pictured heaven as a kid, LT, it definitely looked a little like this. A lot cleaner and, well, you know, with some nice landscaping and shit, but it sure does bear some resemblance," Marcel said from the passenger seat of Devon's truck as they pulled over at the side of the driveway. Devon had deliberately pulled over a little further from the house than was necessary so he could get a real good look at the place.

Reaper leaned forward from his position between Maddox and Sam in the back seat of the Ford Expedition they were traveling in to get a better look at the house. "When you said your grandmother left you a house, I pictured a little old house with a small flower garden at the front of it, somewhere in the burbs. This place is so far removed from that it's not fucking funny!"

Dev was still shocked as hell that his grandmother's homestead in Redwood Falls was now legally his. There had been a five-year waiting period after her death while a distant relative she had wanted to give the property to had been unsuccessfully searched for. But hey, all was well that ended with him being given a two story, eight-bedroom homestead on fifteen hundred acres of reasonably fertile farmland in the heart of agricultural Wyoming. It even came with three large outbuildings which were perfect for what he and Bravo team wanted to do.

Dev shrugged as he stared up at the house. "It's just a house on some land, with a fancy name, but with some time, the buildings and grounds will be one of the country's leading tactical training facilities. Not much has changed since I left eight years ago." He was almost crippled by the guilt that struck at that statement but refused to think too much on the sequence of events that had driven him from Wyoming and into the welcoming arms of the US Marine Corps. "It needs some work, but it will eventually be what we want it to be. We have the plans, we just have to get things in motion and start getting organized."

The mission to eliminate al-Hassan had been their last as enlisted Marines. All of them had decided they'd done their time, ridding the world of some seriously large assholes, and it was time for them to think about their own futures. It was irony at her spiteful best that had their last mission as the one that nearly killed them. When the dust had settled after that RPG round slammed into the floor above them, they had each had to crawl out from a pile of debris. They'd each been left banged up and bleeding from that, but it was the firefight which followed that really caused the damage. None of them had come away injury free, and it had been a damn miracle they'd been able to make it to the extraction point alive. For Reaper, it had been touch and go, and without Sam's medical training and the fact the man was basically a fully trained surgeon, it would have been a very different story.

Shaking his head to clear the dark memories of that day, Devon looked more closely at the homestead his great-great-grandfather had given the name, Three Pines. Damn, that name was one of the first things that had to go. The place was surrounded by cottonwoods for starters, not a damn pine tree in sight! Dev had always thought the property was better suited to the name Cottonwood Farm than Three Pines, and he guessed now he could actually make the change. His grandmother had always prided herself on the property, ensuring the house and grounds were immaculate. It was obvious no one had been looking after the place in the five years since her death.

The driveway curved around in front of the house with a large car port and garage off to the left. The fountain and grassed area in the center of the curved drive had always made an impressive statement as you drove in, but now the grass and weeds almost completely obscured the base of the fountain. The large white house, with its wraparound veranda on both levels, and large floor to ceiling windows looked dirty, badly in need of painting, and completely unloved, which was appropriate given how little love there had been in that house in the years he had been forced to live there.

"Dude, that place looks fucking haunted," Maddox growled from the back seat and Devon had to agree with him. And although he would never admit it to the boys in the truck with him, he wouldn't have put it passed his grandmother to come back and haunt his ass given the great disappointment he had been to her when she had been alive.

"You're not afraid of a few ghosts, are you Maddox?" Sam asked, humor clear in his tone.

"Fuck you, Sam," Maddox muttered, but when Devon looked in his rear view mirror, he could see the smile on his friend's face. "You just wait until you wake up one night and your bed is floating six feet in the air and the LT's grandmother's floating above you with a knife."

Laughing, they all climbed out, opting to walk the last one hundred feet or so to the house. Dev felt the ache and pull of his injuries, and had to bite back a laugh as they all seemed to mutter curses and stifle groans as they moved out of the truck, sounding like men three times their age.

"Come on, let's go up to the house and see what we've got to work with." Devon led the way to the stairs up to the front veranda. He was assaulted by memories the closer he got, most of them that featured his grandmother were ones he would rather forget. But there were the happy memories he'd called upon to help him through the lonely nights and danger filled years that had passed since the last time he had been here. These memories were filled with laughter, and desire, and a pair of soulful green eyes that were so damn mesmerizing, Devon had found himself drowning in them on more than one occasion.

It was the happy memories that took place in the small bedroom just off the main hall that he treasured the most. But they were also the most painful to remember.

****

Someone was in the house. The creaking noise of someone treading on the loose board of the third step leading up to the porch was unmistakable. Oh God, had Silas come looking for him?

Finn's heart began to pound at the thought of his father finding him and fulfilling the threat he had made earlier that morning. Sliding off the bed he had been resting on, Finn silently pulled the dust cover up over it again. He had been doing this ever since the old lady who owned it passed away. Every time Silas had beat on him in the past five years, he would come here to this house and this bedroom. It was the only place he could remember ever truly being happy as a child.

Ignoring the pain in his ribs from the body shots Silas had given him, Finn pressed his shaking frame back against the wall nearest the door. From here he had a clear view of the entrance, but the angle made it difficult to see him. He held as still as he could, trying to make himself as invisible, and peered down the hallway to the front door.

He had to fight to keep the whimper of fear that

was building within him inside. He was surprised to hear a key being slid into the lock and turned. Whenever Finn had come here, he'd had to climb through the window in one of the back rooms he knew was loose. It was the same one he and Devon had used to get in and out as kids. Whoever was coming into the house had a key, and that meant it sure as hell wasn't Silas. Finn's mind filled with scenarios of burglars, squatters, a real estate agent come to show the house to its new owner, but nothing prepared him for who actually stepped into the house.

The door opened and Devon Roberts crossed the threshold and entered the house. Finn's entire world shifted on its axis. He gasped as he hungrily drank in the sight of the man who had taken his heart long before he'd finally taken Finn's virginity. Dev seemed taller and definitely a lot bigger than he had been when he'd left. Devon had once been wiry, tall, and thin, but there now stood a broad, muscular man who definitely knew his way around a set of weights. His hair was shorter too, but there was no mistaking him.

"Come on in, guys."

Finn closed his eyes briefly at the sound of Dev's voice. And there was certainly no mistaking the deep timbre of his tone either. Finn wobbled on his feet, his head starting to spin. Whether it was from seeing the only man he had ever loved again for the first time in eight years, or the injuries he had sustained that morning from his father, he would never know. Either way, the result was the same. Spots formed at the edge of his vision until everything turned black. Fortunately, he was unconscious before he actually hit the floor.

Chapter Two

A muted thud came from down the hall and they all froze. Devon moved forward, his men fanning out behind him in their standard recon formation, and despite the limitations of their injuries, moved silently down the hall. Devon wished he'd thought to grab his sidearm from the locked case in the back of his truck before they'd entered the house.

When they were about halfway down the hall, almost to the door that led to his old bedroom, Devon lifted a closed fist into the air. All of them came to a stop. He signaled that he had eyes on one body, lying prone on the floor. He crept silently forward, until he could see the face of the person on the floor, and as soon as he did, his blood turned to ice.

Forgetting all of his training and everything he should have done next to ensure the safety of his team, Devon ran forward, dropping to his knees beside the prone figure. "Oh, shit, Finn." There was no missing the fear in his voice. With hands that shook, he checked for a pulse and breathed a sigh of relief at the rhythmic thumps he felt against his fingers.

As gently as he could, Devon rolled Finn onto his back, and his breath caught at the sight of swelling and bruising around his left eye. "Jesus Christ, Finn, what the hell happened?" Devon ran his hands over his skull, searching for any contusions or swelling that could indicate a head injury or concussion. He breathed a sigh of relief when he found nothing.

Finn moaned, and his eyes fluttered open, and not for the first time, Devon found himself drowning in his beautiful green eyes and wondering why in the hell Finn was in the house. "Dev?" Finn asked in a weak voice. An ache settled in his chest. He had heard that voice in his dreams on so many nights, but hearing it now, weak with pain rather than passion, just about killed him.

"Yeah, Finn, it's me," Dev answered as he swept a lock of Finn's dark hair from his forehead. "Where else does it hurt, baby? I want to get you up onto the bed so Sam can get a look, but I don't want to hurt you." A flash of hurt that Devon knew had nothing to do with his injuries flickered in Finn's eyes before his anger apparently rose to mask it.

"It's none of your concern where the pain is, and I sure as hell am not your baby," Finn said, sneering the last word and Devon nodded. He understood Finn's anger and accepted it to a point.

"LT, Sam's headed out to your truck to grab his med kit," Marcel said from the door. "You need any help getting Finn up onto the bed?"

Devon looked in earnest at Finn whose eyes narrowed, attempting to read his mood. "No, Marcel, I do not need any help getting Finn into bed. I can do that all on my own," he said with a bit of humor.

Finn growled over the guys' laughter in the background. "Get the hell away from me, Devon Roberts, I can make it to the bed myself." Finn gritted his teeth and rolled to his side, a groan of pain caused any humor on Dev's part to evaporate. Frowning, Devon swiftly swept Finn up and into his arms, wincing at his quick inhalation of breath.

Devon moved swiftly to the bed, waiting while Marcel removed the dust cloth, then laid Finn down on the quilt, absently noting that it was the same damn one he had used all those years ago. "Stop it!" Devon ordered as Finn started to struggle to stand. "Stay there, Finn, and let Sam have a look at you." Sam put his med kit on the bed and opened it, but Finn kept trying to stand. Devon reached out a hand and gently gripped his chin, tilting Finn's face up so that their gazes locked together.

"I mean it, Finn. Stop trying to move around, and let Sam have a look at you. Once we have you all squared away, you are going to tell me what the fuck happened." A red hue rose up Finn's face and his gaze slid away, but Devon gently turned his face so Finn had no choice but to look at him once more. "You are going to tell me who did this to you, Finn. I know what being beaten looks like, and you will tell me who turned their fists on you."

"What do you care, Dev?" Finn's expression turned bleak and he kept his voice low, obviously uncomfortable with the attention, and Devon's heart ached even more. "You've had eight years to pick up the phone and see how I was doing. Now, last time I checked my cell phone, I hadn't missed any calls so I figure you didn't really give a shit. So why bother now?" Finn sighed, lifted his right arm, and Devon knew he was going to run it through his hair because that was a classic frustrated Finn move. Instead he winced when he got his arm shoulder height and his left arm moved to his side as if to grip his ribs.

"Damn it, Finn," Devon grumbled as he sat on the bed and gently lifted his former lover's shirt. At the sight of the mottled bruises that ran over the ribs on his right side, Devon felt his anger rise even further. "Fuck! Sam, get these ribs wrapped. From the placement of the bruises and how painful they are, I wouldn't be surprised if they were cracked. Finn," Devon kept going even as he saw Finn about to speak, "just let Sam take care of you. Please."

Devon might be retired, but he was and always would be a Second Lieutenant in the United States Marine Corps, which meant he was much more accustomed to giving orders than asking nicely.

Gritting his teeth, Finn searched his face and Devon kept his expression as open as he could. Finally, Finn exhaled deeply and nodded his consent. "Thank you." On impulse, Devon leaned in and pressed a soft kiss to Finn's cheek, his heart cracking when Finn flinched away. Devon's senses filled with the feel, smell, and taste of the man who still haunted his every dream, and he had to fight the sudden urge he had to slam his mouth to Finn's and take him in a kiss he knew would send them both skyrocketing into arousal. Mindful not to act on this, he slid off the bed but couldn't bring himself to leave the room. Instead he moved to stand at the foot of the bed.

A barrage of unanswered questions ran through his head as he watched Sam gently urge Finn to a sitting position and then help him to remove his shirt to make it easier to tend to the injuries. Finn's frame was thinner than Dev had ever seen it, but it was the sight of what looked like a knife wound scar low on his left side that had him seeing red. He had to bite the inside of his mouth until he could taste blood to stop from bombarding Finn with questions. High on the list was where that knife wound had come from, who the hell had treated him like a fucking punching bag, and where could Devon find that fucker. There was one more question that Devon needed an answer to, but he had no clue how on earth to ask it. He needed to know if Finn believed in second chances, because Devon sure as fuck was here to see if Finn would give him one.

****

Finn heard Dev's growl as the man, Sam, helped him to remove his t-shirt. As much as Finn would like to think it had something to do with a banging physique, he knew it was more about the bruising and the scar low on his left side. Finn knew he was thinner than he had been eight years ago, and he definitely could do with gaining more weight, but hell, no one was perfect. Despite the fact Finn could actually hear Devon's teeth gnashing together, he refused to look up at him.

"I don't think they are cracked, LT," Sam said as he gently palpitated the areas around Finn's ribs. "But they are definitely bruised. I'll wrap them so he can move better."

Finn scowled at the blond man in front of him who looked like a surfer and way too damn good looking. "*He* is sitting right in front of you, pretty boy, so if you have anything to say about me, grow some balls and say it directly to me."

"Pretty boy?" Someone repeated from beyond the doorway to the bedroom, laughter in his voice, but Finn never took his eyes off Sam whose face began to redden.

"Sorry, Finn, you're right." Sam winced. "The LT is—or shit, was—I guess, my CO and I am used to keeping him apprised of everything I am doing. I apologize." Finn nodded and then sat still as Sam used a thick tape to wrap the right side of his ribs, and even though he hated to admit it, as soon as there was a constant pressure against them, the pain subsided a fraction and he was able to breathe more freely.

Dev moved closer to the bed. "Finn, what are you doing here in the house? Don't get me wrong, I am not complaining about finding you here, I was planning on coming to see you as soon as I could anyway, but I am curious why you would come here instead of seeking medical help."

Finn glanced around the room, noting that the other men in the room looked anywhere but at him, as if picking up on his discomfort at being the center of attention. "I had nowhere else to go." He mumbled in answer. How could he tell Dev that he always came here to the house when he was hurt and bleeding? That this was the only place he truly felt safe.

Sam gave him some ibuprofen for the pain and Dev held out a glass of water. When Finn reached for it, Dev held on to it for a moment, waiting until Finn raised his eyes to meet his.

"Are you sure you're okay?" Finn shivered at the deep timbre of Dev's voice. "Do you hurt anywhere else?"

"Not physically," Finn replied with a pointed look. He had no idea what made him answer that way, and from the regret that filled Devon's eyes, Finn knew he understood what he'd been referring to.

"Yeah, I can understand that, Finn." Dev sighed as he released the glass, and Finn took the two pain pills. "But if you'd let me, I'd like to talk with you and hopefully explain about what happened eight years ago."

Finn's breath caught as he stared into Dev's eyes. There were a range of different emotions swirling there, but the one that had Finn's heart racing was hope. Devon was hoping for an opportunity to talk about whatever had driven him from Redwood Falls and Finn had to think about whether the risk of him being hurt, again, was worth it. Before he could say anything in return, they were interrupted by someone banging on the front door.

"Boy!" Finn's eyes widened at the sound of his father's voice. "I've looked for you everywhere, so I fuckin' know that you're 'ere. Open this damn door." From the way his voice was slurred it was clear he had been drinking. Again.

Devon's brown eyes darkened until they were almost black, and his jaw tightened. Finn watched in fascination as the anger on Dev's face morphed quickly into rage. "Your father?" Dev snarled. "Your fucking father was the one who beat you? Was Silas also the one who took a fucking knife to you?"

Finn tried to hide his expression, thinking of a way to diffuse the situation, but as Devon stood and turned to walk out of the room, Finn knew he had failed.

Scrambling up from the bed, and groaning at the sharp pain the sudden move caused, Finn ran to follow Devon from the room, but was stopped by a firm hand on his upper arm. "You might want to let the LT take care of this one, Finn," Sam said gently, and when Finn turned to look at him, he saw understanding and anger in the man's eyes. "I've known the LT for a few years now, and when he gets that look on his face, someone is about to be ripped a new asshole. From the marks on your body and the signs of older injuries, I'd have to say your father deserves it."

Finn extracted his arm and nodded, even as he walked out of the room. "You're right, Sam, he does. No one deserves it more. But if he doesn't hit me, he takes it out on my mother and my little brother. And that is something I simply cannot allow."

Finn stumbled past the three men who stood in the hallway, all with faces like thunder, no doubt having heard Finn's secret. He didn't have to turn around to know they followed him. When he got to the front door, he opened it quickly and stepped out onto the porch. Devon stood on the top step, his arms crossed in front of his chest, and his legs shoulder width apart, staring down at Silas who stood at the bottom of the stairs.

Still dressed in his Sheriff's uniform.

And there lay the problem. Finn wasn't an idiot, he knew what his father was doing was wrong, and he had tried on more than one occasion to go to the authorities. It was just really fucking difficult when the person you were accusing of domestic violence against you, your mother and your twelve-year-old brother, was the county sheriff.

Silas's hate-filled eyes fell on him and Finn's stomach began to turn at the sight of it. "There you are, you piece of shit. Get the fuck down here and get into my car. I am taking you home."

Everything within Finn screamed for him to turn around and run back into the house, but he made himself step in the direction of the stairs. Dev moved at the same time, effectively blocking his exit from the house. "You aren't going with him, Finn." Dev spoke loudly, wanting Silas to hear every word, but he never stopped looking directly at his father. "Get the hell off my property, Silas."

Silas sneered in their direction. "Well now, isn't that fucking sweet? Your childhood fuck buddy returns to Redwood Falls and you turn up here like a fuckin' pussy to beg him to take you back? That's pathetic! He fuckin' left you behind, Finn. Now, stop being a pussy little queer and get in my damn car!"

Devon's body seemed to tense and Finn could almost feel the anger roll off him in waves. "Why don't you come up here and make him, Silas? I see the years have been unkind, or is it the fact that you're still killing yourself slowly with the fucking whiskey? If it is death you are after, come at me now and I will be more than happy to introduce you."

Finn's eyes widened in shock when he saw a flicker of apprehension sweep across Silas's face before it fell into his familiar mask of vile hatred. "You think just because you went off to war it makes you a man, Devon? It takes more than that you little cock sucker. I would be more than willing to show you exactly what it does take to be a man, but I wouldn't bother wasting the fucking time to educate you. Finn! Move your fucking dumb ass!"

Devon's arms dropped to his sides, but his hands remained clenched into fists. "Marcel!"

Finn jumped at the shout and turned to watch the taller man with the olive skin walk out the door of the house. He winked at Finn as he moved to stand just behind Dev's right shoulder. "LT?"

"Educate the Sheriff here about what the charges would be for an officer of the law caught drinking on duty and in uniform."

Marcel grinned and folded his arms across his broad chest. "Well, now, as a licensed lawyer in the state of Wyoming, I can officially tell you that as we happen to be standing in the state of Wyoming, you would be immediately relieved of your service weapon, booked, taken into custody and charged with drunk driving. Until your hearing, you would be suspended without pay and if you were indeed found guilty of drunk driving, that automatically makes you guilty of drunk on duty, and that would cost you your badge."

Silas sneered. "You think my fucking deputy is going to come out here and place me under arrest? Fuck no. I'm the law in this county, boy, the only power higher than me is God, and he certainly ain't listening to anything that gay little fucker says. Now, Finn! Get in this fucking car or I promise you, you are not going to like what happens when I get home."

Finn felt all the color drain from his face and he swayed on his feet. He hadn't missed the fact that Silas had said "when I get home". The only one home at this time of day was his brother, Nate. Two hands grabbed him from behind. "You okay, Finn?"

"Not really," Finn whispered as he took a deep breath, shrugged off the hand, and then moved to step around Devon.

Devon turned to face him, his whole body tense. "Finn, don't do this, man," Devon whispered.

Finn smiled sadly. "It's okay, Dev. Things are different now, and I don't think that what I do is any of your concern. You managed to walk away from here eight years ago, and you never looked back. You need to let me walk away this time." Finn couldn't lift his gaze to meet Dev's, he simply waited until Devon moved out of his way. Then, with a heavy heart and thoughts of what was to come filling him with fear, he walked down the steps, passed his father, and climbed into the back of the cruiser.

He missed whatever parting remark his father had said, and ignored him when he climbed into the driver's seat, started the car, and roared out of the drive. Despite how much he wanted to, he refused to turn and look back. The only positive was that no matter what Silas dished out to him when they got home, it would be nothing compared with the pain he was in right now.

Chapter Three

"Fuck!" Devon roared as the police cruiser tore out of the drive. He jumped down from the stairs and marched around the side of the house, looking at the oak tree that stood beside the house. He snarled in satisfaction. The old punching bag he had secured by a chain to the largest branch in the tree still hung there.

As soon as he reached it, he started swinging. Head shots, upper cuts, body shots—all of them in quick succession as he fought the demons within him. Demons of his own making. There had been no love in that house, and his grandmother had been an epic bitch to him even when his mother had still been alive. Once she'd passed, his grandmother turned the full power of her toxic nature on him.

Hell, the bitch even managed to get photos of him and Finn having sex in his room. When Finn had left, she had confronted Dev with the images, calling him and Finn foul names and screaming that they were an abomination against the church. She threatened to send them to the recruiting office where he had enlisted, and give them to Finn's father and paste them all over town. Devon had feared for his own future but he also knew that Silas was a homophobic asshole and hadn't wanted Finn to have to face that. Hell, Finn still had a year to go to finish high school, and he would have been bullied incessantly.

So, Devon had allowed his grandmother to drive him away, and had taken the coward's way out and left. Oh, he'd told himself at the time that he was going to come back for Finn in a year. Then it was when he made more money … when he had a place to live … excuse after excuse until too much time had passed. After the first time he had been seriously injured, he wanted Finn with him, but he had convinced himself that too much time had passed, and that Finn was probably living a happy life with someone else.

And in the meantime, Finn apparently had no idea why he had left, and somehow his fucking father had found out he was gay anyway and had been beating him for it ever since.

"LT! Fuck, Devon!" The sound of Reaper's voice penetrated the red haze that had descended over him, and he stopped. A wave of nausea had him swaying on his feet.

Breathing heavily, trying desperately to draw in enough oxygen to stave off the nausea, sweat pouring off his body, he leaned heavily on the punching bag. "What?" he asked, his voice cracking.

"LT?" Sam asked hesitantly.

Grunting, pain radiated through his fists, arms, and his own cracked ribs, not to mention the gunshot wounds he had taken in his back and thigh. "Why would Finn do that? Why would he go with that fucked up bastard?" The tense silence behind him made Dev turn and the strained looks his men shared made his heart fill with dread. "What?"

"Silas shows the classic signs of being an alcoholic." Sam told him nothing he hadn't known before. "Tiny blood vessels on his skin that look like spider webs, redness on the palms, his hands that trembled and redness around his nose and cheeks. They're all classic symptoms. He also has the signs of a man who is more than willing to use his fists against the people he should love and protect above all others. That look I know well because my own father had the same damn look." Devon inhaled sharply at that revelation. Sam had never been one to talk about his family life, and now he understood why. "If Finn didn't go, who would cop the brunt of his drunken rage?"

Devon's blood again turned to ice in his veins. "Shit, Nathan? That fucker would hit a kid? He was four when I left so that would make him, what, twelve?" Even as he asked the question, Devon knew it was true. Finn loved his brother and adored his mother. He would never leave if it meant his father's anger would be turned on them. His anger dulling the pain, Devon stood tall, then he started for his truck.

"We going for an extraction, LT?" Reaper asked, excitement clear in his tone.

"Yep," was all he said as he swung the door open and started the truck. His men clambered in behind him, and then they tore out from the yard. When he looked at his hand on the steering wheel, he saw that his punching had torn the skin across his knuckles to shit and they were bleeding sluggishly.

"I'll sew you up when we get back, LT," Sam advised when he saw Devon's fists. "But you might hurt them more if you punch the Sheriff. You'd better let one of us take care of that pleasure."

"Me!" Maddox shouted from the back. "Let me take a shot at the good Sheriff. I have never liked bullies."

"No," Devon snarled. "That fucker took his fists and a damn knife to the man who has been mine since we were in high school. It's my right, my privilege, and my goddamn job to pay that prick back."

****

"He's gonna kill us this time, isn't he, Finn?" Nate asked on a breath of air, making very little noise. Finn's heart bled for the fact his little brother's tone held no fear, just a resigned acceptance that this was going to be the day their father finally went over the edge and killed them.

Finn had no answer or any words to comfort Nate, so he simply held him tighter. They were squeezed into a hidden crevice behind a couple of loose boards in the wardrobe of the room they shared. Finn had forced the boards out and made it for them years ago. It had kept them hidden and safe on many occasions over the years until their father had slept off whatever drunken binge he was on, or gone to work. Whatever came first.

When they had arrived home from Devon's after a harrowing and high speed trip in the cruiser, Finn had remained in the car until Silas had opened the back door. There was no handle on the inside of the back seat, and Finn had chosen this seat deliberately. Not just because it meant he didn't have to sit beside his father, but also because his father had to open the door for him. Silas didn't anticipate Finn punching him as hard as he could in the nuts, then knocking him to the ground.

The move hadn't knocked Silas out like he'd hoped. The cursing and groaning coming from behind him as he ran into the house told Finn that, but had given him enough time to get into the house. Now, they could still hear their father cursing and swearing outside, and then shots sounded as he fired his service weapon into the house. With the report of each shot, he and Nate flinched, each of them waiting for one of the stray bullets to enter through the thin wood and hit them. Although they hadn't been hit yet, surely it was only a matter of time.

A high pitched female scream had Finn moving out of their hiding spot, whispering urgently for Nate to stay where he was, and putting the boards back into place. It occurred to Finn that this might be the last time he saw his brother, but he couldn't dwell on that now. Spinning around, he ran outside to where he had heard his mother scream.

His heart leapt to his throat when he saw that his father had his mother, Rose, on the ground. He straddled her hips, holding her down with his weight, and his hands were rapped tight around her throat. His mother's fingers clawed at his father's hands in a desperate fight for air, but she was no match for his strength.

Leaping off the porch with a scream of rage, he ran straight at his father. He had the satisfaction of seeing Silas's face fill with shock moments before he ploughed into his side, pushing him off his mother and rolling with him onto the front lawn.

Silas had at least one hundred pounds on him, and even though Finn fought to get the upper hand, it was him who was held to the ground in a similar position to that of his mom. Finn fought to pry his father's fingers from his throat, but he couldn't find any purchase.

"Get the hell off my son, you bastard!" His mother roared as she threw herself against her husband, but she didn't have the weight or the momentum Finn had, and wasn't able to move him. But he did let go of Finn's throat to swing his hand back, catching Rose on the side of the jaw, and knocking her back a few feet to where she lay stunned on the ground, a thin thread of blood sliding down her chin.

"Get off me, you whore! Don't think I don't know who you've been fucking!" Silas snarled. "The whole fucking town is laughing at me behind my back because you can't keep your fucking legs closed! That damn baker is going to find himself on the wrong end of a bullet very soon."

Now that Finn had managed to pull in enough air to stave off unconsciousness, he gripped his right fist with his left and swung them both as hard as he could into his father's chest. Silas grunted, but didn't move.

"You even fucking hit like a girl!" Then his hands were wrapped around Finn's throat again, squeezing the very life from within him.

Finn's gaze met his mother's and there was so much regret and sadness there that his heart hurt for his mom. He reached out a hand to her, trying to tell her that it was okay, but then Silas was suddenly lifted from him, and it looked like he kinda flew through the air a few feet before he hit the ground with a thud.

Finn was so busy gulping in air, and watching his father flail around on the ground winded, he failed to notice the man who knelt down on the other side of him. "Finn, baby, are you okay? Can you breathe?"

Finn turned his head, his eyes wide with shock as he looked into Devon's concern-filled face. Devon's gaze flickered over Finn's face then seemed to narrow on his throat. Devon's gentle hands pushed Finn's head to the side and he snarled at the bruises that were no doubt forming from Silas's fingers.

Devon's gaze lifted to look at Silas, his face filling with rage and then he was pushing up and heading for Silas, just as he was getting to his feet. Without a word, Devon gripped him by the collar, hauled off and punched him in the face. Once, twice, three times. The only reason Silas kept his feet beneath him was because Devon refused to allow him to fall, showing a staggering amount of strength as he held him upright and at arm's length. "You fucking piece of shit coward. You hit someone half your size? A woman? A goddamn child? I bet you think that makes you a man, huh?"

"You just hit an officer of the law, you stupid shit." Silas spat blood to the ground, his voice slightly slurred, and Finn wondered if Devon hadn't broken his jaw. He certainly hoped so. "I've got witnesses who will fucking swear in court you attacked me unprovoked, and you will see the inside of a fucking prison cell for a very long time!"

Finn fought his way to his feet with the help of one of Devon's friends, noticing for the first time they'd come with him. Sam and the one called Marcel were helping his mom to her feet, the blond guy helped Finn up, and the fourth one was headed into the house. Finn tensed and was about to charge forward when the guy behind him whispered, "Maddox is just going to go in and get your brother. Devon wants all of you out of this house. Today."

At those words, Finn felt a strength he hadn't known he had, flow through his body. It was stronger than anything he had felt before, and it eclipsed the fear he'd had of his father all these years. It was funny, but being held up by Devon, with a fear of his own shimmering in his eyes, Silas looked old, and small.

Finn put his shoulders back, lifted his head and walked to where his father was still trying to bluster his way out of Devon's hold. He certainly couldn't break it any other way. "You are pathetic." Finn's voice was hoarse but there was no missing the disgust in his tone as he addressed the man he no longer considered his father. "You have hidden behind that uniform for years, terrorizing your wife and your own sons. And for what? To make yourself feel like a man? I said it before, you are pathetic." He looked up at the sound of footsteps on the porch and he almost sighed in relief when he saw his brother exiting that house with the man called Maddox right behind him. They each carried one of the bags he and Nate had packed in case they ever got the chance to get away.

His father struggled for a moment before giving up. Devon was just too damn strong. Then he glared at Finn. "Where do you think you're going to go? You have no money, no home, nothing! Who is going to look after you and your brother?"

"I am!" Rose roared, coming from nowhere to punch his father in the side of the face, snapping his head back. Finn's jaw hit the ground. He had never seen his mother like this, but he definitely approved. "I have stayed with you because you threatened to kill my babies. But no more. Know this, you arrogant prick. I have documented records of your abuse against me and my sons and I will use it if you come anywhere near me or my babies again, you hear me! I will lay charges against you in a federal court, not here in this county, but somewhere I know you will be held accountable for your actions. Now, me and my boys are leaving, I don't know where we are going to go, but—"

"To stay with me." Devon interrupted, and when Finn turned to look at him, Devon's gaze was intense and focused completely on Finn. His father went to say something, but Devon hauled back and punched him again, this time knocking him out before dropping him to a heap at his feet. "Come home with me. Please, Finn. Say yes."

Chapter Four

The steady *thud, thud, thud* of a gloved fist hitting the solid mass of the punching bag was fast becoming an all too common sound around the newly named Cottonwood Farm in the last week. Finn sat in the porch swing, listening as Devon pounded his fist into the punching bag over and over again, wondering if he had made a mistake by bringing his family here.

On the first night here at the house, Devon had tried to talk with him, but Finn had refused to listen. Whether that was born from the shame of having his dirty little secret aired before the one man who at one stage in his life had meant more to him than anything else, or a deep seeded need to punish Devon for leaving, Finn couldn't say. After that one attempt of trying to explain, Devon hadn't tried again. But he was always there making sure Finn had anything and everything he needed. On more than one occasion, Finn caught the pain and need in Devon's expression before he was able to blank it out, and Finn had to leave the room. *God, could he forgive Devon?*

"Do you know why he's out there night after night pounding the shit out of that punching bag?" Finn turned to see Sam standing in the doorway, holding a bottle of beer in his hand.

"No, but since you're out here in the cold with me, pretty boy, I figure you're going to tell me." Finn and Sam had formed a fast friendship, but he wasn't sure if Sam could be objective with his advice where Devon was concerned.

Sam walked over to the rail that ran around the veranda and leaned against it, crossing his feet at the ankles. "Remind me to shoot you later for calling me that in front of the rest of my team. I'm never going to shake that handle. Now, back to Devon. He's doing two things. The first is he's imagining that bag is actually that douche bag Silas, because he never got to pound on him as much as he'd like. And to be honest, every man on the team has had a round with that bag in the past week picturing it was your father."

"Don't call him that." Finn snapped. "Silas—or hell, better yet—douchebag, is perfect."

Sam grinned, doffing his head in acknowledgement. "Douchebag it is. The second is that he is imagining the bag is him."

Finn started and frowned, not understanding what Sam was getting at. "What do you mean *him*?"

Sam shook his head and gave a small sigh. "Jesus, you really don't get it, do you? Devon wants to punish himself for leaving eight years ago. He blames himself for everything that happened to you during that time. He left you alone, vulnerable to that prick's attacks."

Finn frowned. "But that's ridiculous, he was only nineteen years old. He couldn't possibly have had the foresight to see Silas as he truly was." Finn heard his own words, and felt a kernel of guilt ignite within him at the realization that he had resented Devon all this time, and had let that color his behavior toward him over the past week.

"That is true, but he left none the less, traveling to a distant land, hell bent on saving the world from terrorists and an evil few can truly comprehend, but all the while the person he loved most in the world was being bullied, beaten and terrorized by an evil much closer to home."

Finn sat up. Was that really why Dev was pounding on that bag? "But he didn't love me. I was just a childhood friend, who, over the course of a couple of summer months, became more for a while. He always talked about enlisting with the Marines, getting out of here, and he did that the first moment he was able to. Hell, the week before he left for good, I went with him to the recruiting office. I knew he was leaving. I wasn't enough to keep him here."

"Do you truly believe that was all it was?" Sam asked incredulously. "I have known and served with Devon for almost six years. Anytime we were pinned down, when our lives were in danger, and it looked like there was a very distinct possibility things were going to get FUBAR very damn fast, we had a ritual. We would tell each other what we would say to our loved ones if they were there with us. You were the only one he would want to talk to."

Finn pressed the palm of his right hand against the ache in his chest. "Me?"

Sam nodded as he pushed up from the rail. "Finn, ask yourself what it is you want for your future. Devon is hoping and praying you'll give him a chance to explain and probably apologize for a few things, but he is not going to come to you. He doesn't think he's worthy of you and it's killing him seeing you turn from him every damn day."

"I don't—"

"Honey, you do," Finn turned to watch as his mother stepped out of the house and onto the porch. She hadn't been downstairs much since the day they arrived, and she hadn't spoken much at all. "Whether you realize it or not, every time Devon steps into a room, you look for any opportunity or excuse to leave. He's taken to eating in the kitchen so that you don't get up and walk out before you've finished eating."

"How do you know that, Ma? I haven't seen you

downstairs much at all."

"Because I sit and eat with him. We talk because we both have our regrets, our sins and our hopes and prayers for you and the future." Finn felt the sting of tears when Rose came and knelt down beside him, tears falling swiftly down her cheeks. Vaguely, he noticed Sam slipping silently back into the house. "I should have kept you and Nate safe, Finn. It was my job and I failed you, baby. I failed you and Nate so damn bad I don't know if I'll ever be able to forgive myself."

Finn fell off his chair, landing on his knees beside his mother and pulling her into his arms. "No, Ma. You didn't. Douche bag threatened to kill us if you left or if we all took off together. He'd have stopped at nothing to get us back and make us pay. I knew that. He's the damn Sheriff, it's not a large leap to think that he would see that threat through, and hell, he never would have faced any charges for it either. Not here." Finn took a breath to calm himself and saw Nate standing in the doorway, silently crying. Finn held out an arm and Nate dropped down beside them, and Finn hugged his mother and his brother tight in his arms. Thanking God they were all safe. "Ma, we're safe for now, and I know that Devon and his team are working on something to ensure that man is out of our lives forever. Have faith in them, Ma."

Rose sniffed and lifted her face from his shoulder, pressing a kiss to Nate's head before she reached out and cupped Finn's face with her hands. "Finn, my darling boy, you need to do that too. Have faith in Devon. Trust that huge heart of yours because it will never let you down. Son, hear me and what I'm saying. Have *faith* in Devon. Put aside the past, and listen to him."

Finn stared into his mother's eyes, looking for answers he knew he wouldn't find there. He needed to look into a pair of wounded dark brown eyes to find those answers. So far tonight had been the night for jumping emotional hurdles, so why not one more?

****

Devon leaned against the wall of the shower, letting the hot water rain down over his shoulders and back. Sam had already told him he was risking doing more damage to himself with his need to pound the punching bag night after night, but Devon couldn't bring himself to stop. He let his mind drift through the day, lingering on the moments when Finn actually seemed to talk with him before he shot from the room like a wounded rabbit. Aside from the fact Finn was pretty much ignoring him, it had been a decent day.

Marcel had been talking with a friend of his who was a state's attorney and things were progressing with making Silas accountable for his actions. Apparently, he had a few other complaints against him, and those were only the ones people were not too scared to actually lay against the man. He and his deputy had both been suspended from duty without pay, awaiting investigation into a whole list of charges. A lot of that had come from Finn and his mom thanks to her diligent documentation of his abuse and his actions.

Devon and his team were making progress on the outbuildings, stripping one completely so they could create a self-contained special situations training area, where they could build and simulate real life situations for SWAT and sniper teams who came to them for training. The large barn structure at the back of the property would be perfect for an indoor small caliber gun range, with a special sniper training area in the surrounding forests that Reaper had already planned out. The garage at the side of the house would be turned into on-site living quarters for those undertaking the training, and they were currently looking at plans to add a gym and pool area to it.

They had reached out to a specialist contractor who could manage the new builds and the conversions, but before they'd had the opportunity to meet with the specialist, an alternative contractor had come to light. A company in Montana called Marksmen Construction. They'd all liked the name so had made contact with the owner, Riley Marksmen, and he was heading out their way in a couple of days with some site plans he'd drawn up after a lengthy phone conversation with the team. Devon was excited to see what became of it.

Sighing deeply, he shut off the shower, stepped out, and grabbed a towel. He made a few cursory swipes of his body with the towel, wincing when he raised his hands to dry his hair, his muscles protesting the movement after punching the bag for over an hour.

He pulled the towel off his head, wrapped it low around his hips, and looked at his fist. At least his old pair of sparring gloves gave him some protection. He walked over to the sink and looked at himself in the mirror. He had to fight the urge to punch his fist through his reflection. Averting his eyes from the mirror, he quickly brushed his teeth and rolled on his deodorant before he opened the door, strode out into the bathroom, and came to an abrupt halt.

He blinked a couple of times to make sure he wasn't seeing things. He wanted to pinch himself to check he wasn't dreaming either, because Finn was in his bedroom sitting in the arm chair against the wall.

"I don't remember ever coming into this room before," Finn murmured as he waved an arm around the room. "It's very … kitsch."

Devon stayed where he was. He didn't want to scare Finn away. "Kitsch, huh? Gaudy and tacky. Yeah, that describes my grandmother perfectly." When they had divvied up the rooms, he couldn't bring himself to use his old room, not when every time he looked in there he was plagued with memories of him and Finn and happier times he didn't deserve to think about. He also felt that he couldn't subject anyone else in the house to this particular hideous room so he took it as his own.

It was the master bedroom and came equipped with its own bathroom which was useful. Especially in the middle of the night when he awoke from dreams of Finn, heart pounding, his hand wrapped hard around his dick and he needed to step into the shower to take care of things.

"True," Finn said with a grin, and Devon's heart stuttered at the sight. "Not that I remember her much. She didn't leave the house a whole hell of a lot after you left." Finn's eyes cast down when he said that and Devon threw his own feelings aside and went to him, dropping to his knees beside the chair.

"I'm so sorry. So fucking sorry, Finn." Devon's voice was hoarse with emotion and he didn't even try to hide the moisture gathering in his eyes as Finn looked up at him. "I don't know what to do or what to say to make it up to you, but know that I am not going to give up trying to find a way to do just that."

Devon bit his lip when Finn shook his head. He couldn't forgive Devon, and there was nothing he could do to earn that. The really shitty thing was Devon couldn't blame him. He pushed up to his feet, turned and walked to the window, tears falling freely as he realized the thing he wanted most in this life was beyond his reach.

"Devon," Finn's soft voice came from just behind him, and Devon flinched. How lost in his own misery was he that he hadn't even heard Finn get up from his chair and follow him? "Why did you walk away just now?"

Devon heard pain in Finn's tone and spun around to face him. "Because I knew you couldn't forgive me, and I had no fucking right to ask that of you. I let a poisonous bitch drive me from this town, and I should have taken you with me. You shouldn't forgive me, Finn."

Finn reached up and pressed his warm palm to Devon's cheek and his touch nearly dropped him to his knees. "Dev, that's not why I was shaking my head, it's not that I can't forgive you. I had somewhat of an epiphany this evening and realized that there is nothing really to forgive anymore. Not really. We were kids. Oh sure, I was pissed off for a while there because you did leave without saying goodbye, and I thought it was because of something that I did."

"No! God, Finn, I—" Finn pressed the palm of his other hand over his mouth, effectively stopping his tirade. Not used to submitting physically in any way to a person, Devon's eyes narrowed.

Finn grinned. "Yep, I am gagging you, and you are going to let me because you need to hear what I have to say. If we are ever going to get over this and move on, in whatever capacity that may be, you have to listen to me now."

Hope and hesitation bloomed within Devon, but he nodded and held still.

"All I knew at the time was that you left after a night with me, and I was so young and everything was about me, so I figured it had something to do with that. It wasn't until I came looking for you a couple of weeks later, refusing to leave when your grandmother told me you didn't want to talk with me like I had the multiple times I had come before. I had hoped I could beg you to forgive me for whatever I had done. On that day, your grandmother told me that she knew about you and I, and that if I didn't want her to tell the whole town that we were gay, including my father, then I would leave and never come back."

Finn removed the hand that he held against his mouth and used it to cup the other side of Devon's face. "And I am ashamed to say that I left. I gave in, not wanting to have to face my father or anyone in town knowing that I was gay. I am just as guilty as you of letting that hideous woman make me feel guilty about loving you."

Devon reached out, placing his hands gently on Finn's hips and pulling him closer. "But grandmother told your father anyway, didn't she? Despite the fact I let that bitch drive me from my home and from you, she did what she threatened to do and took those photos to your father, didn't she?"

Devon felt Finn flinch as his hands dropped away and his eyes widened in shock. "No! Dad found out about a year later when I was admitting everything to my mother, and he flipped the fuck out. What did she threaten to do exactly?"

"She threatened to take the photos to your father, the town, and even the goddamn recruiting center."

"That fucking bitch! She would have put what you had been dreaming about all your life in jeopardy?" Finn asked incredulously.

Dev smiled wryly. "You did meet her right? Of course she did. Anything that could and would hurt me was absolutely something she wanted to do. Ultimately, it cost me what I wanted most for my future anyway." Devon hoped that Finn could read the open expression on his face.

Finn looked into his eyes for a long moment and Devon felt like this was the turning point. Finn could either choose to forgive him, or decide that forgiveness was beyond him. When Finn finally offered a small smile and his expression softened, Devon felt a weight lift from his chest and he could breathe.

"I didn't know she had photos of us." Finn frowned. "How in the hell did she manage that?"

Devon shrugged. "I found a drill hole in the ceiling above my bed. And, she'd used a fucking spy camera she'd bought online that had a flexible scope. Bitch was nothing if not hell bent on getting me to leave."

Finn's jaw dropped open in the cutest way, and he shook his head. "Jesus Christ, that's like something out of a movie. One starring Kathy Bates as her, because damn she plays a great crazy woman." Devon laughed and felt more of the weight of guilt he had carried on his shoulders since learning of the horror Finn and his family had lived through over the past eight years dissipate a little. Devon didn't think it would ever go away completely, but it was a start.

Realizing he still had his hands on Finn's hips, he dropped his arms to his sides and moved back as far as he could. Watching him closely, Finn's head tilted sideways as if he were trying to figure out a complex math equation. "So," Devon cleared his throat when his voice came out sounding rough. "Do you think we can move on from here as friends?"

Finn's eyes narrowed again. "Is that what you want?"

Devon lifted his arms, running a frustrated hand through his hair. "No! Yes! Shit, Finn, I'm fucking trying so hard to be stoic and not make this about what I want."

"But that's what I'm asking you, Dev. I'm asking what *you* want." Finn stepped closer until their chests were almost touching, and Devon's tenuous hold on his control snapped.

Yanking Finn into his arms, he slid his hand up his back and into Finn's hair to cup the back of his head. Holding Finn still, he lowered his own head until their foreheads were pressed together. "I want it all, Finn. I want a second chance at the forever kind of love I know that you and I can have together. I want everything and anything you're willing to give me. I want to go to bed every night with you by my side, and wake up the exact same way in the morning. I want to be the man you need in your life and the lover that you crave and reach for in the still of night. I want it all, Finn. With you, I want it all."

Devon felt like he had just ripped his still beating heart from his chest and laid it at Finn's feet. And in a very real way, he just had.

****

Finn's heart pounded in his chest while his palms itched with the need to feel Devon's skin beneath his fingertips, and in that moment, the question became clear. He could allow the past to dictate his future, or he could work on accepting the past for what it was and move on. "Dev, I'm not sure who we are together anymore." Dev's face crumpled and he was about to drop his hands, so Finn reached up and wound his arms around Dev's neck. "I'm not sure if our second chance could lead to a forever kind of love, but I want to see where it will lead. I don't think we will ever be who we were eight years ago, but I would very much like to see who we are together, now."

This time, Dev's face filled with disbelief and wonder. Then his handsome face transformed into the most amazing smile that had Finn grinning back. "You are not going to regret this, Finn," Dev promised as he lifted Finn off the ground, and his legs lifted naturally to wrap around his hips. "I swear to God, you will never doubt my feelings for you, or wonder where you stand with me from now on. I am going to make this place a home, for me, the team, and … well, you if I can convince you to stay."

Finn smiled as he swept Dev's hair from his forehead, loving that he had the right to touch him. "Let's not move too fast, Dev. Let's just take things slow and see where things are going. I want to explore who were are now, and get to know the older you."

Dev took a deep breath then smiled softly. "I want that too, baby."

"Then take me to bed, not to have sex, but to explore each other a little and just sleep in each other's arms. Okay?"

Finn remained locked in Dev's gaze, then Dev grinned as he walked them toward the huge bed against the back wall of the room. Dev surprised Finn by turning and sitting on the foot of the bed so that Finn straddled his hips, and he was sitting in his lap. Finn reached up a hand and gently stroked Dev's face, softly wiping away the lines of stress and tension that had lined his face for the past week.

Dev closed his eyes briefly and sighed. "I love the feel of your hands on my skin. It makes me feel alive."

Finn leaned in and pressed his lips to Dev's ear, relishing the shudder that rocked him. "And how do you feel about my lips against your skin?" Rocking his hips forward, Finn rubbed his jean clad erection against Devon's which was now tenting the towel he wore. "Or the feel of my cock grinding against yours?"

With a desperate growl, Devon pulled Finn's shirt up and over his head, then tugged him close so that they were skin to skin. "I fucking love all of it!" Devon slid his hand up Finn's naked back, making him shiver before he plunged his hands into Finn's hair. He slammed his mouth against Finn's. With his hand in Finn's hair, Devon could direct the angle, the pressure and the intensity of this kiss.

Finn moaned as Devon bit gently on his bottom lip before swiping his tongue over the sting. When he plunged his tongue into Finn's mouth and teased his own tongue into an erotic dance that almost mimicked the act of making love, Finn felt his arousal spiral to new heights. Devon had always been able to drive him to the brink of sanity with just a kiss. Devon pulled back but not too far, moving his mouth to Finn's neck, finding with unerring accuracy the spot below his jaw that always made him shiver.

"Damn, Finn," Devon murmured against his neck, "you taste so fucking good." Dev moved an inch lower, and when their position stopped him from being able to continue, he simply lifted Finn, turned, and rolled them onto the bed. Then his mouth latched onto Finn's nipple. Finn cried out as he arched his back, offering more of himself to the man currently shorting out his brain circuits. "And you are still as responsive as you always were."

Dev sat up, yanking away the towel that was caught around his hips and threw it away. Finn's arousal dulled at the sight of a puckered, angry looking scar on his right thigh. He sat up, reaching out a hand to touch it gently. "What happened?"

Dev shrugged, "I took a bullet to the thigh on our last mission. It's all good now, though."

Finn bit his lip as he took a longer look at Dev's body. He had been struck with nerves when Devon had first strolled from the bathroom and hadn't taken too close a look. Then, as soon as they started talking, he had needed to look into his eyes. Devon often said more with his eyes than he ever did with words, but now, Finn took some time to really look at him.

The gunshot wound to his thigh wasn't the only fresh wound on his body. There were signs of contusions and long gashes around his shoulders, and much too damn close to his head for Finn's liking. There appeared to be what looked like another gunshot wound to his lower back. His rib cage was bruised, not like the fading marks Finn had, but a solid block, like he had fallen onto something or something had crashed into him.

"It was more than that, though, wasn't it?" Finn lifted his gaze to Dev's, who was diligently studying the back of his hand. Finn's gaze followed and he saw the scabs over his knuckles, a few that were still bright red as if they had been opened again, and there was quite a bit of swelling there too. "Jesus, Dev," he muttered as he lifted Dev's hands to cup them between his own. "What the hell have you done to yourself? Night after night you're out there pounding the shit out of that damn bag, and now look at your hands." He lifted one to his lips, pressing a series of small kisses to the knuckles. "You're not punching that damn bag again until these are healed."

Devon laughed. "That is the first time anyone other than my CO has given me an order. But I will do as you have so nicely asked, baby. Now, if you've finished cataloging my injuries, I'd like to get back to what I was doing. I want to love on you a little, and then sleep with you in my arms. You will never regret giving me a second chance, I promise. Going slow is fine with me."

Chapter Five

"Going slow sucks!" Finn moaned as he threw himself down on the couch, wanting to reach across the coffee table and smack Sam in his laughing mouth. "I swear to all that's holy, pretty boy, if you keep laughing I will do something that will hurt you and make your nickname nothing more than an ironic statement!"

Sam coughed into his fist, obviously trying to stop from pissing himself laughing. The bastard. "Finn, from what you've told me, the 'let's go slow' thing was your idea."

Finn frowned and slouched further into the couch. "I know that! But I didn't think it would be so fucking frustrating!" It had been four days since his and Dev's *come to Jesus* moment when they'd cleared the air. Since then, they had spent hours together rebuilding their friendship and were discovering their desire for each other was just as explosive as it had always been, and Finn wanted to take it to that final step.

Sam sat back in his chair, mirth still shining in his eyes. "You have to know that Devon is walking that thin edge of desire too, Finn. One word from you and I'm sure you'll both be shouting it from the rafters and the rest of us will be hating on you just a bit. Hell, it probably won't even take a word, one come hither look from those green eyes of yours and you'll find yourself up those stairs in a heartbeat!"

Finn sighed. "But what am I supposed to say? Dev, going slow is fucking killing me, let's go upstairs and get our groove on?"

"Thank Christ for that!"

Finn's eyes widened with shock as Devon's voice came from the door that led to the kitchen and he strode into the living room with a singularly focused intent the likes of which Finn had never seen. In the next second, he was pulled up from the couch and placed over Devon's shoulder. Finn placed his hands on Dev's hips to keep his face out of Dev's ass. Devon braced a hand across his thighs to hold him in place.

"You taking charge, huh, LT?" Sam asked and Finn was spun around until he was facing the opposite direction.

"Don't I always!" Dev's response had Finn grinning. "The boys are going to need help out in the barn this afternoon. Keep Rose and Nate busy too. Finn and I are going to, how did you put it, love?"

Finn giggled, turning his head slightly so he could see Sam. "Get our groove on?"

Devon laughed and ran a hand down Finn's calf. "That's right, get our groove on. See you later, pretty boy!"

Finn laughed as Dev turned to leave the room and Sam narrowed his gaze at Finn, raising his hand and mimicking shooting him. It would have been a lot more believable if he hadn't been grinning like a lunatic!

Dev took the steps two at a time, and in no time at all, they were walking into Dev's room, locking the door behind them. He pulled Finn over his shoulder and encouraged him to wrap his legs around Dev's waist, a position that was fast becoming a favorite for Finn.

Finn's breath caught at the desire in Devon's gaze, but he didn't miss the hesitation that swirled there too. "Are you sure, baby? I don't want to rush you if you don't feel like this is the right time."

Finn wrapped his arms around Devon's neck and snuggled close, loving that the position pushed his cock tight against that of his lover's. "Oh, this is most definitely the right time. Remind me what it is to be loved by Devon Roberts, and I will remind you what it is to be adored by Finn McGregor."

Dev's grin turned hot and wicked. "Oh, babe, that would most definitely be my pleasure."

Finn squealed when Dev practically threw him on the bed. Then Devon stripped before him so quickly, Finn could do nothing but admire the speed, and he only had time to strip his t-shirt off him. Then he laughed as a now naked Devon pounced on him, pushing him back to the mattress, and moving so that he lay over the bottom half of Finn's body. Devon kissed and licked his way down Finn's abdomen. When he reached the waistband of his jeans, Devon moved to kneel between Finn's thighs. The sight of Devon's cock bobbing against his abdomen made his mouth water and he licked his lips, anticipating the moment he would get the chance to take him in his mouth again.

"Fuck," Devon groaned. "I can almost feel the heat of your gaze on my dick, baby. You'll get your chance to get your mouth on me, and really fucking soon, I promise. But I need to take care of you first." Devon quickly dealt with the buttons on his jeans and moaned out loud when Finn's throbbing erection pushed up through the gap. "Damn, I love the fact that you have always hated wearing underwear."

Finn bit his bottom lip as Devon pulled his jeans completely off, then simply knelt there, looking down at him. "You are so fucking beautiful." Finn grimaced at the word, and Devon barked a breathless laugh. "Yeah, not the manliest of terms, but for you, lover, it is extremely accurate." As Devon shuffled back off the bed and dropped to his knees, Finn squeaked as he was pulled to the edge of the mattress so that his legs dangled almost to the floor, and his butt rested near the edge.

With no warning, Devon took him into his mouth

and didn't stop until his lips touched the tight curls at the base of Finn's cock. Finn arched, groaning Devon's name before pushing up on his elbows, not wanting to miss another second. He watched as Dev worked his cock in and out of his mouth, using his hands to stroke him while his tongue swirled around the head, dipping into the slit at the top. When his mouth would slide almost to the base again, Finn would use his hands to mold and roll his balls, before pulling back with just the right amount of suction.

Finn's ability to form coherent sentences regressed to the point where he simply groaned constantly, panting to get air into his lungs. He felt the familiar tingle at the base of his spine that told him he was moments away from release.

"Dev," he forced out on a groan. "You've got me. I'm gonna … you need to let go, Dev… Dev!" Finn dropped back against the mattress as he came hard down Devon's throat. Finn had expected him to stop, but when he simply tightened his jaw and sucked him stronger, Finn was helpless to hold back. Wave after wave of pleasure rolled over him as Devon swallowed everything he had to give, even drawing deeply on the sensitive head to ensure he had every last drop. When the force of the orgasm finally released him, Finn collapsed back on the mattress.

When the feeling returned to his legs, he pushed onto his elbows and almost swallowed his tongue. Devon stood at the end of the bed, his hand shuttling up and down his sheathed swollen cock, working a handful of lube from root to tip. And just like that, Finn's own cock began to thicken, which was nothing short of a miracle after the orgasm he had just experienced.

"If this is not something you want," Devon said through gritted teeth, his voice strained, "then tell me now and I'll take care of this in the shower, then come back and hold you for a while. We can still take it slow if you need to. There is no pressure here whatsoever."

Finn looked up at Devon and saw the vulnerability shining in his eyes. With a wicked smile, he lifted his legs up onto the bed, completely baring himself to Devon's hungry gaze. "I think we can safely assume that what you have in your hand there is exactly what I want, every glorious inch of it."

****

Devon stood for a few moments, gripping the base of his cock and willing the orgasm he was now hovering on the edge of back. The sight of Finn laid out before him, welcoming him with a smile, was almost more than he could take, but the anticipation of being buried balls deep inside him was more than enough to bring him under control.

He stepped up to the side of the bed and grabbed one of his pillows. "Lift up, baby." Finn lifted his hips and Devon gently pushed the pillow beneath his them, lifting his ass to just the right height and angle. He stepped to the end of the bed and used his lubricated hand to gently massage the ring of muscles around Finn's back entrance.

Finn sighed, lifting his legs and letting them fall to the side, opening himself completely for Dev. Using the lubrication to gently push his fingers into Finn's ass, Dev made them both groan. "Holy fuck, Finn. You're so damn tight, baby, you're gonna have me coming before I truly get to take advantage of you."

Finn grinned wickedly and Dev's dick twitched. "I figure you got, at least, a couple of rounds in you this afternoon, Dev. You can always make it up to me later. Or are you trying to tell me you're a one shot wonder and I should just lay back and enjoy it while it lasts."

Dev shot back a wicked grin of his own and stepped in to press the blunt head of his cock against Finn's ass, pressing in just slightly. "Baby, you should know that words like that to a Marine are like waving a red rag at a bull. One shot wonder my ass. Let's just see who calls uncle first, hmm?"

Then, locking his knees, he leaned in, placing his hands on the backs of Finn's thighs and slowly worked his cock past the ring of muscle, gently pushing inside him, watching Finn's face for any sign of discomfort. But he should have known better. The only look Finn had on his face was one of impatience. With a sharp snap of his hips, Dev was buried to the hilt within him. Finn cried out once, then rolled his own hips—the look of joy and pleasure on his face was hypnotic—and Devon stayed still a while longer, letting him get used to the feel of him again. He also allowed Finn to move, taking his own pleasure anyway Finn wanted to.

"Fuck, you are strangling my cock, baby," Dev groaned as he finally withdrew, then pushed home once again, Finn's hungry little asshole pulling him in and fighting against his withdrawal. The sensation of Finn's body pulling him back, not wanting to lose him, was like nothing Devon had ever felt before, and there was no way he could articulate it.

He moved in and out of Finn, setting a steady rhythm, watching the flush of arousal sweep up Finn's chest and into his cheeks. He leaned forward even further, pushing Finn's thighs against his chest, and this time when he pushed forward, he felt Finn shudder beneath him and he knew he had the right angle to slide against his prostate.

"There it is," Dev whispered, his voice sounding harsh, "hold on tight, baby, this is the hard and fast portion of tonight's program." Then with no further warning, Devon began to shuttle his hips back and forth, harder and faster until he was slamming into his lover. Finn cried out with each thrust, telling Devon without words that he was still right on target. Looking down, he saw Finn's hands feverishly working his own cock, and the restraint and control he'd wielded over his own orgasm disappeared.

"Fuck!" Devon roared as he slammed into Finn and jerked against him, filling his ass with his cum. His entire body tensed as he was held in the grip of his orgasm, helpless to do anything but surrender everything he had and everything he was to the man beneath him. Vaguely, he heard Finn shout his release to the room as well. After the last shuddering role of his release, Devon gently let go of Finn's legs and slumped forward onto his arms, breathing heavily like he'd just finished a five mile run in full gear.

When he felt like he could function again, he looked up at Finn, and saw that he was still struggling for breath, his arm flung across his eyes. Devon stood up on shaky legs and gently pulled his still semi-hard cock from Finn's body, making them both moan. Dev wobbled as he headed to the bathroom, and from the breathless laugh that came from the bed, Finn had caught that slight sign of weakness.

He went into the bathroom and turned on the shower, making a mental note to add a bath when they gutted this room and the bedroom to update them. He disposed of the condom then turned to the mirror and almost did a double take. This man was not the same man who had looked into that mirror every day for the past two weeks. This man was one who stood tall, who looked younger, and who had a future he actually wanted to be a part of. With a wry smile, he grabbed one of the face cloths from the pile on the shelf, rinsed it with warm water, and then returned to the bedroom.

Finn hadn't moved, but he lay there with a satisfied smile that had Devon feeling ten feet tall. "Laughing at a man who has lost the feeling in his legs is a little low, babe." Devon used the cloth to gently clean up the mess the lubricant left behind in Finn's ass, and the mess Finn had made on his own stomach.

"I couldn't help it," Finn answered, his voice sounding hoarse, "it looked funny. Here was this huge man, a Lieutenant in the Unites States Marine Corp, stumbling across the floor like a drunk."

Devon chuckled as he helped Finn up and led him into the bathroom then into the shower, angling the shower head so that it soaked Finn's body but didn't hit his face. "Well, what can I say, fucking you almost took my knees. Besides, it's been a long fucking time for me." He grabbed the sponge and body wash from the shelf in the shower, squeezed a small amount of gel on the sponge, and pleased himself by washing his lover's body.

Finn sighed and his head fell back on his shoulders as Devon pressed a little harder across his shoulders and back. "It can't have been that long," Finn argued. "From where I was lying it felt like you'd had a lot of practice since the last time we were together."

Dev remained quiet, dropping to his knees to clean Finns' legs, not really wanting to continue the conversation, but Finn must have caught something either in his expression or from his lack of response. "Dev?" He asked softly and when Dev looked up at him, he saw understanding written on his face. "It's okay, love. You don't have to tell me about your other lovers. The only thing I'm concerned about is that I'm the only one from now on."

Dev shook his head as he stood up, cupping Finn's face in his hands, pressing a firm, opened-mouthed kiss to his mouth. Devon kept up the sensual assault until Finn was completely compliant against him before he pulled back. "Finn, when we made love for the first time as teenagers, I took your virginity just as surely as you took mine. I knew then that you were it for me. Despite my actions eight years ago, that never changed for me. You're not just my last, babe, you're my fucking only."

Dev watched as shock filled Finn's expression before it changed to joy. "Your … only?"

"Yeah, my only. I have never wanted to be with anyone else. Christ Finn, I was always going to come for you. Snipers have a term we use a lot, it's called *line of drift*. These are the paths across terrain that are most likely used when going from one place to another. I have been traveling my line of drift from the moment I left this town, and the destination was you. It has always been you. I wish to God I had fucking come for you sooner, but I would have always worked my way back to you."

Finn's eyes narrowed and filled with mischief. "What if I was with someone when you got back?"

Jealousy ripped through him, and it must have been clear on his face because Finn laughed.

"I am the leader of a team of highly trained sniper specialists that government and military organizations alike are approaching to train them once this facility is up and running, baby. I would have taken the fucker out and been right there to comfort you through your loss."

Finn smacked his arm and they laughed together, and holy shit, it felt good. It felt normal.

"The funny thing is," Finn admitted as he slid his arms up and around Devon's neck, "I never felt the need or desire to take a lover either. Hell, Redwood Falls isn't exactly known for its large gay community, and besides, with Silas being … well, Silas and a douchebag, I never wanted to give him more of an excuse to kick my ass."

Devon growled and his anger rose at the mention of the fucker who had terrorized Finn and his whole family. His team already had a plan in action to get Silas taken care of legally, but sometime, in the not too distant future, that fucker was going to be dealt a lesson he would never forget. Devon had already started making a mental list of every scar Finn's body bore, and he was determined to give them back to Silas in return.

"Hey," Finn's voice broke through his revenge-soaked thoughts. "Stop thinking about Silas and get to the part where I have just admitted that you are *my* only, too." All thought of Silas evaporated, and one hundred percent of his attention focused on Finn. "You say your line of drift would have brought you back looking for me, well you would have found me here waiting for you."

Devon's heart swelled to the point it ached. He pressed the palm of his hand against his chest. He had to lock his knees to keep from falling when Finn dropped to kneel in front of him. Devon quickly moved the shower head so that his body protected Finn.

"Now, it's been a really long time since I've done this," Finn murmured as he gripped Devon's cock firmly and stroked him hard, adding a delightful twist at the end which made him groan. Dev leaned forward and pressed his arm against the wall of the shower. "Why don't we see if I've still got some oral skills that make you shout my name, hmm?"

Dev was about to say he had no doubt that Finn still had those skills, but lost it when Finn leaned in and swallowed him, taking him and sucking so strongly on his dick. Devon growled as Finn ran his tongue over the head, fluttering it against the sensitive vein along the underside of his cock.

Yeah, Finn still had the skills, and Devon figured he'd be shouting Finn's name a hell of a lot sooner than Finn had shouted his.

Chapter Six

"What about the bedrooms?" Devon asked as they sat around the dining room table the next morning, all staring down at the schematics of the main house Maddox had drawn up on his laptop. Despite the fact they had all lived, worked, bled and fought beside each other over the last few years, it was easy to forget these talented soldiers and second to none marksmen had a whole shit load of talents that had nothing to do with war. "I want to pretty much gut the master bedroom and bathroom. Hell, all of them probably need some updating."

Riley Marksmen was coming with the plans for the facility, but they had yet to fill him in on what they wanted to be done to the main house. They had spent the morning drawing up a list of their goals and as soon as Devon mentioned the bedrooms, the conversation fell quiet. "What?"

"Well, LT," Reaper's Texan drawl thickened which told Dev that whatever he was about to say, it was going to be some smart ass comment. "Whatever you plan to do with the bedrooms, you might want to consider some soundproofing."

The rest of the team snickered like school children and Devon frowned, missing the joke completely. They had discussed the need for sound proofing around the shooting range, but this was the first time anyone had mentioned it for the house itself.

"What the hell for?" His question met open laughter now, and he turned to a blushing Finn who rolled his eyes at him.

"Christ, Dev, you never were very good at translating smartass." Finn sighed as he stood up and moved to stand beside him, placing a hand on his arm. "Glenn is telling us in a smart ass way that because of the age of this house, and how loud we were last night, they heard us when we were making love."

Devon's grin turned wicked with the realization, and he slid his arm around Devon's waist to rest his hand on his opposite hip. "Oh that had nothing to do with the age of the house, baby, and everything to do with how fucking explosive we are together." Devon took Finn's mouth in a hard and intense kiss, not letting up until he moaned and softened completely against him.

He released his mouth and turned to his team, grinning. "Yeah, soundproofing sounds like a really good idea. Then Finn and I don't have to try and be quiet all the damn time." That sparked a round of jokes, jibes and smartass comments that had them all laughing.

"If you're going to soundproof the rooms," Sam added, pointing at Marcel, "make sure you add a double layer to his room. He snores like a fucking chainsaw."

Marcel stood up quickly, no doubt to do something to Sam, but whatever it may have been was stopped short by the sound of a gunshot. The glass in the window opposite them shattered almost at the same time. Devon spun quickly, dragging Finn to the ground and under him, but watched in horror as Marcel fell backward, red blooming on the shoulder of his t-shirt.

"Sam! Man down!" Devon shouted, immediately falling into the familiar pattern of what his team did best. Assess the situation and figure out an attack plan and egress route. His mind immediately ticked through exits, strongholds, and points of weakness in the house and the room. Sam scuttled into the next room, no doubt going for his med kit. Glenn had already reached Marcel, but from the way the man was swearing the air blue in French, he was going to be fine.

"Colt, M4," Reaper said from his position, crouched by the door leading to the kitchen.

"That shot was fairly loud. The shooter was close, he had to be. The wind is up, he's not overly confident in the high wind," Maddox added as he guarded the door that led into the living room and front door. Devon cursed the fact they had locked their weapons away in a strong box upstairs. Right then and there he swore they were going to build strong boxes and fucking panic rooms in multiple areas of this house. Finn was in danger and that was un-fucking-acceptable.

"Finn!" Nate's terrified voice came from upstairs, quickly followed by his mother telling him to be quiet.

Finn looked up at him in inquiry and Devon nodded. "I'm okay, Nate! Just stay quiet and let Devon and his team see what's going on."

"LT." Devon turned as Sam came back into the room, crouching and keeping low, his medical kit in one hand, and handed Devon his Sig with the other. As soon as he palmed the butt of the gun, the familiar feel and weight of it calmed him even further. Sam handed weapons to both Maddox and Glenn and everyone seemed to relax a little.

"Reaper, you and Maddox go out the kitchen door, flank left to the garage. I'll go out the front, draw this fucker's fire. Let's see if he actually knows what he's doing."

Maddox and Reaper moved in unison toward the door and Finn suddenly reached up, gripping his t-shirt. "Please Dev, don't go out there. It has to be Silas. If you go out there, he'll kill you. He was always bragging about his marksmen scores."

Devon frowned. Did Finn honestly believe he could be taken out by a piece of shit like Silas? "Finn, I've faced down and survived firefights with tougher sons of bitches than Silas, and I sure as hell am not going to stay lying here in my own damn dining room wondering if that fucker is out there. Besides, Marcel has taken a bullet to his shoulder. He might need to be taken to a hospital."

"Bullshit!" Marcel snarled from where he was now sitting up against the sideboard. "I'm not fucking going to some hospital. I'm going hunting! It is open fucking season on bigoted fucking Sheriffs who think they are above the same goddamn law they took an oath to protect."

Sam chuckled from his spot beside Marcel, pushing a pressure bandage to his shoulder. "Lucky for you it's not lodged in too far. I'll be able to get it out. Go, LT, we'll keep an eye on your man for you."

Devon looked down at Finn, cursing Silas for the millionth time for the fear he saw shining in his beautiful green eyes. "Finn, I'll be fine. I'm just going out to make sure we're good, and then we'll set up a guard rotation. We'll keep you and your family safe until this shit blows over. I promise."

He waited until Finn nodded, then he moved toward the door that led to the hallway. He took one final look over his shoulder, his heart aching at the look of worry on Finn's face. In an attempt to make him feel better, he shot Finn his cockiest grin. "Be right back, lover."

Finn rolled his eyes with a slight shake of his head. "Oh, get over yourself, Devon Roberts. Go play soldier then get your butt back in this house safe, and you had better make damn sure you are unhurt. Or there will be hell to pay."

Devon mock growled at him as Marcel and Sam both hid their laughter behind a cough. Then he headed into the hallway. As he approached the door, everything within him stilled, his focus narrowed and he cracked the front door open just enough. He whistled low, checking to see if his men were in place. When the answering low whistle came, he took a slow, deep breath, then pushed the door open and ran like hell.

****

Finn thought he could quite possibly be experiencing a heart attack. The organ was certainly pounding hard and fast enough, and hadn't he heard somewhere that sweaty palms were a symptom too? He heard two low whistles coming from outside, and then the front door slammed open. He heard Devon step twice on the veranda then nothing as he no doubt launched himself off the steps. A split second later, the sound of another gunshot split the air, and Finn was up and running for the door without even thinking.

Just as he was about to reach the door, he was grabbed from behind and dragged to the floor. "Goddamn it, Finn!" Sam muttered as he dragged him back from the door. "Stop being a pain in my ass. Sit back down and wait for Devon or I will fucking sit on you and hold you here myself if I have to, but, either way, you are staying inside this goddamn house!"

Finn struggled briefly but froze when he heard another gunshot, this one not as loud as the other two. "Devon!" he shouted, moments before Sam slammed his hand over his mouth.

"So help me God, if you don't shut up I will knock you the hell out!" Finn glared at Sam, daring him to even try. Sam sighed, and removed his hand. "That second shot was from a Sig, not the M4. Maddox or Reaper got a shot off, and unless he was already legging it in a vehicle, then this is over. They never miss. The boys are just going to sweep the area, find where the shots came from, and then they'll come back in."

Finn took a few moments to try to gain control of his breathing. "Get the hell off me, Sam. I'll stay here."

Sam looked at him suspiciously, as if judging whether he meant it or not. "Sam," Marcel added dryly, "think about how the LT is going to react if he comes in here and sees you lying on top of his man."

Finn had to laugh out loud at the wide-eyed look of horror on Sam's face before he scuttled backward and moved over to Marcel.

Finn moved to sit with his back against the wall, counting to one hundred in an attempt to calm himself. His brother and mother came and sat with him just before he finished counting. He started over in Spanish when Devon was still not back and he was in the eighties by the time Devon and Maddox walked into the room. With a sigh of relief, Finn scrambled up from the floor and ran to Devon.

"I'm okay, baby," Devon promised as he wrapped an arm around Finn and pulled him under his shoulder. "But the shooter got away. He had an ATV waiting for him. Glenn got a shot off, but we're not sure if he caught him or not. Either way, he's in the wind now."

"I still think I saw the fucker flinch," Maddox said as he moved to help Sam get Marcel up off the floor. "Glenn never misses. I'd put money on the fact that whoever that was, he was hurt."

Finn looked up at Devon. "Do you think it was Silas?"

Devon sighed and nodded. "Yeah, I do."

"Damn, he really wants to see me six feet under, huh?"

"Nah," Sam said, "the angle was all wrong. He wasn't aiming at you, Finn."

The way Devon looked away made Finn nervous. He turned to the layout in the dining room and tried to picture where everyone had been when the shot came through the window. He walked over to where Marcel had been standing and it hit him. With a gasp, he spun around.

"Finn," Devon said holding his hand out as if he were calming a wild animal. And there was probably something in Finn's eyes that looked more than a little bit wild.

"He was aiming at you." Finn's voice was barely above a whisper. "If Marcel hadn't stood up and taken that bullet, it would have hit you. He could have killed you."

Devon stepped toward him, his face filled with concern, but Finn stepped back. He was undeserving of his concern. Because of Finn, Devon was in his fucking father's sites, and one of his best friends in the entire world had been shot! This had to end. This could not be allowed to continue. Silas had to be stopped and if he couldn't be stopped then he had to be given whatever he wanted to ensure the safety of the people in this house.

"Finn!" Devon's roar penetrated Finn's mind and he blinked as his surroundings came back into focus. All the men in the room were staring at him, their faces masks of concern. Well, all except for Devon. He looked angry. No, pissed would be a more apt description. He looked pissed off and apparently it was at Finn.

"What?"

Devon stared into his eyes for a moment and Finn had the feeling he could see all the way to his soul. Whatever he saw there was apparently not good because he growled, then leaned down, gently placing his shoulder in Finn's stomach and lifted him up and onto his shoulder.

"Devon! What the fuck? You can't keep throwing me over your goddamn shoulder like this." Finn grabbed onto his hips, his world tilting on its axis.

Devon smacked his ass when he wriggled. "Shut the hell up, Finn. You think I don't know what's going through your head?"

"You're not a fucking psychic, Devon, and this caveman display is not appreciated!"

"Like hell it's not. I can feel just how appreciative you are of the move, baby." Finn grimaced at Devon's words and cast his eyes around the room. All the men looked amused, and fortunately his mother and brother had gone back upstairs. "Reaper's taking the first watch, someone trade out with him in three hours. I'll be back down by then and we can put some plans into action. I want this place fucking locked down tight. Sam! Get Marcel fixed up and then I want you on the roof. I want to know where the pinch points are. I want a map and plan in place before nightfall!"

Finn held on tight as Devon ran up the stairs, making sure to hold Finn tightly to his shoulder so that Finn didn't bounce around too much. Finn was struggling to keep his equilibrium and when Devon reached his room and threw Finn down on the bed, his stomach turned. Once he was still on the bed, he lay there for a moment and breathed through nausea. When his gaze caught the arrogant look in Devon's eyes, he contemplated throwing up on his bed just for shits and giggles.

"I am so fucking mad at you," Devon's voice was low and fairly vibrated with emotion.

Finn sat up, leaning back on his elbows. "I'm the one who was just carted around like a damn bag of potatoes. If any one of us has the right to be pissed, it's me."

"Then tell me you weren't contemplating giving yourself up like some goddamn sacrificial lamb. Tell me you weren't thinking that if you were to simply go to Silas and let him hurt you, or worse kill you, in some kind of effort to save the lives of the people in this house. If you can tell me that, Finn, then I will drop to my knees and apologize profusely for manhandling you like that." Finn's face flooded with heat as Devon almost word for word reiterated the thoughts that had floated through his mind downstairs. "Fuck, Finn! What do you think you going to Silas would achieve, huh? You think he'll suddenly forget about your mom? Or Nate?"

"He might!" Finn yelled as he leaped from the bed. If he and Devon were going to shout at each other, Finn was going to do it on his feet. He was already a few good inches shorter than Devon, sitting on the bed made it much worse. "He's always hated me, Dev. If he gets the opportunity to smack me around, that usually calms him down for a while and he forgets about Mom and Nate."

"And if he kills you? What then?"

"Then finally, the law would have to do something about it. He goes to prison for a fucking long time, and Mom and Nate get to live a safer life, somewhere else."

"And me? What about me, Finn? Would I just go on living somewhere else? Take another lover and just move on?"

The thought of Devon with another man ripped Finn to shreds. "Yes."

"Firstly, do you honestly think I will let you go do your sacrificial lamb thing? Hell no. I will tie you to this bed for as long as it takes to eliminate Silas my way, and I will enjoy every fucking minute of having you naked and spread out for my pleasure whenever the hell I want to take it." Finn swallowed as his body responded to the dominance in Devon's tone, but also the bondage scene he'd just described. "You are not dealing with Silas alone anymore. You are *mine*. You have always been mine and now that I have you back, I will stand in front of you whenever there is a threat to you because that's the kind of man I am."

"He could have killed you!"

"Yeah, he could have, but I am one tough son of a bitch to kill. Bigger and badder assholes who were a whole shitload more skilled than him have tried and failed."

Finn groaned and face palmed his hand. "Jesus, Dev, hearing that my father was not the first person to take a shot at you is not helping."

Dev grinned and Finn's heart turned over. "Hell, he probably won't be the last. We might be out of the Marines but there are organizations that know who we are and what we can do. Once we are up and running, they'll come calling."

Finn groaned and looked up at the ceiling. "What the hell have I gotten myself into?"

Devon was suddenly standing right in front of him, pressing up against him and making Finn's breath catch. "You've gotten yourself into a committed and loving relationship with the love of your life." Devon's wink had Finn grinning, he couldn't deny that. "He just happens to be a dominant former Marine, slightly bossy, a leader of a group of exceptional men who know how to take care of themselves and the world at large, and all of whom have a special set of skills that make them extremely sought after by governments, military and security specialists around the world." Devon's joking demeanor slipped away and his expression became serious. "He also happens to be in love with you."

Finn smiled up at his man, immediately wanting to ease the vulnerability he saw in Devon's eyes. "Well, that works for me because I happen to be in love with you, too." Finn sighed and leaned in to press a kiss to Devon's jaw. "I'm sorry, love, I won't think those thoughts again. I will simply wait until my dominant former Marine, who is *hugely* bossy, and leader of a great group of men who will protect me, Mom and Nate, saves me from my asshole dad. Then, I will make a home here with you."

Devon sighed and wrapped his arms around Finn, squeezing him tight to his broad chest. "Well, thank Christ for that. Sometimes, I am just not sure what to do with you. One minute I want to throttle you for being so damn self-sacrificing, and then I want to fuck you blind for the same damn reason."

Finn pushed back so he could look into Devon's eyes. "Do I get a vote? Because out of the two, I would definitely go for the fucking option. As in now."

Chapter Seven

"Then it's unanimous," Devon said, growling as he reached back, and gripped the back of his shirt and pulled it over his head. "The fucking option it is."

Finn laughed as Devon reached out and quickly divested him of his shirt, but when Devon reached for the buttons on his own jeans, Finn's hands shot out to stop him. "Wait, I think I would like to do those particular honors."

Devon's heart started to pound like a jackhammer when Finn dropped to his knees in front of him. *Sweet Jesus!* Was there a more perfect view than the sight of the man you loved on his knees before you? Devon highly doubted it. The muscles in Devon's stomach tensed at the touch of Finn's finger as he released the buttons on Devon's jeans. His breath hissed out almost in relief when the pressure on his engorged cock eased as Finn spread the opening of his jeans, allowing his cock to emerge from the opening.

Finn sighed, and gently tugged Devon's jeans down to his knees. "Have I ever told you that your cock is truly beautiful?"

Devon chuckled then groaned when Finn lifted his hand to cup his balls. "*Sweet Jesus!* Ah, no, I don't think you have, and trust me, I would have remembered that."

Finn laughed softly and he was so close to him, his warm breath washed over Devon's cock, making him shiver. "Well, it's true. It is the perfect length." Devon gritted his teeth as Finn stroked him from root to tip, rolling his hand around the tip. "The width fills me so damn good, Dev, it should be illegal." Finn wrapped his fingers around him, gripping tight, just how he liked it.

"But the thing I love most about your cock, that I crave almost every day, is the taste." Devon groaned as Finn took him deep into his mouth.

Finn used his tongue around the head of his cock, adding a slight tug of suction before taking him to the back of his throat. When Finn swallowed against him, Devon had to lock his knees against the sensual onslaught. Devon growled continuously as Finn fell into a rhythm designed to drive him to the edge of sanity. Not wanting it to end, Devon tried to fight off his approaching orgasm. But when it became clear that only a few more moments in the hot wet cavern of his lover's mouth and he would lose the ability to withhold his release, he reached down, and gently pulled Finn off him.

"Hey!" Finn frowned up at him, an adorable pout on his face. "I was enjoying that!"

Despite the fact his breath was coming in labored gasps, Devon grinned. "Baby, I can assure you that I was too, but I'll be damned if I come before I feel the tight grip of your ass around my dick." The hungry look Finn gave him was almost his undoing.

He lifted Finn to his feet, cupped his face and slammed his mouth against his. When Finn moaned, Devon swept in, licking into his mouth and taking the kiss deeper. Over and over he swept his tongue inside Finn's mouth, tangling his tongue with Finn's and reveling in the unique flavor. When he felt Finn's fingers clench against his biceps, and his body simply melted into him, Devon growled, loving the way Finn would simply give himself over.

Devon pulled back from the kiss and slid his hands down Finn's torso. When he reached the waistband of his jeans, he held still, waiting for Finn to open his eyes. When they fluttered open a few moments later, Devon stared into the brilliant green, reveling in the slightly dazed look in his eyes. "The way you look at me sometimes, cuts me off at the knees." Devon's voice was a harsh whisper as his hands quickly unbuttoned Finn's jeans, releasing his hard cock, and quickly wrapped his hand around him.

"Oh shit," Finn groaned, his head falling back as Devon stroked his hand along the hard length loving the feel of him in his hand.

"I cannot tell you how many damn times I've jacked off to the thought of your dick," Devon said as he leaned in and placed his forehead against Finn's. "One day soon, I am simply going to have you stand before me, all naked and hot, and I'm going to take my own dick in my hand, and show you what just the sight of it does to me." Finn's eyes widened at first in shock then filled with a hungry need that told Devon he was more than happy with the idea. "But for now, baby, I need you to go over to the dressing table, place your hands on the top, and spread your legs for me."

Finn took a deep breath and then nodded, stepping out of his jeans as he followed Devon's instructions to the letter. The dressing table was the only piece of furniture in the room that belonged to Devon. It was huge, made of solid oak, and had a large mirror on the top. He had found the piece at a furniture shop in El Paso a few years ago when he had been called to Fort Bliss to deliver some training. As soon as he saw the solid piece of furniture, he had imagined the very scene he was about to play out.

Devon must have been standing there a little too long because Finn looked over his shoulder, a wicked grin on his face, and rocked his hips side to side. "What's a guy got to do to get some attention around here?"

Devon grinned back and walked slowly in Finn's direction. He wrapped his hand around his dick and stroked it slowly, seeing how Finn's eyes fell to watch in the mirror's reflection, and the flush of arousal swept up across his chest. "Nothing more than what you're doing."

Dev stepped up behind Finn and pressed forward so that his chest lay gently over his back. Looking into the mirror, he held Finn's gaze as he reached around him, slid open the top drawer and withdrew a bottle of lubricant. "When I bought this dressing table, you were very much on my mind. I have imagined the image of you standing in front of me, your gaze locked to mine in the mirror as I take you from behind, a thousand times over the years. But my imagination was never fucking good enough."

Devon pressed a kiss to Finn's shoulder then pushed upright. With hands that shook, he opened the bottle, covered himself and used some on Finn's ass, loving that he groaned in delight at the feeling of Devon running his fingers over, then around, and finally inside the ring of muscle that guarded his back entrance.

Stepping close, Devon pushed gently on Finn's back, encouraging him to arch. He placed the head of his dick against Finn then pushed slightly inside him. When he felt Finn relax, and the head of Devon's cock slipped inside, Devon raised his eyes and locked his gaze to Finn's. His gaze never wavered as he slowly rocked his hips forward, pushing himself inch by inch into his lover. When he finally bottomed out, he held still for a moment. He lost his breath as Finn's expression became one of total rapture as Devon slowly withdrew.

"You love the feel of my cock sliding in and out of your ass, don't you?" Devon asked as he worked himself in and out, his gaze shifting from watching his lover's face, to watching his own cock sliding in and out of his ass.

Finn began to pant. "You know I do, Dev. God, I

fucking love the feel of you fucking me. But lover, I need you to take me hard. I need to feel how desperate you are for me." Dev growled as he put one hand on Finn's hip and the other gripped his shoulder and then he began to move. Pounding into Finn, and giving him everything he had asked for.

Dev couldn't decide which view was best, watching himself shuttle in and out of Finn's ass or the look on Finn's face as his pleasure built within him. When Finn suddenly clenched around him, it threw him into his orgasm without warning. "Fuck, Finn!" he roared as he jerked his hips hard against him, once, twice, three times, as he emptied himself inside his lover.

He felt Finn shudder beneath him but knew he hadn't taken Finn with him. He was close. Probably hovering on the edge of his own orgasm, but holding himself strong, making sure he took everything Devon had to give him. Dev leaned over as the last waves of his release had him shuddering, and gripped Finn's cock in his hand.

"Agh!" Finn cried out as Devon began to stroke him.

When Finn's eyes started to close, Devon barked, "Don't you close your eyes, Finn. I want to watch you as you come. For. Me!" He matched his movement with his words, and Finn's mouth opened on a silent scream as he came hard into Devon's hand. The clench of Finn's ass around Devon's already sensitive cock had him growling and thrusting into Finn again as another wave of pleasure was pulled from him. He kept his eyes on Finn's in the glass of the mirror until the grip of Finn's orgasm released him and he slumped forward.

As the two of them stood there on shaking legs, desperately dragging air into their lungs, Devon whispered the words he had been holding in for years. "I love you, Finn McGregor."

Finn's smile lit the darkest ruins of Devon's soul, blackened by war and the atrocities he had seen. "I love you too, Devon Roberts." But it was his words, those words of love, that had the final untethered pieces of himself finally settle within. Devon was finally complete.

****

"What did your friend at the state's attorney's office say about Silas?" Devon asked Marcel who was sitting up against the headboard in his bedroom, tapping away on his laptop. It was almost midnight and they were heading off to bed for the night but wanted to check in with the injured man before they did. After they'd finally made it downstairs early that evening for dinner, Marcel had been sleeping off the medication Sam had slipped him during the procedure to remove the bullet in his shoulder.

"She reckons without real proof that it was, in fact, Silas who was here, there isn't much she can do." Marcel reached out his arm to close the lid of his laptop, but flinched when it must have aggravated his wound. "Pretty boy's sending the bullet to her in the morning. I can't believe that little shit slipped me a sedative with that shot of antibiotics."

Finn sat on the bed beside his leg and smacked him lightly on the thigh. "Oh, stop being such a baby. You were hell bent on going with Maddox to check on Silas, and we all knew you were going with that rather large rifle of yours, and that meant you were looking for more than a little reconnaissance. Besides, you were shot and you needed some rest."

Marcel made a rude sound and grimaced as he slouched back against his pillows.

Finn hoped they were able to prove that it was Silas who had pulled the trigger, for two specific reasons.

One, it would be yet another charge the bastard would face in court, and two, it would mean there wasn't any other bastard out there wanting to take shots at them.

There was a knock at the door, and when Marcel called for them to come in, Maddox walked in. Finn grinned at what he was wearing. He looked like he'd just stepped out of a GI Joe movie. He wore military wear that Finn had never seen before. It was all black, a belt that would give Batman's utility belt a run for its money with the gadgets and gizmos on it, Kevlar vest with his weapon slung over his back, and he wore a black knit cap and camouflage paint on his face.

"So here's where the party is," Maddox said with a grin as he came in and leaned against the far wall. "I saw Sam outside and just caught up with Reaper in the kitchen."

"What did you find out?" Devon asked and Finn frowned at him.

"Dev, you don't just jump in and start talking about how the mission or task or whatever the hell you Marine types call it went, you say something like you're glad he's home safe or something like that."

Devon flicked him a look and sighed before he turned back to Maddox who was grinning like an idiot. "Maddox, I am glad you are home safe. What did you find out?" Dev deadpanned. Finn rolled his eyes as Maddox and Marcel both laughed at what Dev obviously thought was the height of good wit. Goofy idiot.

Maddox fought his laughter back to a grin. "Shit, I love seeing you take orders, LT." He chuckled once again, but at the clearing of Devon's throat, and the raised eyebrow that anyone who knew Dev recognized meant he was waiting impatiently and he would only wait so long, he continued. "The house is a fucking mess. Anything and everything that could be destroyed has been. I sure as shit hope that your mom didn't leave anything of sentimental value in that house, Finn, because if she did, Silas has pretty much fucked it up beyond recognition."

Finn shook his head with a sad smile. "No, everything in that house, regardless of whether it was purchased with his money or hers, was something he wanted. The only things Mom wanted out of that house were Nate and me." Dev placed his hand on Finn's shoulder, offering support, and Finn reached up to pat his hand.

"The house is also littered with empty alcohol bottles." Maddox continued. "I would have to say that he has been drinking pretty much non-stop since we busted you guys outta that house."

Finn laughed, the sound hollow and without humor. "That's not surprising, Maddox, that's pretty much the state the man has been in my whole life."

"Was he there?" Devon asked and Finn turned to look at him. From the frown on his face, it was obvious he saw something Finn hadn't thought about yet.

"Nope," Maddox frowned, obviously trying to figure out what was bothering Devon as well. "There was no sign of him. The house was a pig sty as I said, and there were dishes and rotting food all over the kitchen countertops, but no sign of Silas."

Devon continued to frown and Finn could almost hear the wheels in his mind turning over. "Spit it out, Devon, the suspense is killing me."

"If he's been on a bender for as long as we think he might have been, then how in the hell was he able to make that damn shot? You know as well as I do, Maddox, that shot required a reasonable amount of skill. Come to think of it, Sam mentioned he was showing symptoms of severe alcoholism, and one of them was shaking hands. Even if he had been stone cold sober, his hands would have been shaking through withdrawal. There is no fucking way that asshole made that shot."

Finn knew his mouth was ajar, but he couldn't bring himself to shut it. There was some other homicidal asshole out there hell bent on killing one, or God, perhaps all of them? "I know my father hates me, that's a given. But I struggle to think of anyone else who could hate me enough to want to off me from the bushes with a great big fucking gun!"

"Whoever was shooting, wasn't aiming at you, Finn, remember?" Marcel reminded him and when Finn turned back to look at him, the man shrugged. "It is more likely that we would have enemies who would go to any lengths to kill us than you do, buddy."

Finn looked at the faces of all three men in the room. They were all nodding as if having someone wanting to kill you was simply par for the course of the life they had chosen to live. "So, let's just recap for a minute here and see what we have? No real proof as to who took that shot, and the person we believed it might have been wasn't physically able to, so that eliminates everyone so far. Oh, except those who could be connected to the people you have all fought against in your service for our country. Does that sound about right?"

Finn heard the hysteria in his own voice, but come on! This was sounding more and more like a goddamn HBO special.

Devon grinned and crossed his arms across his broad chest. "Yes, my love, that does sound about right. I'll contact my old CO and see if the General has anything to say or add to that summary, but to be honest, he would have called and let us know it there were anyone from our past missions states side."

With a sigh, Maddox pushed off from the wall he had been slouched against. "Well, we aren't going to be able to solve this little mystery tonight, and that contractor is due in tomorrow so I'm gonna hit the hay. I'll take the shift after yours, Dev." Then he left the room. It was nice to hear the other men call Devon by his name. But as Devon was quick to point out, once you were a Marine you were always a Marine and rank was often something that was never forgotten.

Devon nodded then turned and reached a hand out to Finn. "If I have to get up and go stand my ass out in the cold in a few hours, I want some time wrapped up in bed with you first. Come on, babe, let's go try not to make too much noise."

Finn laughed over the sound of Marcel's groan. "Give a single guy with nothing more than his left hand for comfort given that his more dominant right hand is out of commission for a while a break, huh guys?" Marcel said, complaining, but Finn saw the glint of happiness in his eyes. Sam had mentioned Finn was the only person Devon reached out to when their lives were in danger, so he figured Marcel knew what he meant to Dev and was happy for his friend.

Dev swept Finn back against his chest, and Finn felt his chuckle rumble through his body. "I'd feel sorry for you, *mon ami*, except for the fact that I've trained and traveled with you for the past six years and know you haven't exactly led the life of a monk."

Finn saw the light extinguish in Marcel's eyes, despite the fact his smile never wavered. "That is true. And now I think I might relive a couple of those moments in my life before I turn in."

After saying goodnight, they left the room, and Finn was quiet as they headed upstairs to their room. "You've gone quiet. What's up?" Devon asked as they stood at the end of their bed.

Finn sighed as he leaned in and rested his head against Devon's chest, wrapping his arms around his trim waist. "It's Marcel. He seems sad."

Devon scoffed, returning the hug. "That man had more lovers than any of the other guys on the team over the past six years. Don't let his *poor me* act fool you."

Finn frowned as he looked up at his amazing but apparently completely oblivious lover. "Dev, people think that being alone makes a person lonely. But I don't think that is necessarily the case. You can surround yourself with the wrong kind of people, or hell, even the wrong person for that matter, and be the loneliest damn person in the world. Marcel acts happy go lucky and like nothing in his life is out of place, but next time you're with him and he watches the way we are together, take a good look in his eyes. That man is lonely, and is longing for the right person to be with."

Devon was quiet for a moment then he sighed, pulling Finn back into his arms. "How could I not see that? In the six years we've been a part of the same team, and that entire year of damn officer training I undertook, how could I not see that one of my men was hurting? Then you come along, and in less than two weeks you see that he's in pain."

"Yeah, well, what can I say? I'm fucking amazing," Finn said with a smile as he snuggled against the warmth of Devon's chest.

"That you are, my love, that you are." Devon sounded happy.

Finn turned his head up, and Devon laid his mouth against Finn's. As always, as soon as Devon's mouth touched his, Finn's arousal skyrocketed, and in minutes, their world narrowed to just the two of them again. And that was exactly how Finn liked it.

Chapter Eight

Finn opened the front door and the smile of greeting slipped a fraction on his face.

"Hi! The name's Riley," the man standing on the porch said as he held out his hand. Finn was a little too shell-shocked to shake his hand. He was dressed in jeans and a blue denim shirt, sleeves rolled halfway up his muscular forearms, black Stetson pulled down low, and black work boots topped off the look. He was one of the hottest men Finn had ever seen in his life, and that probably had a lot to do with the fact he reminded Finn of Dev. Oh, Devon was definitely hotter, but this guy, boy howdy, he definitely came in a fine looking second.

The man's welcoming smile turned questioning as the silence obviously went on for too long. "Dude, this is getting awkward." Even his voice held the same rough timbre that Devon's did. Finn shook his head to clear it.

"Damn." Finn grimaced. "Sorry. Finn, my name is Finn. You said your name is Riley?" Finn finally took the man's hand and shook it. There was where the similarities ended. Devon's touch, no matter how innocent, always left Finn feeling aroused. With Riley, he felt nothing. "You must be the contractor with Marksmen Construction, Riley Marksmen, right? Sorry for zoning out, but you share a lot of physical similarities with my boyfriend and it was a little surprising."

Riley's smile slid even further and his eyes became guarded, and that look fired Finn's anger. "What, you have a problem with me having a boyfriend? I didn't get the you-think-I'm-hotter-than-Channing-Tatum-in-Magic-Mike vibe from you, so I'll ask you straight out, do you have a problem with working for gay men, Mr. Marksmen? Because, Cowboy if you do, you might as well go climb back in your truck and hightail it right back to where you came from."

Riley seemed to stand taller and he got this look on his face that had Finn fighting not to shift his gaze from his. "I think we got off on the wrong foot. I have no problem working for or with gay men. That would be a little hypocritical as I have enjoyed the pleasure of a man's body in my bed as much as I have a woman's. I assume just because you know my sexual preferences as I do yours, we aren't going to have any problems from here on in?"

Finn shook his head. "No, Sir."

"Good." Riley took a deep breath and seemed to shrug of that air of authority or bossiness, or whatever the hell it was, that had Finn acting strange and became the smiling man he had been when Finn had first opened the door. Before he'd opened his mouth and shoved his foot in. "So, yeah, I am Riley Marksmen and I'm here to see Devon Roberts."

"Finn, what the hell is taking you so long?" Devon asked as he came down the hallway and Finn stood for a moment, his head turning like he was watching a tennis match, looking between the two men. The similarities were even more obvious when they were standing in close proximity. "You must be Riley." Devon's eyes narrowed at the stranger and he held his hand out. When they shook hands, Finn could see the muscles in their forearms tense, and he got the feeling there was more than just a slight power play happening in front of him. And fuck him if it wasn't arousing.

It ended just as quickly as it had started. "Come on in. Two of my men are in the dining room anxious to see what plans you've drawn up."

Finn saw the shocked look on Riley's face and couldn't help laughing. "Despite our conversation from moments ago, Devon's not referring to a harem of men all willing and waiting for a moment of his time. He's referring to his sniper team. They are all partners in this little venture." Riley grinned and nodded and followed them down the hallway.

"What the hell was the conversation you had moments ago?" Devon asked as they entered the dining room. Reaper and Maddox stood up and shook hands with Riley, and they all took a seat around the table. Finn noticed Reaper and Maddox shared a look once they caught sight of Riley and knew they saw the resemblances between the two men as well.

"Just a slight misunderstanding between Finn and me, nothing major," Riley answered as he placed a large portfolio case that Finn hadn't even noticed he carried on the table. "Now, I think I've got something here that you guys are gonna love."

Finn sat back and watched as the four men then started talking about the plans for the training facility. From the detailed conversation Riley was able to have, it was obvious he knew a lot about the type of equipment they were going to need, and that made Finn believe he was just as trained as Devon and his team. After about an hour of talking through the plans and only having to make a couple of adjustments to the outbuilding plans Riley had shown them, they had a plan in place and a deal on the table.

Riley had the team and the expertise to deliver what they needed, and Finn nearly fell out of his chair at the price Riley was quoting. It was more money than Finn had even considered it would cost. He shot a quick glance at Devon and relaxed when he didn't seem phased. "That's around what we thought it would cost, especially with the additional structural and proofing required to the outbuildings. There are a couple of other guys we need to talk your plans through, but we'll have a decision for you by tomorrow night."

"So Riley," Maddox asked as he handed some of Riley's plans back to him, "when and where did you serve?"

Riley grinned. "I got out just over seven years ago and I served with the Seals."

Devon shook his head. "Aw, now see? Now you've gone and blown it. No self-respecting jarhead is going to give his hard earned money to a damn frog man."

Riley laughed as he stood up from the table. "Then you won't get the quality you seem hell bent on getting."

They all laughed, shook hands and Devon walked Riley out. As soon as the two of them had left the room, Finn spun around to Maddox and Reaper. "Oh, my God! Their resemblance is uncanny, right?"

Maddox and Reaper both frowned in confusion and looked at each other before looking back at Finn. "What are you talking about, Finn?"

"What do you mean, what am I talking about?" Finn's voice was about an octave higher than normal. "Don't tell me you couldn't see the resemblance between those two? They were so fucking obvious!" When the two men just looked at him blankly, Finn growled in frustration. "Where's pretty boy when you need him, he would have seen it. If you weren't shocked at their similarities, then what the hell was with that look that passed between the two of you when he walked into the room?"

"He had a side arm," Maddox said, like it was painfully obvious to all. "I wanted to make sure Glenn had seen it too."

"Which," Glenn added as he pulled his Sig out

from beneath the table, reinstated the safety and place it back into the shoulder holster he wore beneath his shirt, "I had and prepared for it. Plus, the dude is walking hotness on legs, am I right?"

Maddox sighed. "Yes, he is, but that wouldn't have stopped you from putting a bullet in his heart if he'd made a move."

"Oh, not in the slightest," Glenn said with a grin.

Finn stared incredulously between the two, torn between the need to slam their heads together for being oblivious, and laughing out loud. Devon walked back in and Finn turned to him. "Did he remind you of anyone, Dev?"

Dev frowned and thought for a moment. "Not really. Why?"

Finn's head fell back with an exasperated groan. "How the hell you can all be fucking snipers and able to take amazing shots from like, a bajillion miles away, and not see something painfully obvious when the two of them are standing right in fucking front of you is simply astounding." Finn stomped out of the room heading for Nate's room. He felt the need for some insightful conversation and gratuitous violence, so figured a game of Halo with his little brother was just the ticket.

****

Dev fought the urge to throw his phone against the wall. Although hearing from his CO that there were no threats he knew of to him or his team in the states was good news, it frustrated the hell out of him that they were still no closer to identifying the shooter. And that meant everyone here was still in danger, which just pissed him off.

"Dev," Marcel's voice broke through his frustration and he turned toward the door to the dining room which they had turned into their office of sorts until they were able to refit the downstairs formal living room into a proper office. The look on Marcel's face had Dev's internal threat gauge jumping to DEFCON three. When he walked into the room, with Finn and Rose right behind him, that level went all the way to DEFCON one. Finn walked over to stand with Dev, and he pulled Finn up against him.

"I've just had a call from Jessie." That was the name of the state's attorney who had been looking to press charges against Silas and his deputy. "They moved in on Silas's place today to take him into custody, and found him hanging from one of the struts in the roof of the garage."

Finn shuddered against him and Devon pulled him in tighter. He felt a mix of both joy and frustration at the news. He was more than happy the fucker was gone from this earth, but he wished he'd been held responsible for his actions first.

"Well," Rose's voice shook, "I can't say that I'm too upset by that news, but I will admit to being shocked. I wouldn't have thought the spineless coward had it in him to take his own life."

Marcel shook his head, his eyes wary. "He didn't kill himself, Rose. Oh, someone sure as hell tried to make it look like he'd taken his own life, but he hadn't. The scene examiner found signs of petechial hemorrhaging which can be, but is not solely found in hangings. Due to that and other markings on the body, their best guess is that he was strangled before he was hung."

The room fell into silence as they each processed that information. Dev felt Finn sigh and sag against him. "Well, as much as I would have liked to, I didn't do it." Dev laughed softly and moved so that he stood behind Finn and could wrap both arms around him.

"Finn, my darling," Rose said dryly as she stood up from the couch. "I am pretty sure that the same could be said by anyone in this house. Now, I am going to go upstairs and tell my baby that the monster that haunts his dreams at night is dead." Rose smiled sadly as she looked at Finn. "How I wish you both could have had the father that you deserved."

Finn pulled away and went to his mom, wrapping an arm around her. "I don't miss not having a real dad, Ma, because I had you. I'll come with you. I think Nate should hear it from the both of us."

Once they had left the room, Devon nodded at Marcel who opened the door and whistled a loud and shrill sound. Less than a minute later, Sam and Maddox walked into the room, carrying the radio that would connect them to Reaper at the same time. Dev let his mind trawl through the facts in his head as Marcel updated the rest of the team.

"So, who do you think offed the douchebag?" Sam asked the million-dollar question.

Dev began to pace, something he often did when he was trying to put the pieces of a puzzle together. "It has to be the same guy, right? I find it hard to believe that someone from our past would come here with a bone to pick with us, and at the same time someone with a beef against Silas rolls into town, too."

"Could it be that contractor?" Maddox asked and it was a fair question. He was a new variable in all of this.

"Nah." Reaper's voice came over the radio. "I ran that dude through every database I could find. He's clean as a whistle. And as far as I can tell, there is no connection between him and Silas whatsoever. He'd have no beef with him or us for that matter."

Someone who would have an issue with Silas and

them. Dev stopped pacing as the pieces fell together, and it all became clear. He looked up at his team.

"Aww, damn," Marcel drawled and rubbed his hands together, "I love it when LT gets that look in his eye. It means he's got the target, locked and loaded and we get to go hunting!"

Chapter Nine

Finn sighed as he reached for the TV remote and switched it off. He was nervous and antsy, and neither were feelings he overly enjoyed. The house was too damn quiet and it was driving him crazy! He got up and went to the kitchen to make a cup of coffee. His mother and Nate were upstairs watching TV with Reaper. It turned out Reaper and Nate shared a love of old horror films, and Finn couldn't bring himself to watch Nightmare on Elm Street for the millionth time. Devon, Marcel, and Maddox had gone out, all dressed in their GI Joe blackout gear, and Finn had no idea where they had gone to.

"We're just following a hunch, babe," Devon had told him just before they left thirty minutes ago. "We won't be too long, promise. We'll be back in less than an hour." Finn knew they were going to see someone they believed was the shooter, and no doubt the person responsible for his father's death. Dev might think he was just following a hunch, but from the look on his face, Devon was pretty sure they were looking in the right direction.

Sam was the only one left at the farm, and he was out in something the snipers called tree cancer. It was this hidey-hole thing that attached up a tree, and from the ground, it looked like a shrub or 'tumor' growing from the side of it. There were heaps of shrub-like growths on the cottonwoods that surrounded the homestead, so when Devon tried to get him to spot it, Finn had found it almost impossible to locate.

"Hey Finn, are you there?" Sam's voice sounded over the radio on the table behind him.

Finn grabbed it. "Hey, yeah I'm here, what's up?"

"Nothing, just seems a little quiet is all."

Finn snorted. "Tell me about it! This house is huge and I'm pretty damn sure Dev's grandmother's in here somewhere, making things move and creak around me."

"From what I've heard about that woman, I wouldn't put it past her."

"I'm making a cup of coffee. You want me to bring you out some?"

"More than anything in the world, but no. I've only got another hour and a half then Maddox gets to sleep up this damn tree."

"Well, I'll make sure there is some for when you come in."

"That would be awesome, thanks, Finn."

"Anything for you, pretty boy."

There was a short delay, then, "I really am going to have to shoot you, Finn. To hell with Devon's wrath."

Finn grinned as he popped the radio back on the table and started the coffee maker. While the aroma of the elixir of life that was coffee began to permeate through the kitchen, he poked his head into the pantry, looking for something to snack on while he waited, but stopped when a high pitched whistle sounded from somewhere outside.

Boom!

Finn flinched at the sound and the room shook. He spun toward the kitchen window and looked out into the night in horror. A couple of the trees closest to the driveway had just exploded. "Oh, fuck, Sam!" Heart pounding hard, he ran for the radio on the counter. "Sam! Sam! Are you there?" Finn waited, hoping and praying Sam's voice would come back over the radio, telling him everything was okay. But there was nothing but silence.

"Oh, shit!" Finn turned and sprinted for the living

room. He knew Reaper would be putting his mom and Nate somewhere safe. He grabbed Sam's medical kit, not knowing what the hell he was going to do with it, but determined to do everything he could to save his friend. Lugging the heavy thing into the hallway, he hurried as fast as he could toward the front door. Cursing as he scrambled to get the two locks on the door disengaged, after what seemed like hours but was probably only seconds, he breathed a sigh of relief when the locks disengaged. He turned the handle and opened the door, and his entire body filled with fear as he stared into the barrel of a wicked looking handgun.

****

Dev gripped the steering wheel tight, his foot almost flat to the floor as he pushed his truck to the limit. When they arrived at Deputy Ford's house, Devon had been about eighty percent sure he was correct. The only other man in Redwood Falls who could possibly have a beef with both Finn and Devon, was Harold Ford, Silas's deputy. He was also suspended with no pay, and would have reason to hate Finn and his family for bringing attention to Silas's behavior.

When they arrived at his house, they found the place empty. Ford was nowhere to be found and the boys had the opportunity to do some illegal looking around. He sent Maddox to the barn in the back yard and he and Marcel swept the house. What they found had turned Devon's ice cold. There were photographs of his entire team, Finn, Rose, and Nate, all over one of the walls in the study. There were red circles around Finn, Rose, and Marcel. The day Marcel took that bullet he hadn't taken it for him. Devon was pretty sure Marcel had definitely been the target. Marcel had been the one to call in the States Attorney after all.

"Dev," Maddox called as he came running back

into the house. Dev ran out to meet him. "I found a whole shit load of twenty-two caliber ammo in a locked gun case in the barn." The Colt M4 fired those rounds, so the evidence was just piling up against old Harold. "Dev, he also has a box of single stage HEAT warheads."

Everything within Dev froze. "What the hell is he doing with High Explosive Anti-Tank warheads?" The color drained from Dev's face. "Fucker's got an RPG! Call Sam!" Dev sprinted out of the house, running for the truck they had left further up the drive, hidden in the trees. He heard Marcel calling Sam on the radio but couldn't get an answer.

Now, here they were, only about a mile out from the house, and Dev could see an orange glow in the darkness up ahead. He refused to think he was too late and that Finn was hurt or worse. He was going to get there in time, then he was going to rip Ford's spine out through his throat and make him eat it.

****

Finn stumbled back, dropping the medical kit on the floor. His father's deputy, Harold Ford, walked in the door, leveling his handgun at Finn's head. For one moment, a brief fleeting moment, Finn thought about running but then almost immediately dismissed it. He was neither as fast as Usain Bolt nor bulletproof. Harold closed the front door and waved his weapon toward the living room. Finn walked backward, keeping his hands out at his sides.

"All of this is your fault, you little prick," Harold snarled at him. He directed Finn over so that he was in the center of the room, and Ford stood beside the large window, with his back to the wall.

"After you got your father suspended, and those federal assholes came looking into things here, they found a few things on me that means I'm either going to jail for a very long time, or I'm on the run. For the rest of my fucking life! If you had just kept your mouth shut and had simply been the punching bag your father needed for a few more months, I would have been set for life. But no. You open your mouth to your little fuck buddy and his friend sends the fucking states attorney after us.

"You fucked up my life, Finn! So I've decided I am gonna take yours in payment. I still have money they haven't found, access to assets they haven't frozen yet, and once I'm done killing you, I'm gone. I had thought about simply leaving you alone and running, but I found out something about myself I never knew. I am really fucking vindictive. So, I'm gonna kill you first."

Finn's mind whirled with thoughts of rescue. Reaper was upstairs, but Finn didn't think he would leave his mom and Nate alone. His biggest hope was Devon getting back in time, so he figured stalling tactics would be best. "You really are quite insane, aren't you?" Mentally, Finn rolled his eyes at himself. He was fairly certain that antagonizing the crazed gun-wielding maniac was not exactly textbook stalling tactics.

Ford grinned and nodded. "You know, you're not the first person to say that to me. I had applied for the Sniper training school in the military and failed the psych test. Apparently, it came back that I was a baseline psychotic with just enough narcissism in me to make me dangerous. So I was discharged. Your father hired me despite the fact I had blatantly lied and fabricated my resume. All he needed was someone who would turn a blind eye to his drinking and penchant for domestic violence and he found that in me."

Finn caught movement in the darkness out the window, but ignored it, not wanting to bring it to Ford's attention. "Okay, so I get why you want to kill me, but why did you off my old man? Don't get me wrong, you did me and the world a favor, but I am curious."

"He grew a fucking conscience! Can you believe that?" Ford asked incredulously. "I went to his house to try and get his help with killing you, and he starts fucking lamenting about his life and the fact that he had lost his wife. The same woman the bastard had beaten on more than one occasion. He started rambling on about how to get the bitch back, and you know what he came up with?" Finn shook his head as the shadow outside the window drew closer. "Coming clean with the feds, and effectively throwing me under the proverbial bus at the same damn time, can you believe that? And he actually told me that while I was sitting with him in the lounge last night trying not to gag at the stench in that house.

"Before I knew it, I had my hands around his throat and he was turning blue. I have to tell you, Finn, it felt really fucking good killing him with my own hands. I think it is something I am truly going to take a liking to." Harold shook his head as he raised his weapon and aimed it at Finn. "It really is a shame that we are under a time constraint here. I would have loved the opportunity to take you out with my bare hands too. Kind of as a last homage to your father, and would almost be poetic, don't you think? Anyway, the time has come. You might want to think happy thoughts, Finn. Maybe God will set it up so that's what heaven is for you."

Finn's thoughts immediately flew to Devon. In that moment, time stood still, Finn's life flashed before his eyes. But it wasn't the life he had led up until this point, it was the future he wanted more than anything. The one that saw him living and loving with Devon for the rest of their lives. Growing old here on Cottonwood Farm together, and watching their children and grandchildren grow and prosper under their love and guidance.

It was a future Ford was about to erase with one simple squeeze of the trigger. And just as Finn was mentally saying goodbye to that future, something came crashing through the large glass window, seconds before the door to the kitchen slammed open and the room came alive in a hail of bullets.

****

The silence of the ambulance as it left the property foretold of the fate of the person within it. There was no reason to go charging out onto the highway with lights flashing and sirens wailing. No amount of speed would help the man on the stretcher inside. He had been alive when Devon ran into the now shot to hell living room, and Devon had leaned down to look into his eyes as he died. He had been shot in the chest as well as in the neck, and from the speed with which he bled out, Devon knew the bullet had nicked his carotid.

He simply couldn't bring himself to care. Harold Ford was a crazy murdering son of a bitch, and as far as Devon was concerned, he was right where he should be. Burning in hell. Sighing, he turned back to the house and saw Marcel talking with the state trooper who they had called. But then Finn stepped out onto the porch, and Dev's world narrowed. Taking the steps two at a time, he was standing in front of him in moments and some of the tension within him eased as he pulled Finn into his arms.

"Mom finally got Nate off to sleep," Finn murmured as he rubbed his face against Dev's chest.

"That's good." Dev kept his arm around Finn as he led him inside and into the dining room, walking past the carnage that was left behind in the living room. Dev noticed that Finn purposely turned his head away from the blood stained carpet, and he made a mental note to check with the trooper whether it would be okay to rip it up. The two walked into the dining room, and Dev couldn't help but smile at the conversation taking place.

"The guy had a fucking RPG. He used an RPG to blow a tree to kingdom come, the same fucking tree I happened to be sitting in, minding my own damn business. Who the hell does that?" Sam complained loudly as Reaper finished wrapping his left bicep where he had been creased by a bullet. The wound above his eye that had bled like a bitch had already been sewn up and Sam pressed an ice pack over it to ward off the swelling.

"Need I remind you that tonight was the second time someone has shot an RPG at you in the last four months?" Maddox said dryly from where he sat sewing closed the nasty looking gash across the back of the arm of the other wounded man in the room.

"Jesus, Sam," Riley shook his head with a laugh, "remind me not to hang out with you too much. Especially if people are going to insist on shooting fucking rocket-propelled grenades at you on a semi-regular basis."

Riley had turned up out of nowhere. Dev hadn't called him that day with a decision so he'd decided to come and see what the happening was, and turned up just as the RPG was launched from the front porch. When he ran onto the property, he came across Sam, who had rolled out of the hide as soon as he'd heard the high pitched whistle of the rocket being launched and hauled ass as soon as his feet hit the ground. The two of them came up with the plan to save Finn, and it involved Riley throwing himself through the window as a distraction and Sam coming in from the kitchen, firing. Crude, but damn effective.

"Riley," Dev spoke and the room fell into silence. "I can't thank you enough for what you did here tonight. You saved one of my closest friends and the person I value above anyone else in the world." Riley shrugged as if it weren't a big deal, and if Dev wasn't mistaken, there was the slight flush of embarrassment on his cheeks. "You have the contract. Even before tonight, you were the right man for the job."

Riley nodded then grinned. "Thanks, Dev. And you never know, this frogman might be able to teach you jarheads a few tricks or two."

When Marcel walked into the room, Riley's intense gaze turned to him. Marcel then did something Devon had never ever seen the man do. He fidgeted. Devon thought that perhaps Riley made Marcel nervous, something else no one had ever done before. Finn's observation that perhaps Marcel was looking for something special came to mind, and he figured perhaps it was closer than he knew.

"Jessie just called." Dev's eyes narrowed as Riley's eyes seemed to flare with an emotion that looked suspiciously like jealousy. "Apparently, Harold was siphoning money off the county through the department that he was using to help fund an expensive gambling habit he'd acquired over recent years. The feds figure he'd taken close to four and a half million in the last five years."

That seemed to fit with what Finn had told them about his conversation with Ford in the moments before the bullets started flying around. When Devon had taken a good look at the room, it had been nothing short of a damn miracle that Finn had escaped unscathed. Devon's need to be alone with Finn exploded within him until it was impossible to ignore. When he looked down at Finn's face, he saw the exact same need in his eyes. Grabbing his hand, they said their goodnights and climbed the stairs to their room, and with each step they took, Devon's need grew until it consumed him, and there was nothing he could do but give in.

Chapter Ten

Finn groaned as Devon's mouth slammed into his and he was backed up against the rear of the door as soon as it closed. He could taste the familiar addicting flavor that was all Devon, but it was enhanced by the need that consumed them both. Finn had thought his time was up on more than one occasion tonight, but by some freaking miracle, he had survived. Despite the death he had seen tonight, he longed to feel alive, and nothing made him feel more alive than being loved by Devon.

Finn reached up and wrapped his arms around Devon's neck, shoving his hands into Dev's hair, and grinding his lower body against him. Dev growled against his mouth and deepened the kiss and rolled his hips in unison with Finn's, building the heat between them.

"Fuck, Finn," Dev growled as he slid his mouth down Finn's neck, making him arch away to give him better access, "when I saw that fucking fire from the road, and then heard the gunfire when we pulled up outside, I thought I might be too late. I don't know what I would have done if you'd been hurt." Dev stopped the sensual assault on the sensitive skin at the side of Finn's neck and simply buried his face against him.

Finn wrapped his arms around Dev and held him close as he shuddered, the memories too damn fresh for both of them. "You weren't too late, Dev. Thanks to Riley and Sam, I'm fine. I'm standing right here in front of you, in your arms, waiting for you to make me feel alive, like only you can."

Dev pulled back to look him in the eye and Finn shivered at the feral heat that shimmered in his eyes. "You better fucking believe I'm the only one who can make you feel alive." Devon reached down and pulled

Finn's shirt out of his jeans, pulling it up and over his head in one swift move. Finn's jeans, socks, and sneakers followed quickly until he stood before Dev naked.

"Look at you," Dev whispered, his voice filled with awe. "You are so fucking hot, and you are so fucking mine!" Devon picked him up, and Finn wrapped his legs around him as he swung around and walked over to the bed. "I am going to take you into my mouth and not let go until you come for me, my love." Finn groaned at the thought of being buried to the hilt in Devon's mouth. "After I've taken all you have to give, and I've swallowed every single fucking drop you have, I'm going to lay you on your back in the middle of the bed, bury my rock hard dick as far in your ass as I can, and then I am going to fuck you until the only thing you can feel, the only thing you can focus on, is me."

Finn's breath came in short bursts and his heart was beating so damn hard he wondered if it might actually beat out of his chest. "That sounds fantastic, lover, but to be fair, you are always the only thing I can focus on." Devon's grin was swift but cocky. He nudged Finn's knees and Finn dropped his legs and Devon lowered his feet to the floor, then he urged Finn to sit down on the end of the bed before Dev knelt at his feet.

Finn's mouth completely dried as Devon gently pushed him down so that he was leaning back on his elbow's watching Dev's every move. Dev's hands slowly stroked down Finn's chest and over his stomach, and his gaze was locked to his own hands. When his hands drifted to the sides, to rest on the top of each of Finn's thighs, Devon's gaze moved to Finn's now leaking cock and stayed there.

"There is no bigger turn on in the world," Dev murmured as his hands tightened on Finn's thighs, "than the sight of your cock, dripping cum, hot, hard and ready for me." Then Dev leaned over and swiped his tongue across the head of Finn's dick, making him jolt. "Fuck, you taste so damn good." Then Dev simply swallowed him whole. He took him all the way to the base, and Finn cried out at the feel of being held in his throat. He groaned when Dev swallowed reflexively against him.

"Oh, God!" Finn cried out as Dev began to bob his head up and down his cock, swirling his tongue over and around the sensitive vein that ran the whole length of him. "Dev! Sweet Jesus, mother of God, that feels so fantastic. Shit!" When Dev reached up a hand to roll Finn's balls in the palm of his hand, Finn's arms gave out and he collapsed against the bed. When Dev used his own saliva and the pre-cum that leaked continuously from Finn's cock to lubricate his ass, Finn's back arched off the bed.

He was so damn close, balanced precariously on the knife's edge between reality and the abyss of all-consuming pleasure, when Dev suddenly thrust a finger into his ass, hitting his prostate and tapping against it rhythmically and Finn was helpless not to go over. He screamed Dev's name as he came down his throat, shuddering and shaking on the bed, his cock swelling and jerking over and over as wave after wave of pleasure had him releasing seemingly endlessly before he finally collapsed back against the bed.

Air sawed in and out of his lungs as he fought to get oxygen back into his body. He lifted a shaking hand to wipe the sweat that had bloomed across his brow, and couldn't help the short self-deprecating laugh that came out. He was as weak as a goddamn newborn.

"I hope that laughter's not at my oral skills," Dev's amused but strained voice came from the foot of the bed. When Finn looked over at him, he saw that somewhere along the line, Dev had managed to strip himself naked and grab the bottle of lube they kept in the bedside table. Seeing his lover standing there, looking all hot and hard, holding a bottle of lube, made his arousal start to stir again.

"Oh, hell no," Finn murmured as he grinned and started to shuffle further up the bed. "There is absolutely nothing amusing about your oral skills, Dev. You fucking destroy me every damn time you put your mouth on me. I was laughing because my entire body was still humming from that epic orgasm you just gave me. But right now, I think there was a little phase two to this particular sex session."

Dev's grin turned wicked as he squirted lube into his hand and rubbed it up his entire length. "Fuck yeah there's a second phase." Finn laughed as Dev leaped onto the bed and crawled between his thighs, but when he met Devon's gaze and saw the desperation and vulnerability shining there, the laughter vanished. "I'm gonna need to fuck you hard, Finn. The memories and thoughts of tonight are too damn fresh and I need you to help me erase them."

Finn nodded, reaching up to put his hands on Dev's broad shoulders and wrapping his legs high around his hips. "I need it too, Dev. Fuck me, lover. Take me hard, and make the world feel normal again."

Dev reached down and placed the head of his blunt cock against Finn's back entrance, and Finn flattened his back so that it lifted his ass slightly. Once they were perfectly aligned, Dev rolled his hips until the head of his cock slipped passed the ring of muscle at the opening to his ass. With a few more quick and careful rolls of his hips, Devon slipped in and worked himself deeper into Finn, inch by glorious inch. Despite a slight burning pinch as Dev slid to the hilt, Finn felt nothing but pleasure.

"You ready for me, Finn?" Dev groaned as he held himself still.

Finn grinned up at his man, who was always going to put Finn's happiness and pleasure before his own, despite his own needs. "Yeah, Devon, fuck me. Fuck. Me. Hard."

Dev's eyes blazed with joy, then he began to move and Finn couldn't quite keep his eyes in focus. Dev powered in and out of his body, and Finn could do nothing but hang on, almost like he was simply an observer to the action, but an active participant in the orgasm that was approaching him fast. Devon tilted his hips and added a twist to each thrust which had him rubbing against Finn's prostate and making him cry out with each thrust.

"Shit! Goddamn yeah, Finn ... that's it ... I can feel your fucking ass tighten on me," Dev growled out through gritted teeth. "Take your cock in your hand, lover, I want to see you come on your stomach for me again before I fill your ass."

Finn groaned as he gripped his hard cock in his hand, jerking on it hard, reveling in the sparks of pleasure that lit within his ass and along his cock as the double stimulation had him hurtling head first into an orgasm before he knew it. He screamed Dev's name to the heavens an instant before Dev jerked against him and he roared Finn's name just as loud. The two of them shuddered against each other as the final waves of pleasure rocketed through them before they collapsed back onto the bed.

Dev held himself up just enough so that he wasn't crushing Finn. After a few minutes, Finn felt Dev's semi-soft cock slip out of his body and they both moaned at the feeling. Dev collapsed on the bed beside Finn and tugged him onto his side and closer so that Finn ended up halfway across his chest. Both of them were breathing heavy and Finn could hear Dev's heart pounding hard and fast against his ear.

"Christ," Dev murmured, awe clear in his tone, "do you think it will always be like that between us?"

Finn laughed breathlessly and turned his head on Dev's chest to look him in the eye. "I think we can pretty much guarantee that, lover."

Dev grinned. "Yeah, I reckon you're right. I'm going to run us a shower in a minute, just as soon as the feeling returns to my legs."

"That sounds wonderful, but for now, I'm quite happy right where I am."

"Forever, right?"

Finn grinned and squeezed his arm tighter around Devon's chest. "Of course forever. Now that I have you back, I have no intention of letting you leave me again."

Dev returned the hug and pressed a kiss to the crown of Finn's head. "I'm not going anywhere, baby. And I realized today that I never even thanked you."

Finn frowned, thought for a moment, then lifted his head to look at Dev. "For what?"

Dev shrugged a small smile on his face. "Giving me the opportunity to earn a second chance with you. I promise you'll never regret it."

Finn pressed a soft kiss to Devon's lips then pulled back with a grin. "I'm sure I won't. I think you were right, we were both traveling our own line of drift, but our destination was always right here, right now, with each other."

And that was a vow they were both determined to keep.

The End

DEDICATION

Is it just me, or has the world gone a little bit crazy lately? Every time I pick up a newspaper or turn on the TV, I find myself falling into a further state of shock and surprise at how dark the world can be. So I dedicate this to anyone affected by the darkness in the world, either directly or indirectly. Here's hoping that sanity and light returns

And for my hubby—my shining light in the dark. Love you, baby.

SNIPER TEAM BRAVO: VOLUME ONE

NO IMPACT

Sniper Team Bravo, 2

Maia Dylan

Copyright © 2016

Prologue

"Shit! RPGs! They've got fucking RPGs. Incoming!"

Marcel turned at the sound of Maddox's warning and watched as the big man moved with a sped that belied his size, gripping the back of Reaper's BDUs and throwing them both against the south wall of the room they had been in, just as Marcel made out the distinct whistle of an inbound RPG.

Marcel was a sniper in the United States Marine Corps, and he and his friends made up Sniper Team Bravo. They were sent in to eliminate targets that posed significant threat to the safety of their nation, but their elimination required the gentle touch of a .50 caliber bullet rather than the mass destruction of an air strike or drone. They were the best at what they did. But even the best were sometimes taken by surprise, and an RPG launched in your general direction was always one hell of a surprise.

In the moments before Maddox had shouted out that chilling warning, they had just taken out their target, and the operation had been flawless, despite having to wait in this fucking derelict and blown to all hell building, at the edge of the Registan desert for more than thirty hours. Devon Roberts was their CO, and he had been behind Marcel, leaning against the west wall. Maddox Devereaux and Glenn "Reaper" Webster were the finest example of a sniper and spotter team Marcel had ever seen, and they were in position by the window to take the shot, about three feet from him. Sam Wilson was a rifleman and their medic and the last man of their team, and he was through in the other room.

As soon as the whistle of that inbound warhead registered, everyone in the room seemed to move in slow motion. All of them dove for points of protection against load bearing walls in an attempt to survive the blast. Marcel was still actually airborne when the damn thing hit, throwing him slightly off course and slamming him into a concrete pillar. He landed with a grunt as pain shot like lightning through his shoulder, and he fell to the ground as the room seemed to implode around him.

One of the things that Marcel had learned during his six years of service was that the mind went to strange places in moments like these. When your life was balanced on a knife's edge, and only God was privy to what the result would be at the end of that day, your mind had a moment of perfect clarity. You saw the people or the moments in your life you were most proud of, the things that exist that made you who you were, and when all you saw were the gaps in your life, it was moments like these where the lack of those anchors in your life, hurt the most.

He was a man with no family, no significant other, a whole slew of men who had held the loneliness at bay for small moments of time throughout his adult life, and the only friends he had were all currently being blown to hell and back. He could only hope that all of them would survive it.

When the world finally regained its equilibrium, Marcel was left with a ringing in his ears, blood dripping into his left eye from a gash on his head, and numbness in his body that he should probably be thankful for. The sound of his own harsh coughing was muted in his ears as a result of the blast, and he drew into his lungs the concrete dust that filled the air around him. The frantic beating of his heart was a welcome sign that he was alive. With a groan he rolled to the left. He was shocked to see that the wall he had been aiming at had crumpled in on itself. The blast of the RPG that had sent him of course had saved his life.

"Marcel!" He turned to see Devon leaning heavily against the far wall where he had last been standing. He was covered in concrete dust and bleeding steadily from a wound high on his arm. "Move! They'll be coming. We need to get to the EVAC point, and we need to do it now."

Marcel nodded before lifting his weapon that he had miraculously kept a hold of, and went in search of Sam. The room he had last been in was completely obliterated. The RPG must have hit the building on the upper right hand corner of that room, because where once there was a concrete wall and ceiling, there was now nothing but open air.

"Sam!" Marcel called as he moved into the room, trying to determine which way Sam would have moved. He looked at the far right hand corner of the room, just as the pile of debris that lay there groaned. Marcel climbed over the other rubble in the room, and started pulling the lumps of concrete away.

After a few moments, another two pairs of hands started to help him. Maddox and Reaper had survived, but not entirely unscathed.

"Sam, you son of a bitch," Maddox yelled, "get

the hell off your ass. Those fuckers are heading here and if you get me killed I'll fucking shoot you myself."

Amazingly, just as Maddox finished speaking, Marcel moved a block of concrete that uncovered Sam's face. For a brief moment no one moved. Sam remained motionless. There was no sign of blood on his face but he was lying at an odd angle, and Marcel felt a wash of fear roll though him.

"Fuck, Maddox," Sam groaned, "do you have to yell so damn loud? Shut the hell up, I have a headache."

Marcel couldn't fight the grin. "Yeah, *mon ami*, I think you'll find that all of us are suffering with headaches after that." He reached down and removed the last of the rubble covering his friend, sending up a prayer of thanks to every deity he knew that all of them had survived.

"Being blown to hell by a piece of shit RPG will do that to a team," Reaper quipped, and the three of them helped Sam from the floor.

"Let's move! EVAC inbound!" Devon called from the other room, and the team moved into survival mode.

Marcel ignored the pain of his injuries and took point like he always did. In single file the team followed behind him. They made it out of the room and down the east stairwell to the main level. Whether it was by luck or design, they didn't encounter any enemies lurking around corners or hiding in shadows. They were able to get to the building's main exit and regroup for a moment.

"Three clicks north to the extraction point," Devon reminded them, and Marcel bit back a groan. Running three clicks was easy even in full gear because they had the fitness to do that and made it look easy. But each of them bore injuries. Devon's arm was pretty much useless. Marcel's shoulder was starting to seize, Maddox was favoring his left leg and not moving as fast as he normally would, Reaper had tucked his left hand into his shirt, which signaled a break or strain in that arm which would make running a bitch, and Sam seemed to be squinting in the light, so Marcel suspected he might have a concussion.

But this was the only way out. So they would do what they always did. Suck it up, get the job done and get the fuck out of this hellhole. This was their final mission, and all of them were determined to see it through. Marcel checked visually with each man, waiting until they signaled their readiness, and it was a tribute to their strength that it came immediately.

Marcel took a deep breath, and lifted his weapon to engagement level. "Well, kids, let's get the hell outta here. I reckon we have overstayed our welcome. On me."

He opened the door, and Bravo team moved out into the alley behind the building in standard formation, moving as one and covering every possible attack angle. As they rounded the northeast corner of the building, they stepped into hell and Marcel knew that either all of them would make it, or none of them. That was just how Bravo team rolled.

Chapter One

Six months later

"Look out! Look out!"

Reflexively, Marcel dropped to a crouch at the shout, reaching for the weapon that should have been in the holster attached to his body armor across his chest. He looked down in shock when he found nothing.

"No, no, no! Move!" Startled, he looked up toward the voice and saw Riley Marksmen bearing down on him like an out of control freight train. The expression on his face was a mixture of fear and determination.

Just as Marcel started to stand, Riley slammed into him. Marcel grunted at the impact but went limp and rolled with him. Marcel might not have known what the danger was or why Riley felt the need to come at him like a linebacker, but he knew it would hurt less for both of them if he just went with Riley's momentum.

They had only rolled once when there was an almighty bang, and the earth seemed to jump beneath them. They came to rest about eight feet from where Marcel had been standing, Riley lay over the top of him, and Marcel couldn't help but appreciate the man's physique, pressed as it was against his own body from shoulder to knee.

His heart beat a little faster, and there was a definite increase in his breathing rate. Marcel couldn't say whether it was the impact and roll from moments before, or because he was lying beneath the star of more than one of his wet dreams of late. Voices and shouts began to register as his focus moved beyond Riley. Marcel was so caught up by in the man who flattened him into the ground he almost forgot that they were surrounded by the rest of the crew.

"Dale! Secure and lock this site down until we can investigate this! I want every fucking man in here to leave me a statement of their actions leading up to this accident and I want it right fucking now!" Riley yelled at one of his team, and Marcel was able to watch him unashamedly and without fear of reprisal.

At least until Riley looked down at him with concern and worry in his eyes. "Damn, Marcel, are you all right?" Riley asked, his gaze wandering over Marcel's face before locking with laser like intensity with Marcel's gaze.

Marcel had to swallow the sudden lump in his throat. "Yeah, I'm good. What was all that about?"

Riley turned his head, and Marcel followed his gaze to a large ridge beam Riley and his team had lifted into place that morning. Marcel had watched fascinated as the crew worked together to secure the large metal I-beam into place. He'd smiled when a shout had gone up once it was in place, and he found out that Riley had promised his men a few beers after work if they were able to get it in before the rain that was scheduled for later that afternoon set in.

"Huh, I guess that means there'll be no celebratory drinks tonight." Marcel had been looking forward to seeing Riley's team let loose a little.

"Are you kidding me?" Riley's voice was quiet, but Marcel felt the anger in his tone like a vibration through his body. "You walk onto my construction site, with no fucking hi-vis or hard hat on, and nearly get flattened by a goddamn five hundred pound I-beam and all you can think about is that there will be no drinks tonight?"

Riley leaped off him like he'd contracted something nasty and glared down at him, making Marcel feel like he was two inches tall. Not something he appreciated at all. He stood up slowly, refusing to drop his gaze from the larger man, or to even dust himself off.

"I have a meeting with Devon at the outside range, and this is the best way to get there. If this is no longer a safe place to walk, then perhaps a sign or some freaking hazard tape would be in order. Besides, I would wager that you have more to worry about than where I walk. That I-beam shouldn't have come down, so either your men or your equipment failed. Perhaps you should concentrate on that."

Riley's brown eyes narrowed. "I will deal with why that beam came down with my men and my equipment shortly. I just need to make it very clear to you that you are not to come into this site without my *express* permission. Do I make myself clear? A man with reflexes as slow as yours should not be walking around a goddamn construction site. You are an accident waiting to happen."

Everything with Marcel turned to ice. "*Fils de puta!* I was a fucking sniper in the United States Marine Corps. I have reflexes the likes of which you will never be able to comprehend."

"Well, if that's the case, the next time someone yells for you to look out, don't drop to the fucking ground in a crouch!"

Marcel's rage red lined, and he stepped up to stand toe to toe with Riley, right into his personal space. "When the army needs a target gone, they send in a team like Bravo. We go where normal army don't because we are just that damn good. If someone yells look out while you are walking through enemy territory, you drop because there is usually some fucker training his weapon on you, and you are standing right in the middle of his crosshairs. Very rarely is there a fucking steel beam about to land on top of you. I dropped because I've been shot at too many damn times for not dropping fast enough. Next time, yell 'move' first and I think you'll find my reflexes more to your liking."

Marcel spun on his heel and would have walked off, but two of Riley's men blocked his path. He stared them down until the two of them stepped out of his way. Yeah, he could have walked around them, or asked them politely to move, but he was over being polite. He walked off the site and made his way over to the outdoor range where Devon was waiting for him, his rage still riding him hard.

Riley Marksmen could kiss his ass, and not in the nice way that he had been dreaming of and hoping for over the past six weeks. Marcel made a note to get out and get laid. Soon. He had been harboring sexual ideas about Riley for far too damn long, and he needed to get back on the horse so to speak. But the thought of simply finding another man to fuck left him cold for the first time in his life. And didn't that just suck great big monkey balls?

****

"Fuck, Riley, did you just diss a decorated Marine sniper and say he had shit reflexes?" Dale Ranger, his construction manager, asked as he stepped over to Riley with Grant Dunn, who was his logistics and safety manager. The three of them stood and watched as Marcel marched out of the site and from the rigid set of his shoulders, Riley knew he was pissed.

Riley cursed under his breath. "Apparently, yeah, I did."

Grant winced and clapped a hand on Riley's shoulder. "Damn, Riley, that was probably not the smartest move in the world." He and Dale knew all about Riley's feelings for Marcel, because from what they told him, he wore his attraction on his face. That seemed fair enough as it definitely wore it in his crotch.

Riley turned to scowl at the man. "You think, Grant? Christ! When I saw that fucking beam rock and the support joist give way, all I could think about was getting to him. Then when I yelled at him to look out and he dropped to a crouch I thought that was it. I didn't think I would get to him in time."

Riley relived the horror of that moment again and felt his stomach turn. Marcel had been seconds away from death, and that had scared the hell out of Riley. Granted, as a member of a sniper team, Marcel had no doubt been seconds from death on more than one occasion. But this time it was much worse, for Riley was there to see this one. He could actually picture the damn thing landing on the man, and that made his chest hurt.

Riley had been working on and off in construction since he was sixteen. There was a portion of his life where he put down his hammer and picked up a gun in the name of his country. He loved both jobs and always invested more of himself than he intended in each job he took. But this job was different. This was personal on a level he hadn't even admitted to Dale and Grant, but it had become something even more the moment he'd laid eyes on the dark haired, green eyed Marcel, with his sexier than all hell French accent that only came out when he was angry. It became a job that just might be the one that led to his future. A future that he hadn't even realized he had been yearning for until Marcel walked into his life.

Grant nodded, understanding in his eyes. "Buddy, I get it. Your reaction was born from fear. The problem is that Marcel doesn't see it like that. All he knows is that you reamed him out in front of people and basically called him an idiot."

Riley started. "No, I never called him an idiot."

"Maybe not in so many words, Ri," Dale added with a grimace, "but I saw the look in his eyes before that mask of his slipped into place, and I can tell you, that is exactly how Marcel took it."

Frustration had Riley tunneling the fingers of both hands through his hair. Fuck, he hated being called out for being a dick. It didn't happen often. "Shit! Yeah, you're right. I'll have to talk with him later and try and get him to see it from my perspective I guess." Riley took a deep breath and turned to face the I-beam on the ground, and the remaining eight members of his team standing around it, all of them with incident forms in their hands, writing their statements in preparation for the investigation.

"We've got something a little more pressing to deal with at the moment. That beam should not have come down. We'll need to report it. Someone or something failed. If it was a piece of equipment then I want it off my site and a new one brought in before we continue with this job."

"And if it's a some*one*?" Dale asked.

Riley's gaze turned cold. "Then the bastard will be lucky if I just fire him. The way I feel right now, I might just be more inclined to kill the fucker and bury him in the concrete we'll be pouring tomorrow. If it was a someone, then he almost killed Marcel, and as far as I'm concerned, there is no greater crime."

Chapter Two

"So, this is where you've been hiding."

Marcel looked up at the sound of the voice, and his gaze locked with Riley's, who was leaning on the door jamb of the room Marcel had turned into a makeshift office. It had been four days since the incident with the I-beam, and Marcel hadn't realized how much he'd missed simply looking at Riley. The cowboy construction worker was dressed in a tight white t-shirt, jeans covered with construction dust, a well-worn pair of steel cap work boots, and the ever-present black Stetson.

Marcel sat back in the kitchen chair he'd snagged to work in and crossed his arms over his chest. "Saying that I was hiding would imply that I either A, had a reason to hide, which could imply guilt of some description. Or B, there was something or someone I was avoiding and was indeed seeking a place in which to hide. Now, as I am neither guilty of anything, nor am I avoiding anyone in particular, then I can assure you that I have not been hiding."

Riley pushed off the doorjamb with a grin and walked into the room. "Then I guess I was wrong." Marcel quirked an eyebrow and sent the man a pointed look, making Riley wince sheepishly. "Yeah, okay, not the first time I said the wrong thing to you. And that was what I wanted to come and talk to you about. And to apologize for."

Marcel grinned back and leaned forward in his chair, placing his elbows on the desk in front of him. "Really? Well, in that case, please go right ahead. I am, as they say, all ears?"

Riley moved closer to the opposite side of the desk and placed both fists on the surface, leaning forward. "That's good, because I wouldn't want to have to do this twice. When you came onto the site the other day, I should have called you back and explained that the site was now locked down. I failed in my duty as foreman to do that, because, well, to be perfectly honest, I was too busy looking at your ass and imagining it bare for my viewing pleasure as you walked away from me to think about what you weren't wearing on the top half of your body."

Marcel blinked slowly as shock filled his system. He had known that Riley was attracted to him. He wasn't blind to the way the man watched him, and Marcel sure as hell wasn't immune to Riley either. But this was the first time either of them had actually spoken about that attraction out loud.

"When Dale called out that there was movement in the chain holding the ridge I-beam and I looked up, I knew it was coming down. From my vantage point, I could see that it was going to land on you. I dropped what I was carrying and sprinted for you. I was so fucking scared that I wasn't going to get there in time. Then, when I tackled you, if you had resisted at all both of us could have ended up seriously injured, but instead you rolled with me, which I am extremely grateful for."

Marcel shrugged. "That's what we're trained to do."

"Yeah, and that leads me into the apology portion of my visit today." Riley leaned in slightly. "I am really sorry for what I said to you. I never meant to imply that you were an idiot and that shit about you lacking reflexes was a total pile of bullshit. All I can say is that I was acting out of fear, and if I had been thinking I would have caught myself before I shoved my foot so far down my throat I could kick my own ass."

Marcel huffed a laugh. "You certainly have a way with words."

SNIPER TEAM BRAVO: VOLUME ONE

Riley sent him a cocky grin that had excitement fluttering in Marcel's belly. "Wait until I'm convincing you to go to bed with me, then you'll get a real good understanding of just how good I can be with words."

Marcel raised an eyebrow. "Are you so sure that you can convince me?"

The grin slipped from Riley's face, and a look of pure need took its place. "I'm sure as hell ready to give it a go."

Marcel looked up at the object of his dirtiest thoughts and the hottest dreams of his life, and for the first time ever he hesitated. Not because he wasn't interested in the man, hell, he was still alive and had a pulse and Riley was the hottest damn thing on two legs as far as he was concerned. The attraction had been instant and all-consuming from the moment Marcel had laid eyes on him.

No, this hesitation was all about Marcel. Over the past six weeks he had spent some time with the man, getting to know him, and at first it was all about the chemistry and physical attraction. Despite the fact that neither of them had acted on it, the attraction was definitely there. But he'd been absolutely floored when he discovered that he liked Riley. A lot. And that excited and scared the shit out of him at the same time. Marcel was more of a "love them hard and with everything he had in him then leave them satisfied" kind of guy. He wouldn't know what in the hell to do in an actual relationship.

Riley's expression turned sad, and Marcel frowned.

"Or we can just forget that this conversation ever took place, and I can get out of your hair." Riley took a couple of steps backwards, and Marcel jumped up from his chair. "I really only wanted to stop by and apologize for the way I spoke to you. It was inexcusable."

"Look, it's not that I don't like you," Marcel said quickly, trying to get Riley to stop and talk to him, but from the pained expression on his face it was obvious he didn't take it that way.

"Right, well, at least now that answers that." Riley stepped through his office door just as Marcel's cell phone rang. The Mariachi music Finn had programmed into his phone for when he called usually made him laugh, but not so much today. "You're busy. I've apologized like I wanted, so I'll catch you later."

"Shit, Riley!" Marcel called, but the man didn't even pause. "*Merde*," he whispered, closing his eyes. When the absurdly happy tune started again, Marcel reached for the phone and had to fight back the urge to throw it through the damn wall. "What?" he all but growled.

"What the hell's got your goat?" Finn responded after a second's silence.

"It might have something to do with that fucking ringtone you set on my phone," Marcel answered. It was better than saying *I might have just lost my chance with a guy I might actually, kinda, sorta, potentially really like.*

"It's fun," Finn said. "Get the hell over your serious self for a moment."

Marcel sighed. "You know, Finn, that might just be the first time someone has ever accused me of being too serious. I am usually the life of the freakin' party."

Finn snorted. "Dude, from where I've been sitting lately, you haven't exactly done a shit load of partying lately. Which is a great segue into what I am actually calling you about. We are going out tonight."

Marcel's brows went up. "Really? We who?" The team had been so damn busy with getting the Cottonfarm Training Facility, or CTF for short, up and running, they hadn't taken much time to unwind. Then that whole episode with Finn's homophobic and bigoted as fuck father happened. Devon and Finn were childhood sweethearts, but due to Dev's bitch of a grandmother, he had left Redwood Falls.

When Dev's grandmother died, the lawyers handling her estate were unable to get the family member she left the farm to, to confirm and take ownership, so after the statue of limitations passed on it, the land went to Dev by default. When he came back, he'd found Finn still here, but living under the iron and violent fists of his father. Bravo team had managed to save the day as usual, but it did end with an RPG being fired into a tree where Sam had been holed up just moments before, a few broken windows in the homestead they were fixing up, and one dead as fuck asshole on their dining room floor.

"All of us. With everything that had happened around here, and the construction and the fact that no one has had the opportunity to just let loose in a long while, I'm invoking my rights as a Redwood Falls local and inviting everyone to the bar for a welcome party."

Marcel grinned. "You're invoking your rights, huh?"

"Hell, yes! I was born and raised in this town, and none of Bravo team has been out drinking with me, and I am damn sure that is against our town's constitution or some shit like that."

When Marcel had first met Finn, he had been beaten and terrorized, but the strength of his character and the man himself has been evident in the way he protected his mother and younger brother from his father. Over the past six weeks, Marcel had enjoyed watching his personality really start to shine.

Marcel ran a tired hand over his face. "You know what, a night out sounds like just what the doctor ordered." He needed a night out with his friends, a chance to relax and download. He needed to get laid. Marcel refused to acknowledge the fact that a certain contractor who had a way with words and a body to die for came to mind with that thought.

Chapter Three

"You know, you've been staring at that man on and off for the past two hours." Devon placed a beer on the table in front of him and sat down. Almost as if it were planned, Dale and Grant stood up from the table they shared with Riley and wandered over to the bar.

Riley grimaced as he grabbed the neck of the beer. "And here I thought I was more of the subtle type." He took a couple of swift chugs of the cold beer. He still got a nervous flutter in his stomach when he spoke with Devon, and it had nothing to do with the man himself, and everything to do with why Riley was here. Pushing that to the back of his mind, he focused on the tall blond man now leaning back in the chair across from him, staring intently at him.

Riley had to fight not to fidget beneath the man's stare. He'd heard Sam talking with Dale one day about how good Devon was at seeing things that others missed. "Eyes like a fucking hawk" were the exact words he'd used, and Riley could see why.

"Being subtle is overrated," Devon said with a grin. "I think there are occasions in life where you simply take the two by four with both hands, and use it as effectively as you can."

Riley grinned back, appreciating the analogy. "Well, you know what they say, 'there is no harm in looking'."

"There may not be any harm in looking, but if you wait until your window of opportunity closes, there is a shitload of regrets. And in my experience, regrets are much harder to live with."

Riley nodded and shot another look across the room. Marcel was sitting at the table with the rest of Bravo team, simply enjoying a night out, but looking hot as hell in a tight black t-shirt and jeans. Men and women had approached the Bravo table, and Riley had tensed when their attention turned to Marcel. Each of them had been politely sent on their way, and Riley had been able to breathe again. He didn't know what the fuck he'd do if Marcel went home with one of them. Following them and beating the shit out of the fucker who thought to touch what Riley was quickly beginning to think of his was fast becoming a serious option.

When Dale had invited him to join the construction crew on an impromptu night out, Riley had initially declined. Then the sly bastard mentioned something about him invoking the rights of the self-appointed site social captain, to ensure the happiness of all staff and added that Finn had told him the Bravo team was also heading out for a drink. Riley found himself saying yes before he'd even thought about it. Marcel had all but told him he wasn't interested, so Riley was nothing but a sucker for punishment.

"Are the regrets harder to live with if you've already crashed and burned?" Riley asked quietly. When there was no response from the man opposite him, he turned, and his gaze crashed with Devon's.

Devon leaned forward, putting his elbows on the table. "I left Finn eight years ago. I told myself it was for the best, I'd be back, we'd make our way back together as soon as we could, all of that bullshit. But bottom line? I walked away. When I came back, on my terms in my own sweet time, Finn rightfully told me to fuck the hell off out of his life. I'd lost that right. I don't think there is any bigger crash than that, my friend."

"How did you convince him to take another chance on you? When I got here, it was very obvious that the two of you were together."

"Persistence," Devon grimaced, "and a whole lot

of beating the shit out of that old punching bag up by the house. But the one thing I didn't do is give up."

Riley took another swig of his beer. "The problem I have, is that I pretty much laid it out for him this afternoon, and he was about to give me the *it's not you it's me* speech. Which, to be honest, would have been a first. I've used it more than once myself, but I have never been on the receiving end of it."

Devon, the bastard, grinned. "Sucked, did it? Ha! Should be good for you, but Riley, let me tell you a couple of things. When I came over here, I told you that I'd caught you looking at Marcel a couple of times. But what I should've also added was that Marcel was doing his fair share of looking, too." Riley felt a small kernel of hope bloom within him at that. "If anyone on my team needs a strong hand, and deserves a happily ever after, it's Marcel. In all the years I've known him, he has never once looked at anyone the way I've seen him look at you."

Well, that was definitely good news. Riley sat back in his chair and smiled at Dev. "Thanks for all of that. My gut is telling me that Marcel is someone special, and I think I deserve someone special in my life. Perhaps I should give it another shot soon, huh? "

Devon stood up and shot Riley a strange grin. "You're welcome. You're a good guy, and you helped save my team, so I owe you more than I can say. But before I go, I'll leave you with this little piece of advice. Don't be like me and wait too long to tell someone they mean something to you," Devon moved slightly so that Riley had a clear view of the table on the other side of the pool table, "because you just might miss your chance."

Riley focused on the table, and his body went rigid. Some guy had approached Marcel and was leaning into him, like he had a right to. Riley was on his feet and striding across the room before he'd actually fully processed what he was looking at. If Marcel needed a strong hand then Riley was just the man to give it to him.

****

"So, are we goin' to fuck or wha'?" slurred the drunken guy currently standing a little too close for comfort and breathing whiskey all over him. Marcel sent a look to his teammates, his eyes narrowing at the grins they all had on their faces. The guy hadn't exactly whispered it.

"As delightful as that offer sounds," Marcel replied dryly, "I haven't drunk nearly as much as I would need to, in order to be even close to the state I would have to be in to take you up on that offer. If you see me later in the night unconscious in a corner, then please, feel free to extend that invitation again."

Marcel watched the man's face went from interest to confusion to fury all in the space of a few moments. "Wha', you think you can do better?" The guy's behavior was distasteful for sure, and Marcel had been willing to let it go. But then the drunken bastard made the decision to actually put his hand on Marcel's right shoulder.

Marcel moved swiftly. He pushed his own right arm back behind him and then rolled it in a swift circle up and over his head, dislodging the guy's arm and knocking him of balance. Marcel stood swiftly, using the man's momentum against him, and had him face first on the table, arm wedged between his, and Marcel had a firm grip on the thumb lock he'd employed.

"Ow, what the fuck, man!"

Sam leaned his elbows onto the table. "That has to be the fastest I have ever seen someone sober up. And all it took was pain radiating up through your arm."

"Fuck you! *Unh*, stop, please!"

Marcel had added a little more leverage to the hold. "If you don't want me to break it, then I would suggest you be a little more polite. Now, say sorry to Sam."

"S-sorry, Sam," the guy gasped in pain, and Sam sat back with a grin.

"Much better. Now," Marcel said in a calm and unhurried tone, "let's you and I have a chat about manners. If you spot someone across a bar that you would like to spend some time with getting to know them, then you approach politely, say hey, I think you might be someone I'd very much like to get to know, then ask if you can buy that person a drink. Approaching them and telling them that you are, and I quote, *fucking hung like a bull,* is not the way to go. Are you getting all this?" Marcel leaned in slightly. Not wanting to actually break the guy's thumb, he added pressure to the man's hyper-extended shoulder instead.

The guy gasped in pain. "Yes! Damn it, yes, I'm getting it."

"Good boy." Marcel's tone was positively patronizing. "I would hate to have to repeat myself." The man whimpered. "Yeah, that's not something I would particularly enjoy either. So, one last little tip before we part ways." Marcel dropped his voice, his tone turning deadly, "Never put your hands on a man unless he invites it. If you want to know what it feels like to have your asshole pulled up through your esophagus then by all means, keep doing it, but I would suggest, for your own health, that you not."

Marcel released the guy and stepped back, giving him room. The man stood up slowly, and from the sound he made he'd had to bite back a cry of pain the move had caused. Limiting the blood supply in a hold like that hurt like hell, but it burned like a mother when it came back to you.

The guy threw him a filthy look then marched out of the bar. Marcel was surprised when the people around him started applauding, egged on by the men who shared his table.

"Check you out, Marine," Finn yelled with a grin, "still got the crazy moves."

Marcel grinned back, then bowed like he'd just finished a Broadway show, waving his arm theatrically before bowing low. He turned to face the room behind him and would have moved to do the same bow, but he stood still when he saw Riley.

He was standing only a few feet away, wearing black jeans and a tight white t-shirt that showed off the muscles he'd earned working the job he did, his cowboy boots and ever present black Stetson adding to the visual delight. Standing like he was with his hands in his back pockets, legs spread shoulder width apart and cocky smile in place, he looked like sex personified.

"Hey, I think you might be someone I'd very much like to get to know. Can I buy you drink?" Riley asked with a grin.

Marcel couldn't help but chuckle. "If only that guy had stuck around to see that didn't get you in a thumb lock and your face driven into a table. It might have reinforced the message."

Riley walked forward until they stand a little closer. "But did it get me the opportunity to buy you a drink?"

Standing this close, Marcel got an understanding of not just how tall Riley was—and for a six foot tall man like Marcel that was saying something—but also how broad he was. His torso was molded perfection, and Marcel had enjoyed the view of Riley working in nothing but a sweat soaked singlet stuck to his rock hard body on the site on more than one occasion over the past six weeks. His shoulders and arms were chiseled works of art that often glistened in the sun, covered lightly in the sweat earned through hard work that had Marcel longing to run his tongue over the definition just to draw the taste of him into his mouth.

Marcel found himself nodding, and reveled in the quick grin Riley flashed him. "Only if I can buy the next round."

Riley dipped his head in acceptance, and the two of then moved toward the bar. Marcel caught the grins on the rest of Bravo team and responded the only way he knew how. He flipped them all off, much to their raucous delight. When he and Riley were each settled on stools at the bar, a cold bottle of beer in front of each of them, Marcel's mind turned to how easily tonight could have gone a different way.

"What's that grin for?" Riley asked, and Marcel chuckled.

"I almost didn't come tonight, but Finn invoked his rights as a local or some such shit," Marcel watched as Riley's expression turned to shock, and then he grinned with a shake of his head. "What?"

"Are those the exact words he used? Invoked his rights?"

"Yeah, it was. Made me laugh, and the next thing I know, I'm saying yes."

Riley threw his head back and laughed, a sound Marcel found he enjoyed a lot. "Those scheming sons of bitches."

"Who?"

"Finn and Dale. Dale used the exact same line on me to get me to come out tonight. After our talk in your office this afternoon, I had gone back to work and might have been a little quieter than usual I guess. Dale hit me with this impromptu night out." Riley grimaced slightly. "I gotta be honest, although I was keen on a drink, I was more than likely going to take my wounded pride back to my quarters and drown my sorrows a little."

Marcel leaned in slightly and waited until Riley met his gaze. "The hesitation I had this afternoon had nothing to do with you, or how I feel about getting to know you on a more intimate level. It was all about me."

Riley took a slug of his beer, without taking his gaze from Marcel's. "Are you going to tell me what your hesitation was about?"

"Not right now, no."

Riley nodded, his gaze assessing. "That's fair enough, but you should know that I won't stop trying to work out what it is. The sooner I have an idea what the barriers between us are for you, the sooner I can work on breaking them the fuck down."

Marcel barked a short laugh. "Spoken like a true construction worker, huh?"

Riley grinned. "Hell, yeah. I've been a nail bender most of my life, and that ain't about to change."

"Okay then," Marcel agreed, "you can keep trying to work it out, and when I feel like I can tell you without feeling like a giant ass, then I will. Deal?"

"Deal." The two of them clinked their beers together in a silent oath, before taking a drink. "I'll also be trying to get you into bed as soon as humanly possible. I just thought it was better to forewarn you."

Micah laughed, almost choking on the beer he had just swallowed. "Well, thanks for the warning. I have to admit, that's probably the first time anyone has advised me of their intentions so blatantly."

Riley's expression turned serious. "This ain't about what feels good for now, or trying to rush either of us into anything too damn fast. From the moment I met you, I saw you as something more than just a casual fuck. I've had those, a lot of those. Men and women." Marcel felt a stirring of jealousy in the pit his stomach at those words, but it was quickly quelled by the hypocrisy of him feeling it, when his past was the same. "But I want something different, something … more. And my gut is telling me that I might get that with you, and it's something I'm willing to try for. The only question is, are you?"

Marcel felt the hesitation of that afternoon retreat, and he was able to answer swiftly and honestly. "Yeah, I am."

Chapter Four

"Fuck!" Riley roared, throwing his hard hat against the wall of the mobile free standing construction office he'd built for the business when he first started. It housed everything he needed to do his job, a small break room for him and his team, and a conference room they used every morning for their kick start meetings.

He was so fucking angry he was actually shaking. The incident with the I-beam that had nearly taken Marcel out could have been passed off as a site accident. The investigation Dale had completed had pointed to it most likely being equipment failure. He hadn't been able to pinpoint the exact equipment that had failed, and it looked as though it may have been a weak chain link in more than one place, but there had been nothing that had pointed to sabotage.

Riley's stomach revolted at even the thought of the word, but now, with today's discovery, it was becoming more and more obvious that was what they were dealing with. Dale walked into the office, his face a mask of rage that no doubt mirrored his own.

"This is going to set us back by at least three weeks, but more like a fucking month," Dale spoke through gritted teeth, and Riley saw the tick in the side of his jaw that said he was gnashing his teeth together.

The frames they had ordered for the custom build of the housing facility Bravo team had requested had arrived that morning. His crew had got to work getting everything in place, but nothing fit within the confines of the concrete foundation they had poured. No matter how they looked at the pad, it was hard to miss that it was too small for the frames that had been delivered. Someone had moved the goddamn survey stakes, not by much, just enough for it to affect everything they had ordered for it.

"Fucker knew what he was doing," Riley muttered as he threw himself down in his chair. "Those markers weren't out by much, just enough to fuck us over, but not enough for us to immediately notice. Whoever did this knew the plans, and that means they are on this team."

There was a knock at the door, and Devon and Marcel walked into the office. Riley's stomach dropped, despite the fact his heart beat a little faster. It had been three days since they had cleared the air at the bar, and he and Marcel had agreed to get to know each other and see if they were compatible for something more. They had driven back to CTF in companionable silence. It had been a long time since Riley had walked someone to their room and kissed them goodnight, but he had done it that night. The kiss was the hottest damn one of his life, and he had gone back to the temporary quarters they'd set up for him and his team in the large barn to the right of the main house, to relive it over and over again as he jacked off in his shower.

He and Marcel hadn't been able to find a lot of time to spend together, but that had simply added to the anticipation of what was to come as far as Riley was concerned. And from the heat in Marcel's eyes when their gaze met as he entered Riley's office, it was going to be soon.

"What's happened?" Devon growled as he stood on the other side of Riley's desk, his hands on his hips. "You said you needed to see me, and Marcel 'cause he's a lawyer. What fucking law did you break?"

Riley quirked an eyebrow and shot him a withering look. "I'm not going to dignify that with a fucking response. Someone is going to need a lawyer, but Marcel will be the prosecutor in this one. We were moving on the accommodation build. The frames arrived this morning, but they don't fit."

Devon frowned. "What the fuck does that mean? Someone didn't measure shit properly?"

"No," Riley growled, "we have processes that negate the possibility of that happening. It means that some fucker moved the survey pegs on the build. They only moved them a foot or so, and tried to make the new 'positions' look convincingly real. That way we didn't know about it until the prefabricated elements of the development arrived and they didn't fit."

"The bastard had some time to do it, too," Dale added. "If he didn't have a lot of time to map it out properly he would have just ripped up all the survey markers, which would have delayed us, but not by as much as this is going to."

Devon leveled Riley with a glare. "Someone on your team fucked us over? Is that what I'm hearing?"

Gritting his teeth so damn hard he thought he heard them crack, Riley said, "Yes, that's what it looks like."

Devon seemed to swell in size, and a growl of frustration erupted from within him. "Son of a fucked up piece of shit! First I get notice that there is some fucker trying to mess with my right to this place, some prick constantly calling me from some firm in Cheyenne, and now one of your fucking team is fucking everything up for us."

"Dev, we'll speak to the lawyer and get to the bottom of the estate issue, but this is more serious," Marcel said as he pulled up a chair, reaching for the notebook and pen on Riley's desk. "This has legal implications. We're going to need to call in the Sheriff's department. I will need to speak to each member of your crew, Riley. We will need to inform them of what it is we are investigating, and I'll need to look over their employment contracts. Any historical information you might have on them will need to be reviewed. We're going to need to do that sooner rather than later."

"And in the meantime," Devon asked, his voice filled with an anger Riley could appreciate, "what the hell is going to happen with the build? Are you going to be able to fix this?"

Riley nodded, his brain moving into problem solving mode, and he turned to Dale. "Once Marcel has met with each man on the site and cleared them, I want you to send everyone we hired on for this build to our site over in Jackson. If I haven't worked with them for the last two years, I don't want them on this build. Warn Terrance that we are sending some new hires to him and to watch everything that they do. If anything untoward is to happen, then he's to come to me directly and immediately."

Riley then turned to Devon. "We'll be behind. We'll need to rework and relay the foundations and that will take time, but I'll absorb the additional cost."

"What? Wait—" Marcel went to intervene, but stopped when Riley shot him a glare. This was between him and Devon.

"My core crew and I can get everything finished for you." Riley raised his gaze to Devon's meeting the man's stare. "You will have everything you requested at the price we quoted and not another penny. That I promise you." Riley held his hand out, in the age old symbol of honor. He waited, never taking his gaze from Devon's, and just as he was starting to feel like he was standing there with his dick hanging out rather than his hand, Dev finally reached out and clasped Riley's hand in his, shaking it firmly.

"Okay then," Dev shook his hand firmly. "Maddox will call the contracts we have lined up and tell them there's been a delay. We'll push everything back a month and make it up to them with additional classes they hadn't requested."

With that Dev walked out of the office muttering. They had all worked hard to get this facility operational, and after everything they had been through and worked for it wasn't right that someone could screw it all up for them. It had Riley seeing red that it was someone he had brought into their lives that had done it.

"I bet I can guess what's got you looking so pissed off." There was a definite thread of humor in Marcel's tone.

Riley turned to look at him. "It's not that hard to guess. Dale, go round up the guys and get their recruitment files together for Marcel." Dale left the office, and Riley leaned back on his desk, crossing his arms across his chest. "If you find the prick that did this, or even if you just get a bad feeling about one of my guys, I want you to let me know."

Marcel stood up from his chair with a sigh. "Yeah, I can do that, but, Riley, you have to know that anything you do to him could be detrimental to any legal action we take against him."

Riley scowled. "Well, what the hell kinda lawyer are you? Surely you can get me off for temporary insanity or something."

Marcel laughed as he moved to stand in front of him. "I'm not sure even I can pull that off. No jury in their right mind could ever find you as anything but sound mind and hot body."

Riley reached out and tugged Marcel closer, widening his stance so he could bring the man to stand between his legs. Despite the fact he was sitting down slightly, they were eye to eye. "I've been feeling pretty fucking crazy these last few days, wanting you, seeing you but not being able to do a damn thing about it."

Marcel's arms rose to lie over Riley's shoulder. "Trust me, I share your frustration."

"Good. Let me come to you tonight." Riley heard the plea in his tone and didn't give a shit. He wanted Marcel so damn badly. He was done waiting.

Marcel stared at him for a while before a smile swept over his face. "I was about to say the same thing to you."

"Let's get this afternoon out of the way, and then I will meet you in your rooms after dinner." Riley pulled Marcel, wrapping his arms around his waist. "Your room will provide us with the privacy I'm going to need to have that conversation with you."

Marcel's expression became quizzical. "What conversation?"

"The one where I convince you to not only let me get you into bed, but to also let me fuck you the way I've wanted to for so damn long." The last word Riley practically whispered against Marcel's full lips before he claimed them.

Riley was a dominant man. He was used to taking charge, being the one to control all things in both his professional and his personal life. But when Marcel was not only an active participant in this kiss, but actually dueled with him, both men vying for control of that kiss, Riley growled in arousal. As hot as it was, this was not a battle he was prepared to lose.

Sliding his hand up Marcel's back, Riley plunged his fingers into his hair, using his grip and just the slightest tug to angle Marcel's head to where he wanted it. then he took control. He thrust his tongue into the hot wet cavern of Marcel's mouth, licking into him, loving the suction Marcel applied to his tongue that had his dick twitching in his jeans.

Riley sucked Marcel's bottom lip into his mouth, and bit down gently. Marcel groaned in pleasure, and Riley knew he'd won this round when Marcel softened against him, submitting to Riley's dominant nature. Marcel seemed to melt into him, and Riley felt his arousal start to spiral out of control. He pulled back, sipping from Marcel's lips a few more times before slowly bringing the kiss to an end.

"Damn." Riley's voice was little more than a growl. "Your mouth should come with a warning. Any more of that and I'll have us both naked in a mere second, and that could be embarrassing when the team start coming in for their interviews.

Marcel laughed breathlessly as he stepped back and pushed a hand through his own hair. A hand that Riley was pleased to note had a slight tremble to it. "Agreed. *Mon dieu*, you sure know how to kiss a guy."

"I know how to do a whole hell of a lot more to a guy, Marcel. But you are going to have to wait until tonight to experience that."

"I'll look forward to that, and you should know something about me." Marcel walked over toward the door to let Grant in, but turned with his hand on the doorknob, and shot him a hot look over his shoulder that would have Riley hovering on the edge of intense arousal for the rest of the afternoon. "If you think my mouth should come with a warning from just that kiss, wait until I get my lips around your cock."

There was a knock at the office door. Riley wanted to growl in frustration even as his dick swelled to painful proportions behind the zipper of his jeans. "Who is it?" His question came out more of a snarl than anything else.

"Sheriff Nick Jones," a man answered from behind the door. "I'm here to follow up on the incident form that's just crossed my desk. An issue with an I-beam that came down on your job site?"

Riley groaned as his head fell back on his shoulders for a moment. "Sure thing, Sheriff, come on in." The door opened, and a large man walked in wearing a country sheriff's uniform. "Welcome, my name is Riley Marksmen, and this is Marcel Cross, part owner of this facility."

Nick smiled at both him and Marcel. "Nice to meet you both. I won't take up too much of your time, I have a couple of questions then—" He was interrupted by another knock on the door and Grant calling out that he was ready for his interview. Dale obviously needed him back on the site as soon as possible so had sent him in first.

"Interview?" Nick asked.

"Yeah, Sheriff, there's been another incident on site today." Riley figured it would be best to be completely honest with the new sheriff. "Nothing but time lost, but deliberate in nature."

The sheriff drew out a notepad from his shirt pocket. "You guys sure know how to spice up a country cop's day."

Marcel laughed as he moved to open the door for Grant. "That we do, Sheriff, that we do. Now, I am going to go prepare statements with Riley's team, and I will make sure that your office gets a copy." Nick nodded as he started scribbling madly on his notepad as Marcel let Grant into the conference room.

Riley's eyes followed their movements of the two men as they left the room, one with a look of smug satisfaction and one in confusion. Riley's mind filled with a range of visions of what might happen this evening, but he slammed that closed. He was already sporting a hard-on that was difficult to hide, any more thoughts along those lines, and he was in trouble. With a sigh, he turned back to the sheriff, who was grinning at him in a way that had Riley thinking he saw more than most, and settled in for the longest damn afternoon of his life.

Chapter Five

Marcel took a moment to take in a deep breath before he opened the door to his suite of rooms. He had been impatiently waiting for Riley to knock on his door since dinner ended over an hour ago. Feeling steadier, his heart no longer in danger of pounding out of his chest in excitement, he opened the door.

"Hey," he said with a smile forming at the sight of Riley standing in the hallway. He was wearing his usual garb of jeans, tight t-shirt, cowboy boots and Stetson held in his hands.

Riley returned the smile as he stepped into the room. "Hey, back." Marcel stood back to let the big man passed and subtly inhaled as Riley moved by him. The spicy hint of the cologne he wore had Marcel's mouth watering. To be fair, it could very well have been that or the sight of the man's ass encased in his jeans. There was nothing better than a man who filled out a pair of Wranglers just right.

"Wow, this place looks great!" Riley cast a look around the space Marcel called home. The work on the main house had been completed first, and Marcel's originally overly huge bedroom was now an almost self-contained unit with a living room area, small galley style kitchen, separate bedroom with its massive king sized bed, walk in wardrobe, and en suite bathroom.

Marcel pushed his hands into the pockets of his jeans and passed a critical eye around the room. "Thanks. It's very much still a work in progress. I've spent the last six years living out of boxes and duffle bags moving from one billet to the next, so it's nice to have a place that's mine."

Riley nodded and turned to face him. "I hear that. I remember when I got out and rented my first apartment.

I went crazy one afternoon and spray painted graffiti on my wall."

Marcel laughed. "Really? How did that work out for ya?"

"Well, I learned two very valuable lessons that day. The first was that I am a shit artist. I have absolutely no artistic skill in my body at all. The second was that neon orange spray paint is an absolute bitch to color over."

Marcel threw his head back and laughed, and it felt good. It had been a stressful couple of days with the sexual frustration riding him hard, trying to get all the legal permits sorted for CTF, and then added to all of that the sabotage shit from this afternoon.

"I'm glad you stuck to white in here. I don't think I have anything to match neon orange. I'm just not that exciting."

Riley's eyes narrowed, and his stare turned intense. "Now, see that's where you're wrong. Everything about you excites the hell outta me." Marcel held Riley's gaze, watching as the man threw his hat down on the two-seater couch against the wall, toed off his boots, and walked toward him. Riley didn't stop until he was standing right in front of him, and Marcel enjoyed the fact that he had to look up slightly to meet his gaze, though not by much.

Marcel felt his body start to react to the man standing in front of him. His heart began to beat just that little bit harder and faster. His cock had filled and was beginning to press against the zipper of his jeans, and arousal began to swirl within him. Riley's intense gaze held his, and Marcel had a feeling that nothing short of an RPG fired into the wall of the room would have made him break that contact.

"I had this all planned out." Riley's voice had

dropped slightly, and the tone was liquid heat. It rolled over Marcel, driving his arousal to another level. "I was going to go for the slow build. I imagined that we would have taken a seat on your couch, drinking wine that as a beer drinker I would have had to choke down, but I know you like it so I would have done it with a smile on my face. I would have started out with some soft touches, perhaps a hand on your thigh, on your knee, a slight touch to your shoulder, and then potentially I would have taken your hand in mine. I would have leaned into you a couple of times, just slow and gentle like, giving you the opportunity to pull away if you'd wanted to, and pressed soft kisses to your lips, your cheek, your neck. I would have built the fire within you and me slowly, until the heat was almost unbearable."

Marcel's mouth had turned dry as Riley painted the seduction scene he had in mind and his entire body started to hum. The seductive picture was weaving a spell around Marcel that had him hanging on Riley's every word.

"When it got to that point," Riley continued, "I would have taken your mouth in a proper kiss, one that would coax you into pressing your entire body against mine. You would roll your hips against mine so that I'd know just how fucking hard you were for me, and you sure as hell would be feeling how damn hard you had me. Then, I would stop with the coaxing and just take what you would so sweetly offer me. Your mouth, your body, your cock, your ass, all of it would be mine."

Later, Marcel wouldn't be able to pinpoint the moment one of them made the move toward the other, or who actually even made the first move. One minute he was standing there, his body ablaze with desire, his dick harder than it had ever been in his life, his gaze drowning in the heat of the man before him. Then they were in each other's arms, Riley's hands were in Marcel's hair, tilting and turning his head to the angle he wanted. The kiss was a fierce battle of dominance. Marcel thrilled at the play, loving that Riley took control and eventually had Marcel so turned on he simply melted into the kiss and allowed Riley to lead him where he wanted. For the first time in his life, Marcel was happy to relinquish control.

As soon as Marcel acquiesced to the kiss, Riley removed his hands from Marcel's hair then tugged his own shirt up and over his head. Seconds later he was pulling Marcel's from his jeans and removing that. Marcel's mouth watered when he looked down over Riley's chest and abs. There were scars and signs on his body that he had seen his fair share of battle, but Marcel had them, too, so he couldn't complain. Not that he would, Riley had a body that made a man want to explore every inch of skin with his hands and then his mouth.

Riley reached up to cup Marcel's face, but he stopped him. There was ink high up on the left hand side of his ribcage that he had never seen before, and Marcel wanted to see it clearly. There were words in what Marcel expected was Latin written in a swirling cursive.

"*Nunquam obliviscere, nunquam ignosce,*" Marcel murmured as he gently swiped his fingers over the words, and froze when he felt the unmistakable feeling of ridged scar tissue under the writing. He cast a questioning gaze to Riley and was taken aback at the shuttered, cold look in his eyes. "So I am guessing there is a story here, and it's not one you want to share."

Riley frowned and put his hands on his narrow hips, tension radiating from him. "That's right. Is that going to be an issue for you, Marcel?"

There was a tone that Marcel had never heard in

Riley's voice before, and he didn't like it. "As you and I both know that there are things in my past and about myself I am not ready to share with you yet, it would be hypocritical as all hell for me to have an issue with it, Riley. But you can take the defensive attitude you are giving me right now, shove it up your ass, grab your shirt and get the hell out if you think you can speak to me in that tone."

Marcel held Riley's gaze and waited. He watched as the man's eyes darkened, and an emotion he couldn't quite name swam within the man's beautiful brown eyes.

"Goddamn it!" Riley growled as he closed his eyes briefly and took two deep breaths. Still Marcel refused to move, simply stood with his hands relaxed at his sides, watching them man in front of him intently. "Why the hell is it that I always seem to be apologizing to you? I'm sorry for that. I didn't mean to snap. It's just that the tattoo is a reminder and a memorial all at the same time."

Marcel nodded and reached up to run his fingers over the words a second time, not reacting when Riley's body turned to stone beneath his touch. "Thank you for the apology. I know all about reminders and memorials. I have enough scars on my body that act as both for a lot of the shit I have seen over the years. I need honesty in my life, Riley, and as hypocritical as that sounds considering I have my own secrets, it is something I will need from you if we are to go forward with anything between us. I am okay with it not being now, but it has to be sometime. Are you willing to at least try and work up to being able to tell me about the tattoo and the scar it hides?"

Riley's eyes narrowed slightly and Marcel thought perhaps he'd say no, and his heart stuttered in his chest at the thought of this man not finding him worth shining light on something so painful. He almost swayed in relief when Riley nodded reaching up a second time to cup Marcel's face in his hands, and this time Marcel didn't make a move to stop him.

Riley held his gaze. "I've told you on more than one occasion that I think there is something between us beyond just the here and now. That is not something I have ever said to or thought about another living soul. I get that it has only been six weeks, but there is something special between us, and I want to explore it completely. And if that means opening myself to you, and sharing with you the good, the bad, and the downright hideous, then that is what I am prepared to do."

Marcel smiled slowly, lifting his own hand to grin Riley's wrist. "It just so happens that I feel the same way. Everyone has a past, and there is always something in it that you have to overcome, and endure. I look forward to the time when we both can take that step."

Riley exhaled, and Marcel had the feeling he might have been holding his breath. There was relief in Riley's expression, and the heat had returned to his eyes. Riley opened his mouth to say something, but his gaze dropped to Marcel's mouth. Whatever he had been about to say was completely forgotten as he swooped in and placed his mouth over Marcel's. This kiss wasn't about coaxing the submission from Marcel, this one simply demanded it.

Marcel was once again surprised by the speed with which he accepted Riley's dominance and surrendered to his kiss. He felt Riley's hands slide from his face and wrap around his waist, and then he was leading him to walk backward. Trusting that Riley was taking him exactly where Marcel wanted to go, he gave himself over to the kiss and allowed himself to be led. When Riley released him from the kiss that was swiftly getting out of control, Marcel found himself standing at the foot of his bed.

"You know," Riley said in a voice deeper than Marcel had ever heard it, "when we were finishing this room, I would fantasize about the moment I would be here with you like this." Marcel tilted his head as Riley moved to press his mouth against the sensitive skin of his neck, giving him room.

"Really? You were that confident?" Marcel said before he gave a low groan when Riley pressed his teeth against the tendon that ran down the side of his neck.

Riley pulled back with a slight laugh, resting his forehead against Marcel's. "Confident? Is that just a polite way of saying that I was cocky? Maybe, there was a little splash of confidence involved, but there was a definite shitload of lust and desire. It didn't work out that well for me at the time though." Riley reached down to release the buttons on Marcel's jeans, and wanting to be an active partner in the evening, Marcel moved to mirror his moves.

"How so?"

"Well, when you are standing in a room filled with large construction worker type men, all standing around talking about stud levels, support trusses, and architraves, with a hard-on so large it is impossible to hide, you have to think fast."

Laughing, Marcel slid the zipper down on Riley's jeans, loving the fact that as soon as the zipper reached the end of the run, Riley's large erect cock slipped through. He so loved a man who didn't wear underwear. It made for easy access.

"It's the sawdust." Riley's words had Marcel looking up in confusion. "The reason I don't wear underwear, it's the sawdust. It gets caught in your underwear and itches like fuck. So rather than looking like I have something living in my crotch, or scratching it raw in the privacy of my own office, I've taken to simply not wearing any."

Marcel dropped to his knees, swiftly sliding Riley's jeans down the rest of the way. "If you thought that I was in anyway turned off by your lack of underwear, you are very much mistaken." Riley's eyes glittered with need and from the way his hands thighs had turned to rock beneath Marcel's hands, he liked the fact that Marcel was on his knees before him. "There is nothing hotter than knowing that the thing you want most, is only a zipper away."

With that, Marcel leaned in, pulling Riley's cock away from his abdomen, and pulling it into his mouth. Without hesitation, Marcel took him to the back of his throat, before swallowing around the head.

"Sweet Mother of God!" Riley shouted, and when Marcel looked up at him, Riley's head was thrown back, the muscles and tendons in his chest and neck stood out in stark relief, and his hands were clenched at his sides. Riley groaned again when Marcel hummed in appreciation at the sight. Marcel worked Riley's cock in a steady rhythm, alternating between firm suction as he moved up and down the stiff length of him, flattening his tongue against the sensitive underside and working the head between his lips. Riley jerked forward when Marcel flicked the top of his tongue against the mushroomed head.

"You weren't fucking kidding," Riley ground out. "Your mouth is so damn lethal it should come with a warning. Christ! So fucking hot, and so fucking good!"

Marcel started to speed up slightly, taking his direction from the sounds of pleasure coming from the cowboy that was soon to become his lover. When the moaning was almost continuous, Marcel lifted Riley's heavy cock up straight, and leaned in to suck his balls into his mouth, Marcel used the flat of his tongue to play with Riley's balls, knowing it would drive him crazy.

"Shit!" Riley roared, and Marcel felt him shudder and knew he was moments away from exploding, but apparently Riley had other plans. Swiftly, Riley plunged his own hand down, gripping the base of his own cock firmly in his hand, halting what Marcel had a feeling would have been one epic as hell orgasm.

Firmly but gently, Riley pushed Marcel back with a hand on his shoulder, pulling his cock away and leaning a little on Marcel. That in itself told Marcel how close Riley had been to exploding in his mouth. Marcel made the promise to himself that before this night was over, he would have Riley's cock in his mouth again, and he would not be denied his chance to taste his lover.

"Come here." Riley's voice was deeper and harsher than it had been before, and Marcel felt his own dick twitch at the dominant tone. He stood up, never taking his gaze from Riley's. As soon as he was standing, Riley finished undoing Marcel's jeans then moved to draw them and Marcel's boxers off completely.

"No sawdust in my life," Marcel murmured as Riley stood back up after divesting Marcel of his clothes.

Riley grinned as he reached down and gripped Marcel's cock in his hands, and Marcel could have sworn he saw stars. "As long as you aren't wearing them when it is just you and I in this room together with a little time up our sleeve then I don't really give a shit about underwear."

Riley took Marcel's mouth in a kiss once more. Marcel could feel his arousal spiraling out of control as Riley took control of his mouth, using his tongue and his lips to lead Marcel in a heady game of cat and mouse, all while he continued to work his hand around Marcel's cock. Marcel cried out when Riley reached down and began to roll Marcel's balls around in his hand.

In an embarrassingly short amount of time, Marcel hovered on the brink of losing control. His body shuddered uncontrollably, and his heart felt like it was racing away. Riley pulled back, staring into Marcel's eyes intently. The heat and desire of the moment were burning brightly in Riley's eyes, so Marcel knew he felt it, too.

"I want—" Riley snapped his jaw shut for a moment and shook his head. "Hell, no. Want is not a strong enough word. I would say I need, but it is more than that, too. I need to fuck you, Marcel. I need it on a visceral level. I can't seem to find the words to convince you in the moment how damn much I need you, and that is so goddamn unusual for me. You have me in a situation I have rarely found myself in. On one hand I want to fuck you into that mattress until you don't know where you end and I begin, but the other part of me, the protective fucker that wants to make sure that I am not rushing you into this and that you are as ready for this as I am, is telling me to slow down and take a moment."

Marcel took a deep breath, steadying himself, desperately wrangling his arousal into some semblance of control. "Has that protective part of you not realized that you've got my dick clasped in your hand and that I am moments from a release in an embarrassingly short amount of time?"

Riley gave a cocky half grin that Marcel couldn't help but appreciate. "Yeah, he realizes it, but the bastard is too damn stubborn to just step back and let me have my wicked way with you." Riley's smile softened. "But as much as I want to pound that part of me into a pulp for making it necessary for me to give you this option, I will do it anyway. You tell me if this is too fast for you, and I will do my fucking best to pull the dominant portion of my personality back."

Marcel tilted his head slightly, staring at the larger man who seemed almost too damn good to be true. "You know what? I think I like both parts of your personality, but my vote for this moment in time is to tell your protective side to butt the hell out, and let the dominant side of you take over. I am all on board with the whole pounding me into the mattress portion of your agenda."

Marcel had only just finished speaking when Riley swooped in, slamming his mouth against Marcel's and moving them around so that the foot of the bed pressed against the backs of Marcel's knees. Then seconds later, they were lying on the bed, Riley hovering over him. Marcel's feet were still pressed to the floor, and all the while they moved, Riley never relinquished his hold on Marcel's cock or took his mouth from his either. Marcel did so love a man who could multitask.

Chapter Six

Riley pulled back from the kiss to stare down at the man beneath him. *Damn.* Marcel had these sapphire blue eyes that darkened when his emotions were heightened, and right now they were glittering.

With a sly grin, Riley slid down the younger man's hard body. He spent a little time at each and every scar he encountered on the way, kissing the area, or laving it with his tongue. When he reached one of his peaked nipples, he played homage to it for a moment, sucking it into this mouth drawing a gasped moan from Marcel that turned into a groan when he used his teeth. Continuing down he made sure to make note of the areas where Marcel's breathing pattern changed or his body shuddered. Those areas warranted greater attention sometime soon.

When he was kneeling on the floor between Marcel's feet, he looked up and met Marcel's heated stare. He'd pushed up onto his elbows so Marcel could watch Riley's sensual journey down his body, and from the hungry glitter in his eye he was eagerly awaiting Riley's next move.

Riley grabbed his jeans and withdrew the tube of lubricant he'd put there before he left his rooms. "Christ, you have a body made for sin, you know that?" Riley's tone was reverent as his gaze traveled up and over Marcel's chiseled body.

Marcel smiled, but there was no vanity in it. The man was too damn comfortable in his own skin. "I could argue the same for you. But I gotta ask you something."

Riley heard hesitation in Marcel's voice. "Ask me."

"You said that you've enjoyed both men and women in your bed," Marcel asked with no judgment in his tone. "Are you sure that a man is what you want? I mean for beyond just the now?" A slight red flush rose in Marcel's face, and he sat up, forcing Riley to kneel up so that he could remain looking in his eyes. "Not that I am asking for forever. I mean this is only the first time we've been together and … well, we both have our stories we need to tell and … I am not explaining this very well, so I am just going to shut up now."

Riley grinned as he leaned in to press a swift hard kiss on Marcel's downturned lips. "It's nice to know that I'm not the only one that babbles shit when they're scrambling for the right thing to say." Marcel rolled his eyes, but the red flush of color had faded in his cheeks. "Yeah, I have been to bed with both men and women, and I have enjoyed each of them. But what was missing for me, was the connection. I never had a connection with any of the people I've slept with in the past, and as much as that makes me sound like a man-whore, it's the truth."

"I'm not exactly a virgin either, Riley," Marcel said dryly.

Riley continued, not wanting to hear about the other men Marcel had been with. "I've said this to you before, and it remains truer now than ever. As soon as I saw you, there was an instant physical attraction that almost dropped me on my ass. Once I got to know you, especially over these past few days, that's grown for me. I think you and I can have something special, and for as long as this," Riley waved his hand between him and Marcel, "works, then you are it for me. As soon as it stops working, or the connection is broken, then who knows what the future holds for either of us. But for now, and the foreseeable future, you have absolutely everything that I want in a lover."

"Then let's get back to what we were doing."

Marcel leaned back on his elbows, the movement making his erection bob enticingly.

"By all means, let's do that." Riley winked at him then slid down to take Marcel's cock into his mouth. Taking a page from Marcel's playbook, Riley took him as deep as he could on the first pass, flattening his tongue against the underside of Marcel's cock, and applying a steady firm suction.

"*Fils de puta,*" Marcel murmured in French. Riley reached down for the tube of lube beside him as he continued to work Marcel's cock in and out of his mouth, enjoying the explosion of flavor that burst across his tongue as pre-cum leaked from the tip of Marcel's cock, and learning what his lover liked best.

Marcel was responsive, his entire body reacting to the pleasure Riley was building within his body. Riley added a liberal amount of lubrication to his hands. Marcel cried out, his head falling back on his shoulders when Riley reached up to play with his ass. He ran a lubricated finger around the ring of muscle of Marcel's ass, rubbing over his entrance a few times, before he gently pushed his finger inside, not stopping until he was able to feel the small gland within that he knew would drive Marcel crazy.

"*Merde*, Riley." Marcel spoke through gritted teeth, lifting his head to watch, his body shivering at the double stimulation of Riley's mouth and the finger he had embedded within Marcel. Riley pulled off Marcel's cock, until just the head hovered at the tip of his lips. He felt Marcel push his hips forward almost unconsciously, trying to bury the head of his cock back into Riley's mouth, but the movement had Riley's finger sliding back and away from its position against Marcel's prostate.

Marcel began to swear in a steady stream of French when he realized the predicament Riley held him in. Although Riley had no idea what he was saying, it was the hottest thing he'd ever heard.

"Fucking hell," Marcel switched to English. "Riley, I can't take it. Fucking finish me or fuck me into the mattress like you promised. But no more playing."

Riley flicked one last lick across the head of Marcel's cock, taking one final burst of his flavor into his mouth. Then he pushed his finger back into the tight cavern of Marcel's ass, aiming for his prostate, loving the little jolt and moan Marcel gave as soon as he touched it.

"You are so fucking responsive." Riley groaned as he used both hands on Marcel's ass, getting him ready. When he had worked Marcel into such a state of arousal he was only moments from coming, Riley removed his hands, knelt up and placed the blunt head of his cock against Marcel's entrance. They both seemed to hold their breath as Riley pushed his hips forward, slowly sinking inside his lover, not stopping until his hips nestled against Marcel's.

"Fuck," Riley groaned as he rotated his hips. "You feel so fucking good. Hot and tight, gripping my cock. I'm not going to last, Marcel. You've got me so fucking aroused."

Marcel lifted his legs to wrap them around Riley's waist, and held his hands out wide, gripping the blanket tight. "Me neither, so fuck me. Do what you said. I want to feel you in every part of me. Fuck me, Riley!" Marcel's tone was almost desperate, and unable to resist Riley complied, stepping in closer with the foot of the bed, the movement forcing Marcel's hips up and driving Riley even further inside.

He paused for a moment, buried to the hilt, waiting for Marcel to meet his gaze. As soon as he did, Riley began to move. He slid out and in with a couple of firm, steady strokes, making sure that Marcel's body had grown accustomed to him. He watched as Marcel's eyelids dropped a little and he began to nibble on his bottom lip. Then he began to move with more power, sliding his hips back before snapping them forward and driving him into Marcel's body, fucking him in the mattress as he had promised. Marcel cried out as Riley angled his hips slightly so he could hit that swollen gland within him, driving his pleasure even higher.

When Marcel's eyes dropped closed, Riley stopped immediately. "Don't you dare close your eyes," he growled, and Marcel's eyes snapped open. "When I am fucking you, you will look at me and know who is buried balls deep within you, giving you pleasure."

Riley shifted even further forward on his hands, the muscles in his arms locking into position as he pistoned his hips, driving himself in and out of Marcel at a punishing speed. He arched his back with a roar, his orgasm crashing down upon him taking him by surprise. Slamming forward he pulsed within the hot welcoming grip of Marcel's ass, giving him everything he had.

When he was able to draw breath he looked down. Marcel's gaze was locked to his and the sated look of satisfaction in his eyes told Riley that Marcel had come at the same time as he had. "Damn." He groaned as he collapsed against Marcel.

"I second that damn," Marcel said breathlessly, "and add a holy shit."

Riley grinned as he leaned up slightly so he could look into Marcel's eyes. "I wasn't referring to how good it was because I can assure you I could wax lyrical about what just happened between us for hours. I was lamenting the fact that I never got to watch you come. I was so busy losing myself and my mind in you that I never even felt it when you went over, too."

Marcel grinned. "I guess you'll just have to do it

again, and pay attention next time."

Riley laughed. "Yes, sir, I most certainly will. In fact, I have a hankering for seeing you naked and wet, so let's jump in the shower. I had a few fantasies about what we would do to each other in there when we installed it."

Riley moved back, his legs not completely recovered, and he moaned as his still semi hard cock slid from Marcel's body. He looked down and growled at the sight of his cum sliding out of his lover. It fulfilled a decidedly caveman characteristic within him to see that. But it also triggered another thought.

"Shit, I didn't use anything." Riley helped Marcel up to his feet. "I am so damn sorry. I'm clean though, and I can show you my latest medical. In fact, that is the first damn time I have ever taken anyone without a condom."

Marcel grinned as he lifted his arms to Riley's shoulder. "It's okay, Riley. It was a first for me, too. I'm clean, and we can do the whole responsible sharing of tests together over pizza one night. I'm kinda happy that it happened like that though. It means that you were just as into it as I was, completely oblivious to anything except the connection between us."

Relieved, Riley grinned then started to walk backward toward the en suite bathroom, gently pulling Marcel in that direction. "That was most definitely the reason. Getting inside you was the most mind blowing experience of my life, and one I am pretty fucking sure will become an addiction."

They walked into the bathroom, still wrapped in each other's arms, and Riley became sure of one thing. The addiction wasn't just about the sex with this man. It was everything that made Marcel who he was, and it was an addiction Riley couldn't see himself giving up any time soon.

Chapter Seven

Marcel strode out of his rooms with a spring to his step. He and Riley had spent the last three nights together, and it had been everything the sexual chemistry between the two of them had let him to believe it would be. It was more than just the chemistry though. It was exactly how Riley had worded it that first night. There was a connection between them that could prove to be pretty damn special.

This morning, Riley had left before Marcel had been able to drag his ass out of bed, and who could blame him? When they weren't making out, or driving each other crazy with mindless pleasure, they talked about everything and anything. Marcel had never enjoyed talking with someone as much as he had with Riley the night before. Looking down at his watch he saw that he was running late for a meeting with Devon to go over the investigation into the sabotage. He strode forward faster with a curse.

Marcel walked past Maddox's room and performed the perfect comical double take. "What in the hell are you doing?"

Maddox didn't stop or even slow down. He kept taking clothes from his dresser and shoving them in his duffle. He didn't say a thing until he'd emptied the drawers and zipped the bag closed. He slung the bag up and over his shoulder before shooting Marcel a look. Marcel frowned at the empty look in his friend's eyes.

"Do me a favor," Maddox asked in a strained voice. "Tell Dev I'm sorry, but I have to leave. I don't want to fuck up anything for you and the team, so he can keep my portion of the startup money."

Something was wrong here. Very, very wrong and Marcel had no idea how to fix it.

Marcel stood in the doorway, not moving aside even as Maddox stepped closer to him. "I don't think Dev will give a flying monkey's ass about the money, brother. He'll want to know what the fuck is going on. Just like me." Maddox's gaze slipped from his, but not before Marcel caught the pain that glimmered there. "Talk to me, Maddox. What the hell is going on? This was what we worked so damn hard for, and you're just going to leave? Why? And where in the hell are you going to go?"

Maddox let out a sigh, and just when it look as if he might be about to share what was bothering him, a car horn sounded from outside. "That's my taxi. Look, Marcel, just tell Dev that I had to leave and that I'll be in touch soon. It's just not working out the way I thought it would. Nothing is." When Maddox lifted his gaze and met Marcel's, there was no sign of the pain from moments before, just a bitter determination. Maddox pushed past him, and Marcel followed him down the stairs to the foyer. Marcel cursed the fact that he was the only one in the house right then because the others might have thought of a way to keep Maddox there, or at the very least, Devon would have just sat on him until he talked.

"What about Glenn?" Marcel jumped down the stairs that lead off the veranda, just as Maddox opened the rear door of the taxi and threw his bag in the back. "Does he even know that you're leaving?"

Maddox barked a humorless laugh. "No, Glenn doesn't know that I'm leaving, and I don't think he'll give a shit." Maddox climbed into the car, and the taxi driver started the engine.

"Goddamn it, Maddox, you and he are partners, a fucking team! What in the hell should I tell him?" Marcel called out of the sound of the engine, as the car began to move down the drive.

"Tell him he should have locked his fucking door!" And with those confusing words of farewell, Maddox left.

****

"Hey, babe," Riley called with a grin as he spotted Marcel striding toward him. He and his crew were making good time, and all though they hadn't made up for the delays caused by their friendly saboteur they were making better progress that he'd thought. When Marcel's frown didn't lift Riley slid his hammer back into the holder on his tool belt and moved to meet him. "What's happened?"

Marcel sighed. "Have you seen Dev? He said yesterday that he was going to start the day over here with you guys. I need to tell him that Maddox has left."

"What the hell do you mean he left?" Riley said, shock clear in his voice.

"Exactly what I was about to say," Devon's voice wasn't so much tinged with shock as it was anger as he strode from the back room of the accommodation block they were finishing up. "Maddox just up and left?"

Marcel nodded. "Yeah, Dev, he did. I have no idea why. He just told me to tell you that he was sorry and that you could keep the seed funding he'd put in."

Devon growled, his eyes narrowing. "I don't give a shit about the money. I want to know what the fuck would drive him off." Dev spun on his heel. Riley shared a quick look with Marcel, and then the two of the followed the big man.

As they walked back to the main house, Devon muttered about pain in his ass snipers who acted before speaking with him. "This never would have happened when we were still active. I think we need to reinstate that rule. Nothing happens without my knowledge and none of you bastards up and leaves without my fucking permission from now on."

Riley bit back a grin when Marcel rolled his eyes. "I fucking saw that, Marcel!"

Riley couldn't stop the laugh that burst forth at the comical look on his lover's face. "If you think just 'cuz you and the contractor are bumping uglies I won't shoot your ass, you are very much mistaken."

The three of them took the stairs to the porch two at a time, and kept going until they had reached the second floor. When they arrived at Glenn's door, Devon knocked at the same time as he opened the door.

Riley's eyebrows shot to his hairline. Glenn was lying sprawled on his back on the center of his bed, but what made Riley look on in shock was the fact that Owen Taylor, one of his construction team that should have been on his way to Jackson to join Terrance's team, was sprawled out beside him. Both of them were naked, and there was the strong smell of whiskey in the room. Owen's large frame was curled around Glenn's, and there were love bites and marks of possession all over Glenn's body. It was painfully obvious what the two of them had been doing.

"Fuck," Marcel groaned. "Tell him to lock his fucking door. That was what Maddox told me to tell Glenn about why he was leaving."

"Marine! Get your hairy ass outta that bed!" Dev roared.

Owen startled awake, sitting up with a dazed look in his eye.

"Wha'?" Owen blinked rapidly to clear his vision, and when he saw who was standing in the room, his face changed. Not to a look of guilt or good natured humor at literally being caught with his pants down. His expression became smug.

"What? Are you three going to just stand there and stare?" His arrogant tone had Riley narrowing his eyes at the man. "I'm sure Glenn and I can do it again and give you a damn good floor show if that's what you came to see."

Glenn groaned from the bed, and raised an arm up over his eyes. "Wha' the fuck is all the yellin' for?" Glenn's tone was slurred, and for all intents and purposes he still sounded drunk.

Dev stepped forward, and his anger had shifted to concern. "Have you been drinking?"

Glenn raised the arm he had slung across his eyes. "What the hell are you talkin' about, Dev? You know I don't drink."

"You sound drunk. You're lying passed out in bed, your body covered in fucking love bites. There's a naked asshole I have the urge to throw through the fucking window lying beside you, and I want to know what the hell is going on." Devon's voice had risen to just a few decibels below ear shattering.

"I don' drink, Dev, you know that," Glenn repeated in confusion. He turned to look at the man beside him, and Riley grimaced at the look of horror that filled Glenn's face. "What the hell?"

Owen smiled, and if Riley wasn't mistaken there was more smug satisfaction than happiness in that look. "Come on now, lover, don't you go feeling all those nasty morning after regrets. We spent a fantastic night fucking each other like crazy, and I for one will carry the memory of it with me for a long time."

Glenn scrambled away from Owen and turned to look up at Devon. "Dev, I—I don't drink. And I don't remember anything."

Owen leaned forward. "You were hitting the drink pretty hard there, lover. You wanted me to fuck you and—"

"You say one more word," Marcel interrupted, "and you will leave here with a severe limp."

"You can't—"

Riley stepped forward, a move that silenced Owen immediately. "He can. He will. Now, shut the fuck up."

Devon looked into Glenn's face for a moment then nodded. "What's the last thing you do remember?"

Glenn frowned as he thought. "We'd finished up for the day, and some of the guys on Riley's team were going to grill some steaks for dinner."

Riley nodded. The boys did that a lot, as it meant they got to eat mostly meat and drink beer.

"Maddox wanted to stay for a few beers, and I reminded him that this morning we were going to test the long scope we brought the other day. Then I left. I remember grabbing a drink in the kitchen, then nothing more."

"It's like I already said, you hit the whiskey pretty damn hard," Owen interjected, but there was a calculating look in his eye.

Devon snorted a sound of disbelief. "Damn, boy, you are going to have to drink a whole fucking gallon of mouthwash to get rid of the taste of that bullshit out of your mouth. I've known Glenn for six years, and that boy don't drink. He has his reasons, and there ain't nothing in this world that would drive that boy to drink. Not knowingly."

Owen's eyes widened, and he glanced around the room. Riley had seen more than his fair share of assholes looking for a place to run, so he moved to block the door and when Owen's furious gaze met his, he grinned.

"Maybe you don't know him as well as you think," Owen snapped.

"And maybe you're spinning that pile of shit story because you slipped him a little something. Why don't I get Sam in here to run a few tests on Glenn's blood and see what that comes back with? Hell, we should probably call that DA friend of yours, too, Marcel. Seems to me like Glenn has a pretty strong case here." Devon turned as if to walk out and find Sam right then.

"Wait!" Owen called out, and Dev smiled, not in the least surprised. "Yeah, I slipped him something that would relax him. What's wrong with that?"

"What's wrong with that? That's fucking illegal, you asshole," Glenn roared in anger.

Marcel moved to his side of the bed to wrap an arm around his shoulder. "Glenn, it's okay. We can get the fucker charged, and he'll go away for a really long fucking time. Calm down."

"Calm down?" Glenn asked trying to struggle out of his hold. "I'll fucking kill him. *No one* touches me without my consent. He fucking raped me!"

"Hey now," Owen said in alarm, holding his hands out in front of him imploringly, "let's not get ahead of ourselves here. It wasn't an illegal substance, just something that made him relax, and when I brought out the whiskey he was a more than willing participant in what went on between us. There was no rape. It was consensual."

"Owen." Riley's voice was cold and hard as he allowed every drop of contempt he felt for the man show in his voice. "When your advances on someone involve a narcotic, legal or otherwise, it is not considered consensual sex, and why the fuck would you do something like that? These guys are a fucking sniper team, with skills you can only ever imagine. What in the hell would possess you to take a run at one of them like that?"

Owen's entire faced turned ugly, filled with a hatred that Marcel found surprising. "Because they all walk around here thinking they're all fucking shit hot and better that the rest of us! Especially him." Without even looking in his direction, Owen pointed at Glenn. "Every time, every *damn* time I tried to talk to him, or convince him to come and have a drink with me, he blew me off. He never once spent time with any of us, getting to know us. He just walked around with his fucking nose in the air. I wanted to bring him down a peg or two."

Glenn snarled, and Marcel held him as he lunged in Owen's direction again. "And you thought to do that by making it so that I'd slept with you? You better get the hell out of this house, this town, and this goddamn state. You're lucky I have no fucking desire to press charges against you for this. But if I find you once this drug you slipped me has cleared my system, I will fucking *end* you."

Owen looked startled for a moment before he looked over at Riley as if gauging Glenn's sincerity. "You'd better believe him and do what he says, Taylor. He's one of the best snipers in the business. You come within fifteen hundred yards of him, he will take you out."

"Better make that twenty-two hundred," Dev corrected from where he stood with his arms crossed over his broad chest. "Glenn's shot farther than that, but in terms of accuracy at distance, twenty-two hundred is his sweet spot. So you'll want to get the fuck off my property and out of Redwood Falls in the next thirty minutes, or I can't guarantee one of us won't take you out from a distance and laugh while we do it."

Owen grabbed his clothes, hastily pulling on his jeans. Marcel stayed with his friend. Devon stood to the side of the door like a fucked off gargoyle standing vigil. From the tension in his stance, it was obvious he was using every bit of control to keep from beating the shit out of Owen in front of Glenn. No one wanted Glenn to have to endure Owen's presence longer than necessary, but Riley was determined that he'd be leaving in pain. As Owen went to step through the door, a thought suddenly occurred to Riley, and he stepped in front of the man.

"I'm gonna ask you a question, and you are going to tell me the truth." Riley kept his voice low, almost growling his words. "Trust me when I tell you that I will know if you are lying to me, and if you do, it will not go well for you. Did you have something to do with the I-beam falling? Or moving the fucking survey pegs?"

This time Owen's eyes widened in surprise. "Fuck no, Riley. I wouldn't do something to screw you over. You've been nothing but good to me."

"Then let me introduce you to the side of me you are not going to like," Riley snarled as he pushed Owen out of the door, before following him out. "Glenn might not want to press charges, but I am going to make it so you never get work in this part of the county again. Hell, if I can swing it, you will be unemployable anywhere you look for work. Now, because I am responsible for bringing you here, it will be me throwing you off this property. And let me warn you, the landing is gonna hurt."

Chapter Eight

Marcel watched quietly as Glenn pounded the old punching bag hanging in the oak tree beside the main house. Devon had insisted on keeping it for sentimental reasons. Marcel was standing on the veranda with Sam and Finn, and none of them knew how to help their friend. It had been three days since the debacle with Owen Taylor.

Of the five members of Bravo team, Glenn was quietest, but he had completely withdrawn into himself after that. Marcel had learned early on that Glenn did not like to talk about himself or his past. Glenn and Maddox had the kind of partnership that sometimes there was just no need for words. When they were working, and Glenn was sighting a target down his scope, they acted almost as one, and outside of that Maddox would often answer for both of them. Now that Maddox was effectively MIA, Glenn had become even more withdrawn.

"Has anyone heard from Maddox?" Sam asked quietly.

"Dev has his ear to the ground," Finn answered just as quietly, "but nothing so far. He's even gone to your old CO, Colonel Anderson looking for help. But he's got nothing but bupkis. It's like he's just disappeared."

Marcel sighed, leaning down on the railing that ran the length of the whole veranda. "And with his training, he is not going to be found until he wants to be."

Glenn had asked where Maddox was the morning he'd left, and Marcel could still remember the look on his face when Marcel gave him Maddox's message. His friend had gone white. Then his face had flamed red, and Marcel had been positive he had spotted a thread of shame in his expression. After a moment it had turned to anger.

"So he just packed up and left?" Glenn had asked his voice hoarse.

Marcel nodded, looking to Devon for guidance, but his LT had just grimaced.

"I can't believe he would just leave like that," Glenn had murmured to himself, almost as if the rest of them weren't standing in his room. "He didn't even give me a chance to explain. He just what, looked into the room, decided that what he saw was all he needed to know and then he just up and left?"

Dev had tried to get Glenn to go with him to the airport to look for Maddox, but he had refused. It had been hard seeing his friend turn to ice right before his eyes that day. Nothing anyone could say or do could convince Glenn to lay charges against Owen. When he had come downstairs later that day, Marcel hardly recognized his friend. They had all sat down to dinner in an attempt to regain some semblance of normalcy when Glenn finally spoke.

"I talked with Maddox," Glenn's voice had been flat, no intonation or inflection whatsoever.

"How?" Dev had asked, and Marcel knew he had been trying to find a way to get a hold of Maddox all afternoon.

"Burner phone. He and I both have one."

Dev growled. "What the hell is that shit? Anyone else have a secret comms device they wish to tell me about?" Dev glared around the room. "What the fuck is the number?"

Glenn shook his head, and stood up from the table. "I'll give it to you, but it won't do you no good. He'd have destroyed it by now. We all know that."

"Fine," Dev snapped, "I'll just kick his ass when

he gets back."

"He ain't coming back," Glenn said over his shoulder before stepping out the room, leaving the rest of them in shock.

Glenn had downright refused to talk further about it after that. He'd shut down. Marcel had witnessed Glenn do that on occasion over the years. Usually it was when they were in combat and children were involved in the altercation, or whenever someone would talk about their childhoods. This one was slightly different however. In those occasions from their past Glenn's expression would turn blank. Right now, whenever someone mentioned Maddox, Glenn's eyes blazed with rage.

Bravo team was down a member, and there was nothing anyone could do about it. Marcel was pissed off at Maddox. Had Glenn told him what actually happened? It was hard to imagine Maddox leaving if he actually knew the truth. Marcel was livid that the man he'd always thought was infallible, and had DNA that was a fifty-fifty mix of honor and loyalty had left. Not just left Glenn, but all of Bravo team, and that was not something that was easy to forgive.

"Right, that's it," Finn announced loudly, pulling Marcel out of his thoughts. Finn then stomped down the stairs heading in Glenn's direction. Marcel shared a quick "what the fuck" glance with Sam before the two of them leaped off the veranda and followed in his wake.

Glenn didn't even slow down, simply maintained a steady punishing pace on the bag, landing punch after heavy punch on the thing. Marcel had almost cried out when Finn stepped between Glenn and the bag, and it was by the grace of God and Glenn's stellar boxing training that Finn avoided serious injury.

"What the hell?" Glenn panted as he stepped back, and stumbled slightly. Marcel knew muscle fatigue when he saw it, and Glenn was verging on collapse.

"Ding, ding, ding! Give the man a gold star, he stole my line." Finn always had a flair for the dramatic, and Marcel thought that perhaps that was exactly what Glenn needed to help break him from this funk. "Except I would have added more to it. My opening line was going to be 'what the hell are you doing to yourself, Glenn?' You have been out here night after night, pounding on this stupid old punching bag and losing yourself in the pain of it all. Do you think that I wouldn't recognize that move? Hell, G, I basically invented that move!"

Glenn planted two gloved hands on his hips, still breathing heavily. "What are you going on about, Finn? Can't a guy simply be beating on this thing for fitness? Not everyone pounds a heavy punching bag to vent some type of emotional turmoil you know."

"Oh I know that, Glenn." Finn stepped forward until he stood almost toe to toe with Glenn. "Some guys take their fists to their children and beat the fuck out of them instead." Finn knew all about that. Marcel had witnessed what Finn's father had done to him and his little brother Nate, and it made his blood boil that anyone could do that to any kid, let alone their own child.

Glenn's jaw tightened, and his whole face seemed to turn to granite. "I am more than aware of that."

"I know you are." Finn stepped forward placing a hand on Glenn's arm. "Like recognizes like, Glenn, and I can tell you had a few dealings with violent assholes in your childhood, too, but that's not what I am referring to. When you come out here night after night, you are pounding the shit out of this bag in an effort to stop hurting."

Glenn frowned. "That makes no fucking sense."

"Yeah, it does," Sam added as he stepped around Glenn to stand beside Finn. "I could bore you to tears with the statistics and research that all points to Finn making complete sense, but I won't. What it boils down to, Glenn, is that you are using this bag as an outlet for your frustrations and that is healthy to a point, but not when it is your only outlet. Glenn, I hear you pacing in your room at night when the nightmares come, but when I ask you about it you tell me nothing's wrong. You were abused by that prick, and I don't think you've come to terms with that."

"We know that you are hurting, brother. It is clear to all of us," Marcel added as he moved to stand on Finn's other side. "I don't know shit about what happened to you as a kid. You've kept that pretty much to yourself, and I don't need to know what happened to know that you are my brother. You are hurt, and struggling to come to terms with what happened, and the one person you can usually depend on left you to deal with this on your own. Maddox fucked up."

Glenn inhaled sharply, his wild eyes locking to Marcel's. "This doesn't have shit to do with him."

"Bullshit."

Marcel flinched slightly at the shock of Devon's voice coming from behind him. For a big bastard, he moved quietly.

"This has everything to do with Maddox, and as soon as I find him and drag his as back here you can beat the shit out of him for real. I know that's what you're picturing night after night when you come out here." Devon stepped closer, and Finn, Sam and Marcel cleared the way. "Marcel is right. Maddox fucked up. He left you, when I know that he promised he never would."

Bravo team had fought together for six years. Although they had survived their battles, there were times when it was a close call. During those times when death seemed to be reaching its gnarled hand in their direction their conversations turned to their regrets, what they wished they had achieved, and who they would have liked to have said goodbye to. For Devon it was always Finn, and it pleased Marcel and the team no end that he got his happily-ever-after with the man who meant so much to him.

Glenn never really talked about his past, but in those moments he would turn and look at Maddox. The look was always the same, and Marcel likened it to a drowning man looking at his last chance at survival. Maddox would nod, and tell Glenn that he would always have his back, and it would the two of them against the world. "Where you go, I go." Five words that always seemed to calm Glenn, and when he left, the Glenn they knew seemed to shatter on the inside.

"Dev," Glenn whispered, and Marcel could feel the pain in his tone. He knew how private Glenn was, and he would hate to break down in front of all of them. He touched Sam and Finn on their arms and jerked his head in the direction of house. The three of them walked away from their friend just as Glenn took a shaky breath, telling them all he was close to breaking point.

"Goddamn that bastard Owen, and goddamn you too, Maddox," Sam growled as they walked up the stairs to the veranda.

"Once my Dev finds him," Finn said, his voice ringing with a similar anger to what Marcel felt, "and he will, I'm gonna go hunt Maddox down and beat the stupid out of him. Why would he think that leaving would be better than comforting the one person you care for more than anyone else in this world?"

"Finn—"

"Oh hell no," Finn snarled over Marcel, "you don't get to play the whole we're Bravo team and we stick up for each other card on this one, Frenchie. That

Marine decided that rather than manning up and facing the man I know he has feelings for, that it was best to sidle out of this place on his ass. I know he had to have been dragging his ass, because both his feet were firmly jammed down his throat. Anyway he left. All of you are like family to me, and despite not having the best example of family life as a child, I do know this. You don't turn your back on family."

Marcel laughed. "You do have a way with words, Finn. But I wasn't going to say that at all. In fact, if that's your plan, I'll hold him down for you."

Sam snorted. "Maddox is twice your size, Marcel. Hell, I'd better help you. We'll hold him down and you can smack the stupid right outta him, Finn."

"Then it's sorted," Finn announced as he turned to walk back into the house. "Frenchie and Prettyboy will hold the big ox down, and I'll get to slapping the stupid right out of the son of a bitch."

****

"Do you think Dev will find him?" Riley asked as he reached for another slice of pizza.

Marcel had surprised him with homemade pizza that he had made that afternoon when he came in from work. Pizza was Riley's favorite dish, and Marcel had insisted that he hadn't truly had pizza until he'd eaten Marcel's pepperoni and mushroom deep dish pizza. He made the dough himself, and Riley had to concede that it was fucking fantastic.

"Yeah, I do." Marcel sighed as he wiped his hands on a napkin and sat back against the couch. "Dev was known for two things in our unit. His loyalty and his goddamn stubbornness. The reason we were one of the most successful sniper teams in the Corps, was because that man never gives up. And when the person he's determined to save, and not give up on is a Bravo team member, then Devon turns into a damn demon. He'll bring Maddox back."

Riley grinned. "And Finn will slap the stupid out of him while you and Sam hold him down. I will need to organize some beers and popcorn for that. I have a feeling it will be one hell of a show." Riley popped the last bite of pizza into his mouth and moaned at the flavor. "Damn, baby, you should open a pizzeria. I'd be your best customer."

Marcel stood up and cleared away the plates, placing them next to the sink in the galley kitchen. "Now won't that be a surprise to the team. They know all about my toil and struggle through law school and boot camp. They'll fall about in shock when I come out and open a pizza parlor."

Riley stood up and walked over to stand behind Marcel, leaning down to press a kiss to the side of his neck. "I think there might be a way to combine the two. Think about it, you could have a law practice at the back of the parlor, and people can eat your pizza while they are waiting for their appointment."

Marcel tilted his head to give Riley more access, and he made the most of it by opening his mouth against the sensitive skin and nibbling on him. "Jesus, Riley," Marcel moaned as he rocked his hips back against Riley's instantly rock hard dick. "Why is it that you get me so damn hot so fucking quickly?"

"It's the same for me, lover, I can assure you." Riley reached around and tugged Marcel's t-shirt from his jeans. Then Riley pushed his hand down past Marcel's fly to grip his cock.

"Fuck!" Marcel thrust his hips forward convulsively as Riley worked him with his hand.

At the feel of Marcel's rock hard cock, damp at the head with pre-cum, sliding so beautifully in his hand,

Riley groaned against Marcel's neck and turned them both in the direction of the bedroom. "Dishes can wait. I can't."

Riley walked them both into the room, not allowing any space to form between him and Marcel. He continued to squeeze Marcel's cock rhythmically as they walked and he nibbled his way around the sensitive skin on his lover's neck. Marcel reached up and behind him to grip onto Riley's hair, pulling him closer and urging him to take his neck a little rougher. Always eager to comply, Riley attacked Marcel's neck, knowing that he would be leaving marks of possession for all to see, but not giving one shit about it.

When they reached the foot of the bed, Riley pulled his hand out of Marcel's jeans, both of them groaning at the loss. "I want you in my mouth, baby," Riley said in a harsh voice, his breathing heavy.

Riley began to strip, shedding his clothes as fast as he could, his eyes never leaving the man in front of him. Marcel was moving a little slower, his movements so graceful they almost looked fluid. Riley would forever feel like an elephant moving in water next to him, but he could absolutely appreciate the perfect picture Marcel made as he moved.

There was one bonus for moving like he did, he finished first. Marcel was naked from the waist down, and oh what a sight he made. He was in the process of removing his t-shirt up and over his head. Before Marcel's head was free of the shirt, Riley dropped to his knees before him, and swallowed his cock, sucking it down until his lips nestled in the tight, trimmed curls nestled at the base.

"*Mon dieu!*" Marcel cried out, his body rocking forward so suddenly Riley gripped Marcel's hips to stop him from toppling over. There was a mad scramble above him, and then Marcel's head emerged from the shirt seconds before it was flung across the room.

Riley held Marcel's gaze as he flattened his tongue to press it against the sensitive underside of his lover's cock, loving the groan and shudder he was given as a reward. Riley slid his hands up the back of Marcel's thighs, reveling in the taut muscles that led up to the ass that featured so frequently in his dreams, and had from the day he saw Marcel. Riley stared up at Marcel, demanding with just one look that he keep his eyes open and on him. When Marcel's eyes seemed to grow heavy as his cock swelled in Riley's mouth, he used his teeth on him, pressing them around the tight base of Marcel's cock, and his eyes opened wide.

"Oh, fuck! Christ, yeah, use your teeth on me, lover," Marcel said in a voice that shook, and Riley knew he was close. Adding a little extra suction and some serious tongue action when he pulled back, he almost let Marcel's cock slip from his lips. When Marcel's body started to shake, Riley took him to the back of his throat and swallowed. And that was all it took. Marcel reached out, gripping Riley's head between his hands, and roared as he came. Riley groaned out loud as Marcel's cock pumped within his mouth. Riley worked his tongue up and around Marcel's twitching cock, making sure not to waste a single drop.

When Marcel slumped forward, as if his legs were about to buckle, Riley stood up, pulling him into his arms. "Fuck, you are so damn hot when you come like that."

Marcel laughed breathlessly. "I don't think I have ever come like that. *Merde*, Riley, you take my fucking breath away."

Riley pulled back to press a quick, hard, open-mouthed kiss on Marcel's lips, sharing with him the flavor he still savored in his mouth. "And I haven't finished with you yet." He moved them both again, until Riley stood at the head of the bed with his back closest to the wall. Kissing Marcel, loving how pliant his lover's mouth was beneath his, he reached out, slid the drawer of the bedside table open and withdrew the lube they kept there.

Riley released Marcel's mouth and dropped to sit on the edge of the bed, his legs wide, and the backs of his knees pressed tight against the mattress. He clicked open the lube and rubbed a generous amount on his rock hard dick, growling at the pleasure and pain it caused. Reaching out, he tugged Marcel's leg up until he had it placed on the mattress beside him, and he used the lube that remained on his fingers to prepare Marcel to take his cock. He pushed two fingers into Marcel's tight body, watching as a warm red swept into Marcel's face and his expression filled with pleasure.

"You are so responsive," Riley murmured as he added a third finger and began to fuck Marcel with them. "All I have to do is play with your ass for a while and you're hovering on the edge again."

Marcel reached out to lay his arms over Riley's shoulders. "It's your touch. You know just how to touch me to make my entire body go up in flames."

Riley knew all about going up in flames. He was pretty close to spontaneous combustion himself. As if sensing that Riley was close to the end of his control, Marcel slid onto the mattress on his knees, straddling Riley, just how he'd hoped.

Marcel reached down between them, and Riley groaned when his warm hand gripped his cock, hard and with purpose, just as Riley liked it. Then Marcel was pressing the head of Riley's cock against his back entrance and flexed his hips to take him in. Riley tensed every muscle in his body when he felt the scalding heat of Marcel's ass envelop him, and Marcel didn't stop until he had every inch Riley had to offer.

Riley growled when Marcel's taut ass touched his thighs, and he leaned back on his arms and spread his legs a little wider. Taking the hint, Marcel put his hands back to rest on Riley's knees and then he began to move. Riley didn't know where to look. The pleasure that filled Marcel's face as he rode Riley hard was mesmerizing, but the sight of his cock disappearing into Marcel's tight body was so fucking hot he couldn't help but watch.

"Shit. Marcel, you ... I ... shit. Fuck!" Riley spoke through gritted teeth and knew he was babbling like an idiot and cursing like a sailor, but his orgasm was racing toward him so damn fast and try as he might, he couldn't seem to hold it at bay.

"Riley!" Marcel cried out as Riley felt his cock swell. Knowing that his lover was close to coming again, and not wanting to ever leave him unsatisfied, Riley bore down on his pleasure. Then using his stomach muscles to hold him in position, Riley lifted one arm to Marcel's thick hard cock and gripped it tight, jerking it twice, and that was all it took. Marcel's head went back and he shouted out in pleasure and Riley watched as his first jet of cum shot onto Marcel's stomach. Then he lost control and flew into the maelstrom of pleasure.

Roaring Marcel's name, Riley fell back onto the bed, jerking his back and arching his hips as his body released into his lover. Marcel took everything he had to give him, including the last piece of Riley's heart that he had been holding back, afraid to give it all in case Marcel decided to give it back. And once Marcel knew everything about Riley, that was very much a possibility.

Chapter Nine

"Can't sleep?" Marcel's sleepy voice broke the quiet in the dark room, and Riley sighed.

"No, and I had hoped I wouldn't keep you awake. You want me to leave?" Riley made to slide from the bed, but Marcel rolled over and lay across Riley's chest. "I'll take that as a no, and settle back down then."

"You can take that as a hell no," Marcel murmured as he hugged Riley tight, his hand sliding against the scar and tattoo on his left side and Riley couldn't help but tense. Marcel's fingers fell away immediately. "Sorry."

When Marcel went to slide off him completely, Riley held him tight over his chest with his right arm, and used his left hand to draw Marcel's hand back to the tattoo, and the ugly scars it covered. "Don't apologize, love. Everything I am is yours. You might not be ready to hear the words, Marcel, but there is no hiding from the truth behind them. I'm in love with you, and you should know everything about me. The good, the bad," Riley sighed as he pressed Marcel's hand tight against his skin, "and the downright evil."

Marcel pressed a kiss to Riley's chest. "Firstly, I am more than ready to hear those words, Riley Marksmen, and just so that we are clear, I love you, too. If everything you are is now mine, then the same holds true for you. Secondly, I think there was something that both of us were keeping from each other, and now is as good a time as any to share them."

Riley leaned up and pressed a kiss to the top of Marcel's head. "Do you want me to go first?"

Marcel was already shaking his head. "Nope, me. I want to tell you what I was keeping from you and share in the laughter it will no doubt bring you, because now it seems so damn stupid." Marcel propped his chin up on the fist he curled onto Riley's chest, but his right hand remained on the tattoo on Riley's side, sliding his fingers up and over the scars that lay there.

"You've been to war, and you know that there are moments of uncertainty, when you don't know which way things are going to go," Marcel said into the darkness, and Riley tightened his hold on him because he did know about those times. "Snipers have a term, when everything is up in the air. You've planned for the wind, the distance, the velocity, any potential factor that could affect your aim and you've taken your shot, but nothing happens. You've missed your target, you're aim is high and right, or something took your bullet from its true path. Whatever the reason, you're completely off target. We call it 'no impact', and when a spotter or a sniper calls that out, you know that you are now compromised. Your element of surprise and the knowledge that no one knows you are there, let alone that you have a target locked in your crosshairs, is gone. Then everything around you blows up.

"Bravo team has been there before, more times than I care to remember, and more times than we should have survived. When we were pinned down and situations looked dire, we would all talk about who we would want to say goodbye to. And what we would say. The only people I had in my life that would miss me, the only ones that I wanted to say goodbye to, were my team. And it made me sad. I have had sex with a lot of men, Riley. I'm not going to shy away from that. I used sex as a substitute for affection. For me I was looking for a connection, no matter how fleeting. Until I met you, I had fucked a lot of guys, but I had never made love with one."

Riley's heart ached for Marcel. There had been

yearning in his tone when he talked about not having anyone other than his team. Riley didn't want to take a thing away from Bravo team. They were as tight as brothers, but there was something about the love of someone who held your heart and had given you theirs. That was a love that meant a whole lot more to a man, and now that Riley had Marcel in his life and in his heart he knew that better than he had before.

Riley reached up to run his hands through Marcel's hair. "It's the same for me, Marcel. We've talked about this before, I have enjoyed having men and women in my bed in the past, but now I couldn't imagine being with anyone but you."

Marcel made a happy sound and pressed another kiss to Riley's chest. "Yeah, I know, but the guys always ragged on me for having a lover in every port, and it got to me a little. I wasn't a man-whore by any stretch of the imagination, but I definitely sought comfort in the arms of willing partners."

"If I hear them rag on you about it now I'll have something to say about it. And it will involve my fists."

Marcel laughed, and his fingers returned to strumming gently over the scars on Riley's side and he knew it was time to share his own story. "Do you know what the words mean?"

"*Nunquam obliviscere, nunquam ignosce*," Marcel said softly, "I knew the first part was 'never forget' the night I saw it for the first time."

Riley swallowed the bitterness of the memories the tattoo brought. "Never forgive. The last two words mean 'never forgive' and I never will."

Marcel moved his hands gently over the scar, and remained quiet. Riley knew he was giving him time to gather his thoughts and form the words. "My father was a mean son of a bitch. He was raised by a cold heartless woman that threw him out when he was only fifteen years old. I don't blame her, because when I say he was mean, Marvin was an evil bastard, and I am pretty sure he was that way from birth. He met my mom when she was only seventeen, and he was twenty-six, old enough to know better. He turned her head, and she left her family for him. From what she told me, the first time he raised his fists to her was their wedding night."

Riley heard the way his voice caught on that, and he cleared his throat. This was the first time he had ever talked about this, to anyone, but it seemed only right that it was with Marcel. "My mom was one of those women who would do anything for their kids, you know what I mean? She was working two jobs just to keep a roof over our heads and food on the table, and my father never got off his ass to help. He played me, too. For years, I did everything he asked of me, trying to win his love and his acceptance. How fucking stupid was I? That narcissistic son of a bitch was using me to control my own mother, and I let him. I was eight when he killed my mom."

Marcel's head came up off his chest in shock, and Riley was thankful for the darkened room.

"I came home from school and Marvin had her over the kitchen table, his hands wrapped around her neck. He was pissed because she had spent money on a birthday present for me, and he wanted it to gamble or for alcohol or some shit like that. Either way she had nothing to give him, and he took his fists to her. I ran at him as soon as I saw what was happening. However a woman who was about twenty pounds underweight and a scrawny eight year old kid were no match for him. Our neighbors called the cops, and as they were coming up the stairs, Marvin started screaming that it was somehow all my fault. He grabbed a kitchen knife and came at me, but my mom stepped directly into the path of that fucking knife and he never even blinked. I'll never forget the look of madness in his eyes. He stabbed her four times. She was screaming in pain, but she never turned away from me. She was pleading with me to run the entire time, and I couldn't move. I just stood there watching while my father stabbed my mother then dropped her to the floor. He grabbed me as the police stormed into the apartment. Before they shot him, he stabbed me under my arm, two rapid thrusts of the knife, and he twisted the hilt on the second one, taking out a large part of my lung in the process. He nearly killed me, too, that day."

"Please tell me that they shot that fucker thirty-six times after that?" Marcel snarled and Riley stroked a hand down his lovers back.

"They did shoot him, but not enough to kill the bastard, although he did lose the ability to walk so he paid a price. Marvin served twenty-five years for her murder, with an additional two years for the attempt on my life." Riley sighed.

Marcel was quiet for a moment. "Where is he now, do you know?"

Riley grinned in the dark. He heard the intent in Marcel's tone. His man wanted to hunt his father down and do what snipers liked to do, and as much as he would really love to see that happen, he wasn't about to risk his Marcel.

"I can honestly say, my love, that I have no fucking clue where he is, and no desire to go looking." Riley rolled gently so that he could lean down over Marcel, and he pressed a gentle kiss against his full lips. "I have some suspicions, but nothing concrete. He is nothing to me, not now, not ever again. The tattoo over those scars is a memorial to my mom, because I will never forget her, and I will never forgive my father for taking her from me."

"Why didn't you want to talk about it?" Marcel asked quietly. "It's not like any of that was your fault. Did you think I would think less of you for it?"

Riley leaned down and placed his forehead against Marcel's. Never before had he had the wish that he could crawl inside another human being, but right now he wanted nothing more than to be as close to his lover as possible.

"I failed my mother that day," Riley whispered, shaking his head when Marcel went to speak. "Oh, I know logically that I was only a kid, and he was a grown man. What could I have done, right? When I saw him holding my mom down, strangling her, and she was ripping at his hands so she could draw breath, I thought about going for the kitchen knife. The same damn knife he drove into my mother's body four fucking times. It was right beside me. But I couldn't bring myself to kill my father. I was still that sad, fucked up kid trying to win his father's love, and I didn't want to hurt him. But he had no hesitation in killing his wife, or taking that same damn knife and driving it into my side. If I had been more like my father, I could have saved my mom."

Marcel shook his head, wrapping his arms around Riley and drawing him tighter to his chest. "You wouldn't be the man I love if you were more like that asshole. You take after your mom. Your loyalty and the way you look after your crew tell me that, and it is definitely part of why I love you. That bastard never deserved your love."

Riley felt like a weight had been lifted from a dark area in his heart, and the light from the love of the man beneath him flooded in. He felt relief at having told someone the secret he had harbored all these years. He was thankful that Marcel had understood and not turned from him, but most of all he felt … loved.

Chapter Ten

"Marcel!"

He jumped at his desk at the roar of his name coming from the hallway. He recognized the voice. Dev had yelled at him loud and often over the years, but the tone he used was not one Marcel had ever heard him use before and it had Marcel standing up and running for the hallway. He almost slammed fully into Dev as the man took the stairs up to the second floor at a dead sprint, three stairs at a time.

"What the hell?" Marcel grunted as he gripped onto Dev, both of them teetering on the top step. It was only through their combined brute strength and stubborn will that had them still standing and not rolling in a ball of limbs to the bottom of the stairwell.

"Marcel." Dev's face was granite, and Marcel knew he wasn't going to like hearing what came next. "There's been an accident on the site. Riley, he—"

That was as far as he got before Marcel was leaping down the stairs, heading for the front door.

"Goddamn it, Marcel, wait!" Dev roared from behind him, but he wouldn't. He couldn't. He sprinted for the accommodation block Riley had been working on that morning. Marcel had wandered over to share lunch with Riley and his team an hour ago, and left when they were going back to work.

"He's hurt, but he's okay!" Dev yelled.

Marcel heard him, but he didn't slow down. He leaped up the stairs that led to the wraparound veranda the team had finished that morning. He ran through the open door, and headed toward the sound of voices in the back room of the house.

He turned the corner just as he heard Riley's low groan of pain. "Son of a fucking bitch, Sam, what the hell are you trying to fucking do?"

"Secure the damn thing in your leg so that it doesn't nick any arteries," Sam said calmly. There was one thing about their field medic, he was always cool under fire. "The one in your arm isn't near an artery, but this one is. I for one do not want to have to tell Marcel that you bled out on my watch. I couldn't outrun the bullet he'd send my way."

"You couldn't hide from me either," Marcel said as he walked into the room, not stopping until he had reached Riley's side where he sat in a chair, blood pouring from a wound in his right thigh with what looked like a large nine inch nail sticking out of it, and one in his right bicep.

Riley looked up at him, and Marcel saw the pain in his eyes, but there was frustration and anger there, too. "Damn it, who called you? I was hoping to get this sorted before I told you about it."

Sam snorted. "How the hell were you planning to get this sorted, Ri? I hate to tell you this, but you have a fucking nine inch piece of metal sticking out of your leg. I aced anatomy, and I can tell you that it is really near an artery and if you move and it nicks it, then we will be in a shitload of trouble."

Riley frowned as he stared down at the nail, frustration clear on his face. "Can't I just pull it out? Then you could put a pressure bandage on it and boom! We're done."

Sam sent a pointed look in Marcel's direction. "Control your man, would you?"

Marcel felt a slight thrill ripple through him at the open acknowledgement of his claim over Riley.

"And how do you propose I do that?" Marcel asked dryly.

"Ether?" Dev suggested helpfully from behind

him, and Marcel glared at him.

"Fuck you, Dev," Riley groaned as Sam finished wrapping a bandage tightly about the piece of metal embedded in his thigh, a bandage that Marcel was not happy to see quickly turning red with blood.

"I'll get the truck," Dale said as he moved toward the door. "You are bleeding heavily, and we need to get you to a doctor."

"Aw, now see," Riley said, pointing at Dale. "That is a true friend. Looking out for me, and making sure I get the help and care that I need." Marcel knew he was joking and laughing to try to hide the pain he was in, but the perspiration on his brow told a different story.

"That's me, the caring one," Dale said as he turned at the door a wide grin on his face. "But I don't want blood in my truck so I'm grabbing yours." And with that he was out the door.

Marcel chuckled with the rest of them then turned his attention to Riley, who was starting to try to stand. "What the hell are you doing?"

Riley shot him a glare. "Walking out to the damn truck because apparently you all think I need to see a doctor."

"You're damn right you need to see a doctor," Marcel growled as he stepped up to Riley and tugged his arm up over his shoulder. "But you aren't walking out of here on your own. You can't put pressure on that leg."

Riley grunted. "Don't be ridiculous, a little weight's not going to kill me."

Sam stood up from the floor, grabbing his medical kit to take with him. "Well, I hate to disagree with you there, big guy, but it could. You stand on that leg and shift that metal without knowing where it is in your leg and your leg muscle could shift it as you flex, nicking your artery."

"And you will be in a world of trouble, so shut up and let us help you," Marcel added, waiting until Dev took the other side of Riley and the three of them helped him out to Dale's truck.

"This is so fucking stupid," Riley grumped as they all but carried him down the stairs. "Once I find that sabotaging fucktard I am going to use that nail gun and nail him to the nearest tree and let y'all take pot shots at the prick."

"Sabotage?" Dev growled.

"Yeah, that fucking gun read empty and was rigged to fire as soon as someone opened the loading chamber. Dale opened it, and it fired four times rapidly before he was able to face it to the floor and get the thing turned off."

"And you sure that you only caught two of them?" Marcel asked, checking Riley for any further holes.

"Ah, yes," Riley said in a tone that dripped with sarcasm. "This shit hurts, Marcel. I would have known if I had been hit a third time."

They had reached the truck, and Marcel slid into the back seat first to then help Riley in.

Dale had an arm over the seat and was looking back at them. "You would have been proud of me though, Marcel."

"Shut up, Dale," Riley snapped as he shimmied back on the bench seat, making sure to keep his leg as straight as he could. Once Riley was in, Sam closed the door then climbed into the front passenger seat.

Ignoring Riley, Marcel looked over at Dale where he leaned one arm over the front seat, looking back at them with a grin. "Why?"

"Because the first thing I shouted was, 'move'."

Marcel laughed as he looked at Riley. "And what

was your reaction, babe?"

"I think the medication Sam gave me is kicking in," Riley said as he closed his eyes. "I'm falling asleep."

Marcel wrapped an arm around his lover's chest and pressed a kiss to his forehead. "You jumped aside instead of ducking, didn't you?"

Riley sighed. "Faster than I have ever moved before."

****

"You know, Riley, you really are a terrible patient," Sam mused from his position at the back of the room, and Marcel had to agree with him.

"This is bullshit. They took the nail out, so why the hell am I still in this place?" Riley growled, crossing his arms across his chest and fighting to hide the wince of pain the move caused the wound on his arm.

"Because the doctor said you need to have a shot for something," Marcel answered and stretched back in the chair he was sitting in.

"Well, I wish he would hurry the fuck up," Riley snapped, and Marcel had to fight the laugh that bubbled up at the petulant look on his handsome face. Riley had refused the morphine they had offered him when he was first seen, and if it hadn't been for Marcel he would have turned down the two shots of local anesthetic they gave him in order to sew up the wounds the two nails had left behind. Luckily both had not hit anything vital, and the stitches were the only treatment required.

The door opened, and Dale stepped into the room. "Doc's on his way in, just passed him in the hallway."

Riley swung his legs over the side of the bed, and Marcel leaped up to press a hand against his chest. "What the hell are you doing? Just because he's on his way in, doesn't mean he's going to give you the green light to leave."

Riley frowned. "All he needs to do is shove the needle in my arm and I'm out of here."

Marcel grinned, adding an exaggerated waggle to his eyebrows. "What if the shot is in the ass? Now that would be something I wouldn't want to miss."

Riley threw his head back and laughed as the doctor entered the room.

"Well now, that does a doctor's heart good. You'd be surprised how many people wait in fear when they know I'm on the way with a needle."

Riley grinned at the elderly doctor. "Nah, it takes more than a needle to scare me, doc."

The doctor set the tray with a couple of needles on it and two vials of clear liquid on the bed side cabinet. "Well that is good to hear as I have two shots to give you. One is for tetanus, just as a precaution, and the other is an anticoagulant also just as a precaution. With a condition such as yours it is better to err on the side of caution."

Riley sighed but nodded as the doc went about setting up the two shots.

"What condition do you have that requires a blood clotting agent?" Sam's voice was tight, which had Marcel turning to look at him. Sam was frowning, and moving closer to the bed, staring at the name on the vial.

"Well," the doc answered, completely oblivious to Sam's tone, "your friend here has a very unusual blood disorder, nothing life threatening at all, just something that we need to be wary of when he is injured."

"Hereditary stomatocytosis," Sam said in a flat voice.

"Why yes," the doctor said as finished giving Riley the two shots and turning to face Sam. "It's good that you are aware of his condition, and you will know what to look for if there are any issues. I am positive there won't be, but just to be sure, we will schedule a blood test for three weeks and just check his potassium levels."

The doctor stepped from the room, and an eerie silence fell over them. Marcel looked around at the other three men in the room and tried to understand what the hell was going on. Dale looked just as confused as Marcel felt. When Marcel turned to his teammate, Sam's face was like thunder and his eyes remained on Riley.

Marcel looked over at Riley expecting to see the confusion he felt mirrored there, but was shocked as hell at what he saw. Riley wore the expression he often saw on all his Bravo teammates. It was one that locked down all emotion, and made it seem like their faces were made of granite. Finn called it their poker face.

"Tell me it's just a coincidence," Sam asked.

"Is what just a coincidence?" Riley countered, and Marcel suddenly felt like he was watching a chess match being played out before him.

"Hereditary stomatocytosis is very rare."

"It is."

"And it occurs most commonly in people from the same family."

"That would make sense as the word hereditary is in the name." Riley's tone bordered on sarcastic, and Marcel frowned.

"Then explain to me, how you have the exact same condition as Devon," Sam asked as he lifted his hands to his hips. "Something that I only know about because of my role as medic on his team. Finn has always thought there were physical similarities between the two of you, but the rest of us couldn't see it. So I reckon I'll ask you outright. Are you related to Devon?"

Riley's jaw clenched, and his gaze shot to Marcel for a moment. "Yes."

Marcel felt his entire chest tighten. "Why the hell would you keep that a secret?"

Riley shrugged, his expression falling into a stubborn mask of indifference. "It's no body's business but mine who I am related to."

Marcel looked at the man who had been in his bed and had worked his way into his heart over the past few weeks, and felt like he was looking at a stranger. Then a thought struck him that had his stomach turning. "Are you the relative Dev's grandmother's lawyer was trying to find? The one that was originally supposed to inherit Cottonwood Farm?"

Riley's expression never changed, but Marcel saw the guilt that leeched into his eyes. Marcel moved back from the bed, and only then did Riley's stubborn expression drop. "Wait, Marcel, it's not like that."

"Then tell me what it is like, then, Riley," Marcel said stopping to stand at Sam's shoulder. "Did you find out about the inheritance too late to get your hands on the property? And when you discovered that Devon was looking for a contractor it must have been like all your Christmases had come at once, huh? You could get onto the farm and fuck over Dev's plan for the training facility through all those acts of sabotage. Christ, we all really believed that you and your team were working your asses off to fix those mistakes when really you were simply covering your ass so you could do more damage."

"Dude," Dale interjected, "that was not fake. I have worked for Riley for eight years, and he is totally above board, and we have been working our asses off on the build."

Sam nodded and stepped closer to the bed. "That may be so, but correct me if I'm wrong, Dale, but didn't you tell me once that the training facility build was something you were enjoying because it been years since you had taken on a private and small scale build like ours? Marksmen Construction is world renowned for its large scale commercial builds."

"Yeah, I did," Dale said with a frown, his tone losing much of the indignation of moments before. "But Riley was open with the team from the beginning. He told us that this build was important to him and something he needed to do."

Marcel barked a humorless laugh. "Well, I suppose getting his hands on fifteen hundred acres of farmland in Wyoming would be pretty damn important to him. It was the perfect diversion to ensure it was you hurt with that nail gun, Riley, well done."

Riley growled. "I haven't sabotaged anything. Not on this build or any other in my life. I certainly didn't set it up to shoot myself with a fucking nail gun. Twice! Look, can we just get out of here. Let's go back to the farm, and sit down with Devon. I do have a story to tell, but he needs to hear it, too."

Marcel simply stared at Riley, hardening his heart as much as he could.

"Goddamn it, Marcel, you know me! Do you really think I am capable of all of that?"

Marcel was done. "I don't know what you are capable of, Riley, and I am quickly discovering that I don't know you at all. I asked you for one thing, to be honest with me, and let me see the real you, but you couldn't even give me that. So, don't bother to come back to the farm. We will have your equipment and belongings packed up and delivered back to you as soon as possible. Marksmen Construction is fired."

Riley stood up, wincing when he put weight on his injured leg. "Marcel, wait, I can explain everything if you would just give me a fucking chance."

Marcel turned and walked to the door.

"We have a contract, Marcel. You can't fire us without cause." Riley called out.

Marcel stopped half in and half out of the hospital room, then turned to walk back to the bed. "Check your contract, Mr. Marksmen. There is a clause in their relating to full disclosure of any and all information that could affect your ability to complete this build. Your familial links to the property owner, vested interest in the property itself, and failure to disclose that information at the commencement of the contract warrants your immediate dismissal. The fact that you completely abused my trust," Marcel hauled back and punched Riley in the jaw, cursing himself for pulling it slightly, but cheering internally when Riley's head flew to the side and he sat back heavily on the bed, "warrants more than just a punch in the face, but that is all I have left to give you."

With that, Marcel left the hospital room, Sam on his heels, the pain in his hand nothing compared to the one in his heart.

Chapter Eleven

"Damn, I owe Finn twenty bucks."

Riley put the beer bottle he had been about to drink from back down on the bar and turned around to face the man talking to him.

"And I guess you're gonna tell me why now, huh?" Riley asked hoping for a tone of indifference but not sure if he pulled it off.

Devon shot him a pointed look as he sat down on the empty bar stool next to him and signaled the bartender for a beer. "Yeah, I am. Finn is going to be unbearable about winning that twenty bucks, and I am going to have to live with it. He bet me that I would still find you here in Redwood Falls, and that your ass would be sitting in this bar, drowning your sorrows despite it not even being five in the afternoon."

Riley tipped his beer at the Dev in a toast then took a large swig. "It has to be five somewhere in the world, right?"

Dev grinned as he returned the toast with the beer bottle the bartender placed in front of him. "Too right." After he took a drink he placed the bottle down and turned in his seat so he could stare at him.

"So what is this, Dev?" Riley said when the silence began to creep into uncomfortable. "Some kind of intervention or something?"

Dev threw his head back on a laugh. "If you think you are in need of intervention then perhaps you should look into rehab, but you're a big boy and can work that out for yourself."

"Then why are you sitting in this dingy bar on the other side of town from Cottonwood, drinking a beer with someone who has been banned from your property?"

All humor slid from Dev's face. "Because you need to hear what I have to say, and I think I have the right to say it."

Riley winced as he pushed the half-finished beer away from him and turned to face Dev properly. He figured if Dev was going to punch him, then Riley would sit and take it like a man, He more than deserved it.

"Damn, boy," Dev said with a shake of his head, "you look like a man being led to the gallows. I ain't gonna hit you. Your jaw is still swollen from where Marcel laid into you yesterday. I figure he had more reason to hit you than I do. Besides, I've known you were my cousin from a couple of days after that asshat Ford decided to blow up Sam's hiding spot and tried to take my Finn from me."

Riley frowned. "How the hell did you find out?"

Dev rolled his eyes. "Finn spotted some kind of physical resemblance between you and me from the first moment the two of you met. Then when he told me about it I said he was wrong. There was no way I had a cousin as I was the only child of an only child." Dev smiled and shook his head. "And I have to tell you, Riley, that you never tell that man he is wrong. He had your familial connection to me within a few days."

"Why the hell didn't you say something then?" Riley threw his hands up in frustration. If Dev and Finn had known all this time, he could have come clean a lot sooner.

Dev's eyes turned cold. "I see where your thoughts just went, and best you back the fuck up, pull on your big boy pants, and take ownership of your own actions. It was never up to me and mine to out who you are. You turn up out of the blue, at a time when I am getting hounded by some attorney looking to speak to me about the original beneficiary of the farm but wouldn't give me the damn name. When Finn gets the information on you, he finds out about the fact you changed your name and then all that shit about your father. I knew that the original benefactor had to be either you or your dad or both.

"My first reaction was that it was too fucking coincidental and I was going to throw your Navy Seal ass off my property. But Finn saw the way Marcel looked at you, and he had this idea that the two of you were perfect for each other. I thought I would leave it for a while and see where the two of you ended up. Then all that sabotage shit hits the fan. But by then you've proven yourself to me and the team, and Finn is still on at me about how perfect you and Marcel are for each other, and that you fill a void for Marcel that no one else ever could. Hell, I guess Finn can't be right all the time. Marcel was just doing what he always did. Fucking a guy for the hell of it."

Riley leaned forward, barely keeping himself from leading with his fists. "I'll give you an apology for wanting to blame you and Finn for not calling me on my shit when I should have had the balls to do it myself. That is completely on me and something that I will regret for as long as I live. But you speak about Marcel like that again, and you and I will go a round or two and find out for ourselves who would win in a fight between a Seal and Marine."

Dev stared at him for a while, but Riley held his gaze, and just when it seemed like they were about to throw down in the middle of that bar, Dev grinned, leaning forward and smacking Riley in the arm. "Welcome to the club, man!"

Riley blinked, desperately trying to catch up. "What? What club?"

"The 'I am in love and it is very much the forever

kind'.'" Dev leaned over the bar. "Hey, bartender! Grab us a couple of tequila shots would ya? Me and my cousin are toasting to true love."

Riley sat down hard on the bar stool. "Jesus Christ, you go from hot to cold so fucking fast it's hard to keep up. I gotta feel sorry for Finn."

Dev grinned at him as the bartender placed the shot glasses in front of them. "Nah, no need. When it comes to that man, I am always running hot."

Riley laughed, picked up his glass, and he and Dev toasted with a really shitty brand of tequila. Dev frowned, signaling the bartender again. "Dude, hit us again, but this time don't insult our intelligence." The bartender grinned and moved to the back of the bar to no doubt get the good stuff and not the paint thinner he'd served them.

"So, why have you come looking for me, Dev?" Riley asked.

Dev's expression turned introspective. "All those times in combat, when you start to think about not making it back home, your mind turns to those who mean the most to you. Family is important. Bravo are my family, and I don't like seeing one of them in pain. Then you add in this cousin I never knew I had. I knew that the night you stepped in to help my team and Finn that you were good people. But you remained silent about being related to me, and I figured you had your reasons, so I was waiting for you to either sort it out or come to me about it."

Riley nodded. "Marcel told me about the times you and Bravo team would share the final conversations you would have liked to have with the ones you were leaving behind. He talked about those no impact situations, and I knew exactly what he meant. There were times when I was serving that you went on an op, expecting a particular outcome, but when something goes wrong that shouldn't have, your entire world implodes around you."

Dev looked up in surprise. "Well, if Marcel was sharing that with you, then you mean a hell of a lot to him. He was never one to talk about that side of combat with anyone, even those of us who stood and bled beside him."

Riley sighed, and lifted the full shot glass that had appeared in front of him. "He means everything to me, Dev. He has from day one."

"And that is why I am here." Dev shot the tequila back and grinned at the bartender, waggling the glass for more. "Because me and Finn think that you need Marcel as much as he needs you. Your inability to trust him and tell him everything destroyed that man. He has been stomping around the farm, muttering to himself and refusing to even acknowledge that you exist. Finn tried to get him to talk about it, but he got the short sharp French fuck off, and Marcel headed out to the punching bag."

Riley winced before slamming the tequila back and welcoming the warmer burn of the better liquor. "He told me all he wanted was honesty, and although I never lied to him, my omission was just as bad. I was going to tell Marcel, and you and the entire team, but I was so damn busy trying to get us back on track with the build and find out who the hell has been working for my father, and—"

"Wait, what?" Devon asked. "What do you mean working for your father?"

Riley put the empty glass back, sliding it toward the bartender. "All of this sabotage shit *has* to be Marvin Roberts. Despite knowing that he is still miles away, held in the state he lives in by the law and his parole officer, I know it's him. My father hates me. I have known that all my life. And I am pretty sure that he hates you just as bad. He was the one our grandmother expected to take the farm despite the fact she kicked him out when he was a kid. But he never came forward in time, mainly because he was in jail and didn't even know the old bitch had died. I would bet my left testicle that the sabotage is his doing."

Devon sighed, and leaned back in his chair. "That would make sense then I guess. My mother died before I really got to know her, and I was raised by my grandmother. There was little to no love in that house, but she never once mentioned she had a son. I figured when the lawyers talked about a long lost relative they were talking about a third cousin twice removed kind of shit. Not an uncle or a cousin with a legitimate claim to the land. But, you are my cousin, and half of that property is—"

"Oh, hell no!" Riley interrupted, holding his hands up in the age old sign of surrender, "I do not want any part of Cottonwood Farm. Never have, and never will," Riley thought about that for a moment then clarified, "Except for the six foot French guy who has shares in the business. Him I most definitely want."

"Well, him you are going to have to work for, but I think you know that. And if you ever change your mind about the farm, then I am open to it. It's a valuable piece of land."

"Trust me, Devon," Riley said dryly, "my company does very well for itself, and I work because I want to not because I have to. I don't need that land, but I do plan on living on it so we'll call it even."

"Oh really? Where do you plan on living? Last I heard Marcel had kicked your ass out of his rooms, and all your stuff is sitting on the back of your truck in the car park of the motel down the street."

Riley grinned, his future suddenly seeming a lot brighter. "I am going to build Marcel and me a place in the back quadrant of the property. Out of the line of fire so to speak, but close enough for him to do what he needs to do for Bravo team."

Devon paused for a moment. Then a slow grin formed. "I like that. It would be great for all the team to have their own property on the CTF grounds, and with a contractor in the family, we can make that happen. And you know what the best thing about that is?"

Riley picked up the third shot glass filled with the clear liquid that was starting to give him a little buzz. "No idea, share it with me, cousin."

"You're rich, and you're gonna do it for free."

The two of them laughed like lunatics before slamming back the third shot and ordering another. Looked like the two of them were settling in for a long time, and Riley figured it was well overdue.

****

"Wake up!"

Marcel sat up at the shout that sounded like it was coming from someone in his room, seconds before a pillow connected with his face. He rolled out of the bed, and came up in a fighting stance his Sig Sauer in his hand.

"What the hell?" Finn squeaked as his hands shot into the air.

"*Merde*," Marcel growled as he reengaged the safety back on the weapon and held it down at his side. "What the hell are you trying to do, Finn? Get me killed?"

"You?" Finn cried incredulously, pointing at the weapon by Marcel's side. "Get *you* killed? I was the one who had a gun pointed at him. How in the hell would me waking you up end with you getting killed?"

"Because if I'd shot you, do you think Devon would have let me live?" Marcel put the weapon back in its purpose build holster under his bedside table.

"He's right, ya know," Devon called from the living area of Marcel's room, "I woulda had to shoot ya, Marcel, and my cousin, he woulda not been a happy camper."

Marcel frowned as Devon's slurred voice broke off into laughter, and he looked at Finn in confusion.

"Yep, that's your LT," Finn said as he pointed in the direction of the living area, "drunker than I have ever seen him, and I have to tell you. Devon, he is a happy drunk, and I am not sure how to deal with that. So you had better go out there and see what he wants because I cannot get him to go to our rooms until he has spoken with you."

Marcel walked out into his living room and laughed at the sight of his LT leaning heavily against the wall beside the door. "Hey, Dev, you been celebrating something, brother?"

Devon looked over at him and grinned. "Marcel! There you are. I was telling my Finn that I needed to talk to you and there you is. I was drinking with my cousin."

Marcel's heart contracted at the thought of Riley, but he crossed his arms over his chest determined to ignore it. "Well, that's great, Dev. I am glad you were celebrating with your cousin, but why does that mean that I have to be woken up, and end up nearly shooting *your* Finn?"

Dev turned to look at Finn, who was now standing close by Dev's side, obviously concerned that he might keel over at any moment. "See, love, told ya. You never want to wake up a Marine who's sleepin'. And 'specially not one who's a sniper."

"Yes, baby," Finn nodded with a grin, "you told

me, and I will take that to heart from now on." Dev leaned in, and Finn had to step forward to pull Dev's arm over his shoulder to stop the large man from toppling straight to the floor.

"Good, now, Marcel." Dev's focus slid to Marcel. "You need to go and talk with your man. He's out in the forest, looking at building a house."

"What? Why is Riley building a house at," Marcel looked down at his watch, "two-thirty in the morning?"

"Because it's after five somewhere in the world, and he loves you," Devon replied with a look on his face that clearly said that made perfect sense. "Now, go and talk with Riley, and listen to what he has to say. He's out in the back quadrant, and he took a chainsaw with him, so you should be able to find him."

Marcel's jaw dropped. "Is he as drunk as you?"

Dev nodded, looking not in the least bit worried about the fact that an inebriated man was out in the forest with a dangerous piece of equipment. With a curse Marcel raced back into his room for some shoes and a t-shirt.

"Come on, baby," Finn murmured, "let's get you to bed, and we'll leave those two to sort everything out."

"Yeah, let's get to bed. I have plans," Dev growled in a playful tone that Marcel had never heard before, and he was wishing he wasn't anywhere near them now.

"I'm not sure you're gonna be up for any plans, baby," Finn said with a laugh.

Marcel ran past them, heading out into the hall intent on finding Riley and taking that damn chainsaw off him, but he heard Dev growl something in a low tone that made Finn groan in an entirely sexual way, which made Marcel think that perhaps he'd better knock before he came back into his room later.

Chapter Twelve

Marcel ran through the moonlit forest surrounding the facility, heading in the direction of the rear quadrant. Fortunately, there was a high full moon tonight, and it cast an eerie light over everything but made it easy to see where he was going. When he heard the unmistakable sound of a chainsaw trying to start he cursed and piled on the speed. What the hell was Riley thinking? As he drew closer to where the chainsaw was operating, he heard the machinery splutter once again before falling into silence. He shot out into a clearing, and nearly ran straight into the back of the man who was currently leaning over the chainsaw, cursing it for not working right.

"Riley Marksmen!" Marcel yelled as he slid to stop just feet behind the man on the ground. He saw Riley flinch at the sound of his name then look back at him over his shoulder.

"This was supposed to be a surprise." Riley's voice wasn't as slurred as Marcel had expected it to be. "This means that Dev has opened his big mouth. I was going to get you out here tomorrow and show you this space."

"Riley, it's the middle of the night. Visibility might be good because of the moonlight, but it is still too dark for operating equipment that can take out your legs! What the hell are you doing out here with a damn chainsaw?"

"I need to clear some of the mature trees to make room for the space I have planned. I figured why not get started? The sooner I have it built, the sooner it's finished."

Marcel placed his hands on his hips. "You were fired, Riley. You are not even supposed to be on this property yet alone working out here in the middle of the night with a piece of machinery you are in no condition to be using."

"Dale and my team are still working on the build, baby. I don't think that truly counts as a dismissal in my book. And besides, Dev gave me access to the property tonight, and he is selling me this two acre piece, at a healthy percentage above market value I might add," Riley said dryly.

Marcel blinked as he processed that information for a moment. "It was really only you that was fired, and what the hell do you mean that Devon is selling you some of this property?"

"Well, that seems really unfair, and yeah, he did," Riley said with a shrug. "We're family after all."

"That's it?" Marcel asked incredulously. "Devon finds out that you've been lying to us all since you came here, and that you are after a piece of this land so he, what, just sells it to you?"

Riley nodded. "At a healthy percentage above market value like I said. I'm not sure who taught that man his negotiation skills, but damn, I had no chance. I wanted this parcel of land for us, and I was getting it no matter what." Riley frowned as Marcel's heart dropped to the forest floor, then bounced back into his throat. "I think that is where I went wrong. I shouldn't have told him I was desperate for this parcel of land, then actually shown him the plans I'd had drawn up for the cabin. Anyway, Devon and Finn have known since the day we took care of Ford that I was related to Dev."

Marcel took a deep breath and counted to ten. It was a very surreal feeling to be having a conversation with a man, and feel like there was two conversations going on at once time, and small bombs of information were being continuously dropped. "Riley, I'm afraid all of this is doing my head in, and I simply cannot keep up. I think I am just going to turn my ass around and go back to bed. I'm taking this damn chainsaw with me though because if you end up taking your damn leg off I'll never forgive myself." Marcel collected the machinery from the ground and began walking backward. "You and Dev can sort your shit out in the morning."

Marcel turned and had only taken two steps back in the direction he had come from before Riley ran and moved to stand in front of him. For a man who had a good fifty pounds of pure muscle on him he certainly moved fast.

"Wait, Marcel, please." Riley held his hands out slightly from the side, almost as if he were afraid that Marcel was going to make a run for it. "I need to apologize to you *again*, and there are a few things I want to tell you, and I'm not sure I'll get back on the property without copping a bullet in the ass, so please, just stay. Give me five minutes of your time, please."

Marcel put the chainsaw down then crossed his arms over his chest. "Five minutes then I'm outta here."

Riley nodded. "Then let me start with the obvious. I am sorry, Marcel, so fucking sorry that I hurt you. That was never my intention. I had planned all along to tell you who I was, I promise you."

"Why didn't you just tell us when you applied for the job?"

"Because I knew that the lawyers were looking for my dad. I didn't want you all to think exactly what you thought in that hospital room, that I was after this land. I wasn't. Not then."

"Not then, but you are now?"

"Only this two acre piece and nothing else, I swear. I wanted to work on this build for three reasons. The first is that I knew my dad wanted it. He contacted me five years ago when my grandmother died and tried to play the whole long lost father trying to reconnect with his son piece." The disdain in Riley's tone told Marcel exactly what he thought about that. "And when I didn't do anything to help the son of a bitch, he sent someone out after me with the hope of beating me into submission."

"What?" Marcel found it hard to fathom a father sending someone out to hurt their son.

"It shouldn't surprise you after all the shit I told you about that man and what he was guilty of. Anyway, the prick he sent came at me dressed in black and wearing a balaclava, and I tangled with him in the alley behind my apartment. It was a short sharp fight that we both left with a few new scars. I got a new one on my right side," Riley pointed to the knife wound Marcel knew was beneath the shirt he wore, "and he left with two similar scars on his left shoulder. He never came back, and I sent word to my father that if he came at me again, I would make sure I found a way to have it lead back to him. If he wanted to make it out of that place then he had to simply leave me the fuck alone."

"He never sent anyone else?" Marcel had to ask.

Riley shook his head. "No, not that I knew of. I signed my rights away to this place with the lawyer that was handling the estate, and had him keep me updated with everything. When he rang to tell me that Devon was now the owner of the farm I was over the moon, but three days after that, I got word that my father had been released. The bastard wanted this place, and I knew he would come here with plans to get it. So, when the lawyer told me the plans Dev had for this place, I saw my way in, and I took it."

"You think that your dad is behind all the sabotage, don't you?" Marcel knew he was right, and when Riley nodded he sighed. "Okay, so we need to tell the sheriff's office about your suspicions. Nick was over here yesterday trying to see if we were any closer to finding someone with the incentive to sabotage this build."

Riley winced. "Yeah, I've already talked to Nick. He knows all about my dad, and my suspicions, and he has been in touch with his parole officer. My father is still wheelchair bound and in the halfway house he had been assigned to when he left prison. Nick's had a friend of his on the force in Houston head over to the halfway house and speak directly to Marvin. He didn't get anything, and I would have been surprised if he did."

Marcel frowned. "So you could tell everything to the sheriff, but not me?"

Riley ran his hand through his hair, his brown eyes flashing with frustration in the moonlight. "Fuck, Marcel, it isn't like you are making it sound. It's not that I could speak to him and not you. It was more that I had so much to lose with you that I wasn't sure how to broach the subject. I figured if I could find out who was working for my dad, beat the shit out of him and drop him at your feet that you would listen to what I had to say more favorably. I never had anything to do with the sabotage."

There was no missing the sincerity in Riley's tone, and Marcel heard the undercurrent of pain that lay beneath it, pain that Marcel had no doubt caused when he had thrown that accusation at Riley two days ago. Marcel had been hurt when he had blamed Riley for the sabotage on the building site, but when he had calmed down he knew that Riley would never have been capable of that.

Marcel sighed. "Look, I need to apologize to you, too. I never should have accused you of all the sabotage stuff. I may not have known everything about you, Riley, but I knew that, and it was inexcusable. I lashed out and jumped to conclusions, and that's not the kind of man I am. Just because I was hurt, it did not give me the right to strike out at you."

Riley looked at him, and the longing on his face almost dropped Marcel to his knees. He'd read somewhere once that every relationship had its moments, but if you truly loved that person, then no matter what you'll find a way back to each other. Marcel had no doubt that he and Riley loved each other, and that they were well down the path that led back to each other.

****

Riley felt like his heart was about to beat right out of his chest. He stared into the startling blue eyes of the man who held his heart. He was a retired Navy Seal who had survived hell week and BUD/S training and was known for his nerve. But right now, he felt as if he were standing on the precipice of a cliff that was crumbling beneath his feet.

Riley saw Marcel's lip lift into a smile, and the kernel of hope within him bloomed larger. "Despite that though, the fact that you hid your identity from me is something that I am going to hold over you for a long, long time, and you are going to let me."

Riley's grinned. "Yes. Yes, I am."

Marcel laughed and stepped forward, and Riley pulled him into his arms. The cracks that had formed in his heart two days ago healed instantly. "Thank you," he whispered against the skin of Marcel's neck, inhaling his scent and shuddering at the intensity of his relief. "I don't know what I did to deserve a man like you in my life, but I promise you that I will not let you down again."

Marcel's arms wrapped tight around Riley's waist, and he reveled in the sigh of contentment his lover gave. It was clear that the last couple of days had been difficult on both of them. "Good, because I am not sure I can handle another argument like that one."

Riley pulled back and took Marcel's mouth with his own. He sipped gently at his lover's lips, loving how Marcel melted into him, but his arms were strong around his waist. When Marcel opened his mouth, Riley swooped in, licking into his lover's mouth, swallowing the groan his move enticed from Marcel. Pulling back slightly he ran his mouth and lips along the side of Marcel's face, working his way to the man's neck, biting and nibbling his way down the strong column of his neck.

"Fuck, I love the way you taste," Riley growled between bites. He reached down, grasped the bottom of Marcel's t-shirt and pulled it up and over his head.

"I never liked a lover to use his teeth on me," Marcel admitted breathlessly, "but I fucking love it when you do it."

Riley moved his way down over Marcel's chiseled torso, paying homage to his nipples, nibbling on them a little now that he knew Marcel liked it. While he nibbled and sucked his way down Marcel's abs he pushed the fingers of both hands under the waistband of Marcel's shorts and drew them down to his knees, sitting back to enjoy the sight of Marcel's erection slipping free of the fabric.

"Mmm, I love how ready you are for me," Riley said in a voice filled with need. "It lets me know that you need me as much as I need you."

Marcel's breathing turned rapid as Riley dropped to his knees in front of him. "Yeah, I am most definitely ready for—fuck!" Riley swallowed Marcel back as far has he could, taking the heavy weight of his cock all the way to the back of his throat, using the flat of his tongue against the sensitive underside.

"Jesus," Marcel groaned, his hands falling on Riley's shoulders for support. "Nope, not ready. Holy. Shit."

Riley kept his gaze on Marcel's and continued the oral ministrations he knew would drive Marcel crazy. He alternated between taking him deep, adding an intense suction, to small revolutions of his tongue around the head. Every move had Marcel groaning as his body slowly tensed, and Riley knew from experience that the pleasure was building within him.

"Oh God." Marcel moaned, "Riley, you got me, baby. I'm gonna … I'm coming!"

Riley maintained a steady rhythm right until the moment he felt the first burst of heat in his mouth, the flavor intoxicating and uniquely Marcel exploding across his tongue. Marcel's body shook and shuddered as Riley coaxed every last drop of cum from his cock, swallowing everything Marcel had to offer.

When Marcel leaned heavily on his shoulder, Riley stood up straightening Marcel's clothes, then pulled him into his arms. Marcel exhaled and leaned into him, making Riley feel like he was ten feet tall.

"Um … wow," Marcel murmured as he continued to take calming breaths.

Riley chuckled as he squeezed the man tighter against his chest. "I love it when I leave you speechless."

Marcel laughed as he lifted his head so he could look Riley in the eye. "Yeah, well I look forward to returning the favor."

"Not more than I am, I can assure you." Riley reached up and cupped Marcel's face in his hands. "I'm so fucking sorry for not being honest with you. I promise you that it will never happen again."

Marcel stared into Riley's eyes, almost as if he were searching for something, then nodding. "Okay."

And that was all it took to heal all the cracks within him.

Riley leaned down and plucked Marcel's t-shirt from the ground and helped him to pull it on over his head. "Come on, then, love, let's go back to the house."

They walked quietly through the woods, arms wrapped around each other when Marcel broke the silence. "If we're going back to my rooms, we may need to knock before we go in."

"Why's that?"

"Because when I was last there, I'm pretty sure Devon was hell bent on proving to Finn that there was no such thing as whiskey dick."

Riley laughed. "Well, we did have a fair bit to drink, but I think he'll be more than up to the challenge."

Marcel shot him a sly sideways look. "What about you, lover? You think you'll be up for the task?"

Riley met Marcel's gaze with a heated look. "Without a doubt."

Chapter Thirteen

"Yo, Riley!" Dale called from below, and Riley peered over the edge of the scissor lift he was currently standing in. "There's a sheriff in your office to see you!"

Riley nodded and removed the ear protection he was wearing and placed his nail gun in the safety position, then propped it on the floor of the lift. They were on the final push to get the shooting range finished, and he was putting up the last of the fabricated suspension brackets that held the roofing panels in place. He dropped the lift, climbed out of the bucket and strode towards his office. If the sheriff had come here personally rather than calling, it was obvious something serious had happened.

As he neared the door, he heard voices coming from the office. "All I'm asking is if you were interested in coming out for a drink with me. You're acting like I'm askin' you for your hand in marriage." The frustration was clear in the sheriff's tone, and Riley stopped, curious to hear what was going on behind the door.

"Don't be ridiculous." Now that voice sure made things a lot more interesting. "I know you can't be asking for my hand in marriage, sheriff, because you are already in a committed relationship." Riley's eyebrows shot up at the accusation in Sam's tone. And who could blame him? If Nick was really here asking a man out when he was in a relationship already, then that was taking things a little too far.

"I ain't hiding that I am in that relationship," the sheriff said in a calm tone. "Hell, you've met Aiden. There is nothing about that man that I would hide. He and I both would like the opportunity to get to know you and for you to get to know us again."

Riley mouthed the word "again" and wondered

how the straight-laced, quiet medic was going to take that information.

"I am not that naïve, Nick." Sam's tone said he was pissed. "I know there are relationships that can include more than just two people, but why would I want to get involved with a couple who are already, for all intents and purposes, married? Are you just looking for someone new to play with? To bring something different to the bedroom? Is that I would be for you and Aiden? Because I am telling you right now, that is just not going to work for me. Not with my history."

"What! No." Nick was quick to deny it, and Riley cast his eyes around the conference room to ensure no one caught his very obvious eavesdropping, and wondering what history Sam was referring to. "That is not what we want. It's not what we have ever wanted, Sam. All I want at this stage is an opportunity for the three of us to get to know each other better. There is something there between us, Sam, I have felt that from the first moment I met you, and Aiden said he felt the same damn thing. Now, if you can look me in the eye and tell me that you have never felt anything then we will never speak of this again."

There was silence, and Riley moved closer to the door wishing that there had been a glass pane for him to see what was happening. Then, the door on the opposite side of his office opened and closed, and he heard the sound of someone hurrying down the wooden steps. From the frustrated sigh in the room, he knew it had been Sam that had left. He hadn't answered the question, or at least not in any way that Riley had been able to hear, and he was dying to know what Sam's reaction had been.

He waited a few moments more before he opened the door. Nick rose from the seat against the wall, and the two men shook hands. "Good to see you again, Sheriff."

"Call me Nick."

Riley dipped his head in acknowledgement, took off his hard hat and placed it on his desk before turning to sit on the edge. "So I am guessing that your trip out here today was to share some news?"

Nick grimaced. "Yeah, it is. And it's not great news I'm afraid. I've just been talking with a friend of mine, the guy I sent to speak to your father down in Houston. Your dad was found dead this morning in his room. From the looks of things it was complications due to a bout of double pneumonia he had been ignoring."

Riley remained still for a moment, letting his mind process that information. His father was dead, and surely he should feel some kind of loss, but he didn't. He felt nothing for the man, and hearing that he was dead didn't really change that for Riley.

"Is that all?" Riley asked his voice devoid of any emotion, just like he felt.

Nick looked at him for a long moment before nodding his head. "Yeah, it is. I can understand you not feeling much for the man. I read his file and know what he put you and your mom through, so no judgment here."

Riley nodded and stood up, reaching for his hard hat. "Yeah, he wasn't my favorite person in the world. Then, if that is everything, I thank you for heading all the way out here to let me know."

Nick nodded, as he reached for his hat and moved toward the door. "Not a problem, there was something I wanted to see for myself, so it was a trip I had to make." Nick opened the door and stepped out, but turned back toward Riley. "You and your half-brother will need to decide what you want done with your father's body." Riley froze with his hard hat halfway to his head. "The authorities will want to know what your wishes are."

Nick walked out, leaving Riley standing in a state

of shock.

Half-brother? What the hell was this? He knew nothing about a half-brother. Throwing the hat back on the desk, he ran out of the trailer.

"Wait! Nick!" He jogged over to where the sheriff was climbing back into this truck. "Do you have a name?"

Nick frowned as he close the door. "A name of what?"

"This half-brother you say I have."

Nick's jaw dropped open. "You didn't know you had a half-brother? Shit! I am so sorry, Riley. I thought you had to know because he visited your dad a lot when he was in jail, and has even been to see him at that halfway house. I guess that was a dumbass assumption because if you wanted nothing to do with your dad then why the fuck would you know or care about someone going to see him." He pulled out the notebook from his jacked and flicked through the pages. "He's listed as Ernst der Forster. His mother Ursula married her husband Gerhard der Forster when Ernst was three years old, and he was the result of an affair with your father. He's twenty-nine years old."

Riley nodded his head. He had a half-brother who was born when his father was still married to and tormenting his mother. Did his father beat Ernst's mother as well? "Where can I find him?"

Nick closed his notebook and slid it back into his pocket. "I'm not sure, Riley. He hasn't been to see his father the last few months, although the manager of the halfway house he has been living in told my friend that he received calls from someone he called son on a weekly basis. Now, I am gonna go out on a limb here and say that wasn't you, which means it had to have been Ernst. We don't have an address for him, so the guy at the halfway house is waiting for his call to inform him about his father."

Riley nodded. "If you find him, tell him his br—" No, he couldn't use that word, not yet. "Tell him that I'd appreciate having a conversation with the man." Riley pulled out his wallet and handed Nick his business card.

Nick nodded, as he pocketed the card and turned to climb back in his truck. When he paused, his attention was caught by something over at the main house, Riley turned to see what he was staring at. Sam was pounding on that old punching bag Dev had hung years ago in the oak tree at the side of the house, with a single minded focus of a man with a lot on his mind.

Riley wanted to head off in search of Marcel, to share this information and maybe try to gain a little perspective on the whole thing, but he knew what Nick was feeling. No matter what his personal situation was with this guy Aiden, or what Sam was to the both of them, he knew what it was like to put it all out there and have the man you were developing feelings for tell you to basically fuck off.

"Not that it is any of my business, Sheriff, but I'm gonna pass on a little advice my cousin gave me lately." He waited until Nick turned to look at him before continuing. "He told me that if you wait too long to go after what you really want, you risk the window of opportunity closing on you. And the only thing that exists beyond that is a shitload of regrets."

Nick looked at him for a while before offering a small smile and nodding his head in agreement. "I can totally understand that, but some people just can't see past what they know or think is normal and there is nothing wrong with that. Normal is just a state of mind, and what is normal for one, may be chaos for another."

Riley started walking backward toward the main

house. "You know what they say, Sheriff, all great changes are preceded by chaos. All you have to do is decide if the change you are looking for outweighs the discomfort of a little bit of chaos."

With those parting words, he spun around and jogged over to the house. The steady rhythm of gloved hands striking the punching bags got louder as he approached the house, but he didn't get any closer. Sometimes a guy just had to beat the hell out of something to gain a little perspective. And after this afternoon's revelation, Riley was more than aware of that.

****

Marcel could tell that Riley was still awake. His entire body was filled with a tension Marcel had hoped their frantic lovemaking only an hour before might had helped to relieve. "What's going through that mind of yours?" Marcel asked as he rolled back onto his back and snuggled into Riley's chest. "I've given up trying to fuck you into a restful sleep, so we might as well talk things through a little more."

Riley laughed softly, and Marcel felt the vibration of it against his chest. "There is absolutely nothing wrong with fucking a man into a restful sleep, especially when that man is me. That kind of behavior should be encouraged."

Marcel sighed dramatically. "Okay fine! I'll give it another go once you tell me what is going through your mind."

Riley sighed. "It's just the thought that somewhere out there, a man is walking around with half my DNA, and that is really fucking freaky. I have only just got used to having a cousin in my life, but a brother? I really don't know what the hell to do with that."

"What do you want to do? Because you are going

to have to figure that out soon. We've sicced super sleuth Finn on the trail of this Ernst der Forster, and we all know how good he is at squirreling out a secret, and finding an identity."

"I know he found out about me shortly after I arrived, but I wasn't hiding anything, Marcel. Not really. I changed my name as soon as I as old enough to legally do it. I chose Marksmen because my high school careers advisor said with my eye I'd make a good one in any arm of the armed defenses I chose to enter. It sounded cool and that's what I went with, but there are clear records of who I was before that and who my dad was. What if this Ernst guy doesn't want to be found?"

Marcel leaned up in to press a kiss against the warm skin of Riley's chest. "Then we leave him with his privacy. You tell the manager of that place your dad was living in to tell Ernst when he calls that he has a half-brother and if he ever wants to reach out, you'll be here to connect with him. That is all you can do."

"And the other thing that is bothering the shit out me," Riley continued, "why the hell did Marvin need me to get this property? He had another son. I signed my right away, so why not use Ernst to go up against Devon?"

Marcel frowned. "I was wondering that myself. Maybe this Ernst has a record that would prohibit or nullify his ownership. Or maybe there is a law around children not having as much ownership to a bequeathed property based on being the result of an adulterous relationship. Marvin was married to your mom at the time Ernst was born."

Riley was quiet for a moment, so Marvel pressed another kiss to his chest, a few inches lower than the first. "How did you get so smart?"

Marcel grinned at the affection and love he heard

in Riley's tone.

"That should not have come as a surprise, my love. I am French after all." They both chuckled at that, and Marcel moved further down Riley's body, pressing his lips to any expanse of skin he encountered. When he felt the ridge of scar tissue along his rib cage, he redirected to lave the scars with his tongue, before slipping back up and nibbling on Riley's nipple until he growled.

Marcel continued on his exploration until he was nestled between Riley's thighs, his legs spread enough to allow Marcel free rein and that was something Marcel was determined to make the most of. Just as he slipped his mouth down over Riley's cock, his head was gently tugged off and he grumbled as his treat slipped from his lips.

"Wait, love," Riley said in a harsh voice, "I am not going to be the only one to sleep peacefully tonight. Turn around and bring me something to keep my mind on when you suck me deep and drive me crazy."

Marcel loved the sound of that and moved quickly. Just as he settled with his knees on either side of Riley's head, and was reaching for Riley's hard cock, he groaned at the wet heat that suddenly engulfed his own cock. He groaned at the strong suction Riley applied, almost swallowing him completely.

Not to be outdone, Marcel leaned down and sucked Riley into his mouth, reveling in Riley's groan and the way his hips flexed upward, driving his cock a little further into Marcel's mouth. The two of them then set into a steady rhythm, each of them showing the other what they liked the most, what move they found the most arousing, and then employing the move themselves. Marcel knew he wasn't going to last. But he'd be damned if he was going to go over without Riley reaching his peak at the same time.

He clamped down on the orgasm that was hovering just below the surface, bubbling away building higher and higher within him. He ran his tongue over the head of Riley's cock before sucking him to the back of his throat and swallowing rhythmically around his cock. He felt Riley groan around his own hard cock, and that was all it took. He was going over, and from the feel of Riley's dick swelling in his mouth, he knew he had achieved what he'd hoped for. Riley was going to come at the same time.

With a groan he gave himself over to the pleasure and shot down Riley's throat, just as the first hot stream of cum hit his tongue, and he was treated to the flavor that was uniquely his lover's, and in that moment, everything was right in the world.

****

He knew that something was very wrong. That damn sheriff had turned up today, and he knew immediately that something was up. There was no way he was here for just a social call with that sniper the boys called Prettyboy. No, he had come with a message, and personally it was one that had rocked his world. His dad was dead. He was now an orphan, and the pain of that cut so fucking deep.

It was made worse by the fact his *brother* seemed totally unaffected by the loss. It made him so mad that Riley could just blow off the loss of such a great man as Marvin Roberts. Who did that fucker think he was?

Well, he heard what he'd said to that freak of a sheriff. Riley wanted the opportunity to have a *conversation* with him. Well, he wanted to have a few words with the bastard, too, so all this sabotage shit he'd been doing for his father was now at an end. He and Riley were due a come to Jesus moment, and tomorrow was the day they were going to have it. He had a lot to do in order to get things ready, but one thing was certain. This was going to be one hell of an explosive family reunion.

Chapter Fourteen

Marcel hung up the phone with a growl of frustration and slumped back against his office chair. He had been calling in favor after favor all morning looking for Ernst der Forster, but it appeared the man had simply slipped from sight. None of his bank accounts had been touched. There was no activity on the one credit card he owned, now expired. Nothing. It just appeared that only day he simply stopped being him and started being someone else and that was strange in itself.

Marcel reckoned that there were quite a few illegal reasons for a person wanting to disappear, and not many legitimate ones. But he had never stopped contacting his father, and someone had been paying the bills on the room Marvin Roberts had occupied since being released from prison six months ago. Marcel was willing to lay odds that it had been Ernst who paid those bills.

"Marcel, you seen Riley?" Dev asked from the doorway.

Marcel shook his head. "No, not since this morning. Why?"

"He was supposed to meet me downstairs with an update on completion, but he never turned up."

A thread of unease began to unfurl within Marcel, and he reached for his cell phone. He dialed Riley and frowned when it went right to voice mail.

"You think something's up?" Dev asked.

"I'm not sure, but when has he ever missed a meeting with you?" Marcel stepped out from behind his desk, and he and Devon made their way downstairs. "They finished up the shooting range this morning, and Riley was going to complete the compliance report for the county offices."

He and Dev left the house and crossed the open area that lay between the main house and the sites office block. Marcel saw Dale stepping out of the finished accommodation block. "Dale, you seen Riley?"

"Not lately, Marcel. Not since he and I finished up that compliance report this morning. You looked over in his office?" Dale indicated in that general direction with a jerk of his head.

"Going there now," Marcel said as he started to move faster in that direction. "If you see him, can you tell him to call me?"

"Will do," Dale replied as he collected a large black duffle bag that lay by the door and moved towards his truck.

For the next twenty minutes, Marcel and Dev searched the building site, and with each passing moment when no one was able to find Riley or even say that they saw him that morning, Marcel's unease began to build. He and Dev walked back into Riley's office, and Marcel began to pace in front of his desk.

"What the fuck do you think is going on?" Marcel growled. "His truck is still here, so he hasn't gone anywhere. Yet he is nowhere on the site."

Devon leaned against the back wall of the office. "Something is not right. My left eye is twitching, and that is telling me that something is way the fuck off with all of this."

The sound of feet running up the stairs outside had them both turning toward the outside door as it was suddenly thrown open and Grant came into the room, his face a mask of worry. "Where's Riley?"

"Well, that appears to the sixty-four thousand dollar question of the day." Marcel heard the sarcasm in his tone, but didn't give a shit.

"Shit! I can't find Dale either." Grant started to

fidget where he stood and ran a hand through his hair, and Marcel saw that there was a definite tremble in it.

"What's happened? What's got you so shaken?" Dev asked.

Grant swallowed hard, and if Marcel wasn't mistaken he looked scared. "My inventory audit was due this morning, and some of our equipment is missing."

"You think it is our sabotage douchebag?" Dev asked.

Grant shrugged. "Who knows, man? It could be, and if he is planning on using this shit then we are all in trouble."

"Explain."

"We are missing six explosive tubes, the primers, and the goddamn detonators. Everything the fucker would need to blow us all to hell and back." Grant began to pace as Marcel and Devon shared a look. "Everything was under lock and key, and only me and Riley have the keys. Now, I know where mine is." Grant held up a key he wore on a chain around his neck. "We need to clear this site, the house and bring in the damn bomb squad. If the guy looking to fuck you and your team over has these, Dev, then God knows what he is planning to do with it, but whatever the hell it is, it has the potential to be huge."

Marcel stepped toward Grant. "What the hell do you have explosives for anyway?"

"We use them to clear rock and earth when we are putting in foundations for the commercial builds," Grant explained.

"But this is not a commercial build. Why would you have it here on site?"

Grant shrugged again, and Marcel wanted to punch him in the face. "Dale said something about needing it to clear tree stumps and shit. Hell, I don't know, dude? My job is to order the stuff and keep it safe."

"Well you've done a piss poor job of it, now haven't you?" Marcel complained as he moved around Riley's desk to grab the phone, intent on calling Nick. "Get your team and get off this site. Wait in town until you hear from me." Grant nodded and looked relieved, then ran out of the room. When he had finished dialing he looked down at the desk in front of him waiting for the sheriff to answer, a form that sat on the top of the desk caught his attention, and he froze.

It was the Building Compliance Form that the country needed for the shooting range.

"Sheriff's office, Nick Jones speaking."

"Nick, this is Marcel Cross," Marcel said quickly, "we have a situation out at Cottonwood Farm, and we are going to need you and your team to come out here as soon as you can."

"On our way," Nick said immediately, not bothering to ask any questions, having obviously sensed Marcel's urgency.

"If you have someone who can find explosives that would definitely be good."

There was a silent pause at the other end of the phone. "Fuck me. Okay, funnily enough I have just the man and dog for the job. We'll be there as soon as we can."

Marcel hung up the phone and looked over at Dev. His LT must have picked up on Marcel's reactions before because it wasn't his friend Dev who stood before him. It was very much Bravo team's LT. "Report."

"Riley didn't finish the Compliance report. He never even fucking started it." Marcel handed the form to Dev and moved toward the door. Dale had a lot of explaining to do. Marcel sprinted for where he'd last seen Dale and cursed in frustration when he found Dale's truck gone.

Dev reached for his phone. "Finn, call the team, get them to meet me and Marcel in the dining room in five minutes and tell them we are going down range so come prepared." Marcel fell in beside Dev as the two of then ran back to the house. Telling Bravo team they were going down range was a call to get ready for combat, and Marcel for one was more than willing to gear up and go. Somehow, Dale was involved in Riley's disappearance, and Marcel was hell bent on showing him the error of his ways. And if that happened to also include a glimpse of his own intestines then so be it.

****

Riley came to slowly and immediately knew that something was wrong. He took a moment to assess his situation. His arms were above his head, his hands numb, his shoulders ached, and his feet weren't touching the ground. Somehow, someone had strung him up by the wrists. It wasn't the first time he had risen from unconsciousness in a situation he was uncertain of. But to be fair, when he had left the Navy and no longer went on covert operations he figured the chance of it happening again had been pretty damn thin.

He cracked his eyes open and had to fight the urge to groan at the pain the light in the room caused. Not wanting to bring any attention to the fact that he was awake he took a couple of slow breaths waiting for his head to stop spinning, all the while listening intently for any noise around him. He ascertained that he was alone in this room, but there was someone moving in a room adjacent to the one he was hanging in.

He opened his eyes and lifted his head. The room he was in looked like it was part of an old wooden cabin of some description. There were large timber trusses in the ceiling and the framing was exposed to the roof, but the state of the wood told Riley it was old. There was no other furniture in the space, and the four pane windows were caked in dirt and dust, but clear enough for him to see the forest outside.

Looking up he saw that his arms were tied using a large rope slung over one of the support trusses, and tied off to a spike in the far wall behind him. His feet were dangling about two feet off the ground. The shirt he was wearing had blood down the right hand side, and as soon as he saw that, the thumping headache he'd had since opening his eyes zeroed in on the wound that had caused most of that blood, and with that realization he was flooded with the memory of when it had occurred.

He'd walked out of the main house that morning in high spirits. Hard not to be happy after the night he'd had with Marcel. He was planning that afternoon to show Marcel the plans he'd had drawn up of the house he wanted to build them, and once the sale was complete for the parcel of land he planned to build on he was going to get started. Everything was looking up.

As he neared his office, he saw the locked and bolted front door of his equipment store open. With a frown he had walked over to it and had taken one step inside the door. Then something had hit him hard on the head. It had been lights out for him, and now here he was, hanging like a piñata, waiting to be struck by some bastard with a stick.

The door opened suddenly, and Dale walked in. "Oh, good you're awake. I was worried there for a moment that I had hit you too hard."

Riley frowned at the man he had called friend for the last eight years. "What the fuck is going on, Dale?"

Dale *tsked* as he crossed his arms and leaned against the wall. "I thought you were smarter than that, *brother*."

"Wait, you're Ernst der Forster?" Riley asked incredulously. None of this made sense.

Dale nodded. "Yep, I am your half-brother, and true son to the late, great Marvin Roberts. My mother was a woman by the name of Ursula Dahl, and when I took on this persona to find a way to get to punish you for what you did to my father, I took her last name as my first."

"Why wouldn't you just tell me who you were?"

"Because you *betrayed* my father!" Dale yelled his face turning an angry shade of red. "Because of you, he was taken from me and my mother, and we were forced to fend for ourselves in a country neither of us have residency for. Because of your blind hatred of the man you should have revered above all others my mother was forced to whore herself in order to put food on our table, and she got sick. I promised her on her deathbed eight years ago that I would make you pay for taking my father from us. I would have just taken you out then, but I wanted to make you suffer first."

"How?" Riley asked. "I guess you and dear old dad had it all figured out. How were you going to make me pay?"

"We were coming up with a plan to get you committed," Dale snarled. "We had time. Once you were safely tucked away in a mental institution, Dad was going to come clean about me to his lawyer. I would then be made executor of your estate, and everything you had would be mine."

Riley barked a laugh. "You can't really be that stupid. Did he tell you that? Did you research it at all? I have an iron clad will. Up until the time I found out about my connection to Devon, there were a number of trusts that would have benefited financially from my death, and there were instructions for a governance board to be put into place to keep Marksmen Construction going. Once I knew about Devon, and learned they type of man he was, my latest will left him with full financial control of all my assets."

Dale's eyes narrowed, but Riley saw the doubt that crept into his gaze. "None of it mattered when we found out that grandmother had passed. All we needed from you was to take the land before it went to that prick Devon, but even then you couldn't do right by your own father. Not even when you and I fought in that alley, and I left you with that scar, you were still determined to undermine your father."

Riley felt his own anger building within him. "That was you? Well, from memory I left you with a scar or two of your own, asshole, and that man was a narcissistic, murderer who killed his own wife before stabbing his son. He was insane from the moment he was born, which is why his own fucking mother didn't even acknowledge him when she died. My hatred for the man was hardly blind. It was full blown and clear to anyone who asked me. I have nothing but happy thoughts about the fact that man is dead."

With a cry of rage, Dale launched himself at Riley and slammed his fists into his ribs, once, twice, three times. Riley groaned and flinched with each punch. When Dale stood back again, Riley grunted, trying to draw breath again.

"How dare you talk about my father like that," Dale snarled. "He was the last good thing in this life I had that was worth living for."

"Then do me and the world a fucking favor," Riley said, breathless. "Go join him in the afterlife and leave me and mine the fuck alone."

Dale suddenly grinned, his eyes a shimmer of

madness. "Oh, I will be joining him shortly. We both will, have no doubt about that. I figure he didn't have the chance to kill you in this life, so I will give him the greatest gift I can in death and ensure you are there for him in the afterlife to torture and torment. But not before we hear the explosions I've set at the building site. With each one that is tripped, you will know it was one of your friends or even your lover who has been blown into hell. Then, *brother,* it will be our turn."

Dale pulled something out from his pocket, and Riley's heart almost stopped within his chest.

Chapter Fifteen

Marcel, Sam, and Glenn stood at the ready, just waiting on Dev to give them a target, and then they were in the wind. All of them were armed to the teeth and dressed for combat. Marcel had never been more primed for battle. The stood quietly watching as the sheriff spoke quietly with the man who had arrived with him just moments before. Nick introduced him as Aiden, and the team watched as Aiden let a dog out of the specially designed cage in the back of the truck.

The dog was a chocolate Lab, and as soon as it was allowed out of the vehicle it was leaping around, sniffing the air and doing the things dogs do for fun. But then Aiden gave a hand signal that had the dog sitting still, its ears up waiting for further instructions. The man then put this dog vest on the dog, and it was if that were the signal to go to work. The dog remained stuck to Aiden's side and was completely focused on his handler. Bravo team had seen dogs like these in combat and even owed their lives to a few who had alerted them of hidden explosives in their work quadrants.

"Aiden and Deefer are gonna make a sweep of the compound first," Nick explained as the men stepped closer to Bravo team. "Once we have the explosives contained, what do you want done with it?"

Marcel frowned. "What do you mean? We want it to not blow any of us all over the fucking state. If that could be avoided then we would be most appreciative."

Aiden laughed. "Will see what I can do." He tugged on a flak jacket of his own, with the letters EOD emblazoned on the right side, over the name George. He was part of the Naval Explosive Ordnance Disposal unit and judging by the insignia on the shoulder, the man was a very highly ranked officer.

"Thanks for coming, sir." Glenn must have seen the insignia as well. "According to Grant, the man on Riley's team who was in charge of the equipment used on site, there are six individual charges, primers, and detonators missing."

"I'm retired." Aiden waved his hand nonchalantly. "You can call me Aiden. Do we know what types of detonators were used on site?"

Sam stepped forward. "Non-electric. We don't have to worry about it being set to a timer or the explosion being triggered remotely. We will have to trip these devices to blow them."

Aiden nodded. "Okay then. Why don't Deefer and I take a walk and see what we can see? We will disable what we find and take it from there."

"Start with the accommodation block," Marcel advised, pointing in that direction. "That's where we last saw Dale."

Aiden nodded, and shot a quick glance at Sam who seemed to be overly interested in his service revolver, before stepping away from the group and heading toward the accommodation block.

Aiden had taken only about a dozen steps before Sam asked. "Why is your dog called Deefer? What in the hell does that mean?"

Aiden turned. "Nick, what is D for?"

Nick answered with a grin. "D is for dog, babe, and I still say that is a stupid name for such a kickass dog."

Aiden laughed as he turned and headed back toward the building site. "Deefer loves it, and that is all he and I have to say on the matter. Deefer, seek!" Marcel watched as the dog shot out ahead of his handler, nose to the ground, heading directly for the accommodation block.

"What happens if the dog finds something?" Marcel asked, turning to look at the sheriff, who suddenly looked a little ill.

"Aiden will disarm it if he can. Otherwise we'll have to blow it." Nick started walking back toward his truck. "I've got a team of people just beyond the property line, but I am keeping them back until we know it's safe. I'll radio them now and give them an update."

"Does Aiden need any help? Are you just going to let him go in there by himself?" Sam's voice had a strange tone to it, and it wasn't one that Marcel recognized.

Nick sighed. "I learned a long time ago that Aiden knows exactly what he is doing, and although I hate sitting back and watching him go into situations like that, it's not my place to stop him."

"Then what is your place, Nick?" Sam called out, and Nick stopped, his hand on the door handle of his truck.

"My place is to love him with everything I have," Nick said, turning to look back over his shoulder, and Marcel could see the fear and concern swimming in the man's expression from where he stood. "And to make sure that he never questions that. My place is to ensure that every damn time he puts that fucking flak jacket on, and he and his dog go searching for something I know could take him from me, that he goes knowing I've loved him with everything within me, and I'll be here waiting for him when he's finished. Anything other than that, and it would be a lie. That is my place."

Nick opened his door and sat down on the driver's seat, reaching for the radio attached to the dash. Marcel shot a quick look at Sam and saw a muscle flexing in the man's jaw.

Dev walked out of the house with his weapon

across his chest, and he was wearing an expression Marcel recognized immediately. Devon had a mission for Bravo team and there was a target in sight and a destination, and they had a green light. Finn came down the stairs behind him, with a fierce look on his face.

"Colonel Anderson has come through with a location," Dev said as soon as he was close to the rest of them. "They have Dale's cell phone located less than two miles from here, and the fucking kicker is the little prick is holed up in that cabin on the edge of my land. The Colonel said there were two heat signatures in that shitty old cabin, so that's where he has Riley holed up, too."

Marcel nodded. "Then let's go."

Dev grinned. "We're going in on foot, boys. God help any of you that show you've grown soft in the last few months." Dev turned and dragged Finn for a kiss that said so much, and the intense feeling behind it had Marcel, Sam, and Glenn turning away slightly. "Let's move!"

The four of them took off in the direction Dev had, running as fast as the terrain would allow. The physical exercise allowed Marcel's mind to focus completely on the target, and not on the fact that Riley had been in Dale's hands for most of the morning. Just under twelve minutes later, Dew signaled for them all to stop, and the four of the dropped to a knee, sweat pouring from them.

"Fuck," Sam wheezed, "when this is all over, I am gonna have to take up running. I feel like my heart is about to burst."

"You could always get your ass up when I do and run with me," Dev offered, the only one of the three not drawing in huge gasps of air. *Fit bastard.* "Now, the cabin is only about a hundred feet west of us. It is small, with only two rooms. I'd be willing to bet my left testicle that Dale has Riley in the back room. Sam, Glenn, I want the two of you on either side of that cabin. Report what you see as soon as you are in place. Marcel, take the high road, and find an elevated site that is going to give you eyes on that back room. The hairs on the back of my neck are standing up, so something is off. We go careful, and we go silent."

Marcel moved toward the cabin, moving silently and low to the ground. When he had just set eyes on the cabin he heard Dev ask for a comms check through the earpiece of his modular throat mic. Dev's voice was clear despite the fact that Marcel knew he was barely making a sound. "Reaper."

Glenn's low voice came through clear. "Hooah."

"Rev." With a last name like Cross it wasn't a far stretch for the team to give him the call sign Reverend. Marcel pressed the side of his throat mic and whispered, "Hooah."

"Prettyboy."

There was a silence, and Marcel knew that Sam was currently cursing out the LT's man. Finn had given him that call sign the first day they'd met, and it had stuck.

"Hooah." Although the word was the same, Sam's tone said an entirely different thing, and Marcel grinned.

"Comms all good."

"LT, our Tango has come out onto the porch a couple of times." Reaper's voice came over the comms. "He looks agitated. He keeps pacing and looking in the direction of the facility, muttering to himself, like he is waiting for something."

It only took a moment for Marcel to figure out what that was. "He's waiting for the explosions. When they go, the bastard will know he's hurt someone."

"Hold five," Dev's voice responded, and there

was radio silence for a moment as Marcel made his way up into a tree near the rear of the cabin.

He didn't have to climb too high to get a visual on the room, and what he saw had him filling with relief at the same time he growled in anger. Riley was strung up like a side of beef with ropes over one of the wooden beams in the room. He was struggling to get his hands free, and even from where he was, Marcel could see the blood that was sliding down the inside of his arm. His movements were jerky and seemed panicked.

Marcel pressed against his throat mic. "LT, I have eyes on the friendly, and he seems panicked."

"That might have something to do with what's in the hand of our Tango." Reaper's voice came over his earpiece. "He has a dead switch taped to his hand."

Marcel closed his eyes in dread. That was more than enough reason from Riley to be a little on edge.

"Roger that." Dev's voice came back, calm and in control, just like the man himself. "Be prepared, fire in the hole."

Seconds later an explosion rocked the quiet forest, the birds and wildlife taking off through the trees. Marcel put his eye to the scope of his weapon again and saw Riley had stopped moving and he was looking out the opposite window in the direction of Cottonwood Farm. Then Dale ran into the room, a look of excitement on his face. The two of them argued. Dale waved the dead man switch around threateningly, and that seemed to give Riley pause, looking down at his waist. Marcel moved his scope down and swore violently when he saw the explosives attached to the side of Riley's belt, the primer visible in the top.

"Dev." Marcel's fear drove all thought of military handles out of his head. "Friendly has the explosive tied to him."

"Fuck," Dev came back, not quite as calm as before. "Hold five, I have an inbound friendly who is going to be of help."

Marcel watched as Dale walked back out the room, and Riley seemed to slump in defeat. After a moment, Riley lifted his head, and seemed to fling off the emotions the situation was now churning within him. Then he threw his head back and roared a single word. A benediction of sorts that rang with the promise of retribution, of never giving up, of love and of a thousand words that remained unspoken. It was one word that had Marcel closing his eyes and swallowing the lump that suddenly appeared and threatened to choke him. It was one word—*Marcel*.

****

Riley cursed as his arms felt like they were about to be ripped from his shoulders. He was trying desperately to use the blood that was now flowing down his arms as a lubricant to slip the ropes that held him in place. An explosion had rocked the forest about fifteen minutes ago, and Da—no, *Ernst*—came running in to gloat, questioning which of the men back at Cottonwood had just tripped one of his little surprises. Riley had gone ballistic when he joked about it being Marcel. He had attempted to simply wait and conserve his energy, but that conversation blew his calm out of the water.

Riley was so intent on struggling against the bonds that he hadn't realized there were two voices coming from the other room, until Ernst walked into the room with another man beside him. The guy was slender, but with broad shoulders that spoke of some kind of regular exercise. He had dark brown hair and green eyes.

"Look, buddy." the guy was waving his hands in front of him, staring at Riley in horror. "I don't want anything to with whatever the fuck this is. You can string people up as much as you like, just leave me the hell out of it."

"What the hell are you doing here?" Ernst snarled, pointing a small caliber firearm at the stranger with his one free hand. "This is my private property, and you are trespassing. I am entitled to shoot you for trespassing in this state, you know."

The stranger moved to stand in the window and raised his hands to put them on top his head. Riley frowned at the strange move. "I'm not sure how true that is, but I do apologize for the trespassing. I was out looking for my dog, that is all, nothing more. I heard an explosion a while back and hurried in this direction. I thought if someone was in trouble, I could be here to help. I don't want any trouble."

"Then you should have just kept walking!" Ernst yelled as he moved toward the stranger, still waving the gun, and Riley knew there was more to the scene that what he was actually seeing. The man looked too calm. Almost as if this were not the first time a weapon had been pointed at him. He was staring at the dead man switch, and although it might simply be out of curiosity, Riley thought it looked like he was assessing it more than anything else.

Ernst moved closer to the man, his face a mask of fury. "What? Why the hell are you looking at my hand? If you are wondering what it is, it's a dead man's switch, and if my thumb comes off this button on the top," Ernst held his hand up, the device taped into the palm of his hand, his thumb free of the binding and holding the switch on the top down, "then all three of us will explode into hell and back."

The stranger took his eyes off the device, looked over quickly at Riley and winked, before returning his gaze to Ernst's. "That's what it looks like to me, except there is one thing about that little device you got there that I find interesting. The hollow plastic tube that delivers the firing impulse to the detonator to trigger the explosion, won't work when it's in pieces."

Ernst lifted his hand up in front of his face to look closer at the device and frowned. "But it's not in pieces."

"No," the stranger said as he lowered his hands, "not yet at least." The stranger dropped to the ground just as the window behind him exploded. In slow motion Riley saw the red spray of blood fly into the air from the back of Ernst's hand where he had raised it to look at the device from behind him before Ernst fell to the ground. Panicked, Riley looked at the switch, certain that he would see that the button on the device was up and that his death was imminent. The device was in pieces, still taped to what was left of Ernst's mangled hand. The bullet that had crushed the switch, and saved his life, had also taken Ernst's.

A .50 caliber bullet to the head would do that.

Chapter Sixteen

"Aiden was calm as fuck in that cabin." Riley shook his head. "It was freaky how at ease he was with the whole thing. I had a stick of explosives strapped entirely too close to my dick for me to be anything but nervous, but he acted like this was just an average day."

"For him, it used to be," Nick said with a smile out the window at the man in question. "Aiden and Deefer are still the best bomb detection team in the US, and I would put him against any other team in the world. He is trained, he knows what he is doing, and—"

"And he loves the rush of saving people and the world," Sam finished gently.

Nick nodded. "Yeah, he does. He has lost more to bombs and mad fuckers with a penchant for blowing shit up than anyone ever has. This is the way he reconciles it within himself."

"How so?" Sam asked, as he watched the Aiden play with his dog out in front of the house.

"Now that, Sam, is not my story to tell." Nick stood up from the table, gathering the statements and paperwork he'd filled out since they returned from the cabin that afternoon. "Aiden is not afraid to tell that story, and I know he would love you to take the time to get to know him so he can share it, but that is entirely up to you."

With that, the good sheriff, in a move that had Riley smiling, tipped his hat at the team and stepped out of the house. The sun was starting to set, and the light was beautiful outside. Riley and the rest of the men in the room, watched as the sheriff approached Aiden. The two of them shared a quick kiss, and Riley saw the sheriff lift a hand to cup Aiden's face and pressed his forehead to Aiden's. The two shared a few quiet words then made their way over to Nick's truck. Aiden popped the dog back in the cage at the back, but before he climbed into the car, he looked back at the house, and waved.

"That guy must have balls of fucking brass," Dev murmured from where he sat with Finn in his lap, sipping a beer.

"Yes, yes he must," Marcel agreed

"So, Dale or Ernst or he who shall forever be known as asswipe, was behind everything?" Finn asked from Dev's lap.

Riley nodded. "Yeah, I had some time tied to that roof truss to work this all out, and everything points to him. Ernst was the one in charge of the investigation behind that I-beam coming down, and listed it as equipment failure when it was more likely that he had something to do with it. He was more than capable of moving those survey pegs, and he was the one holding that damn nail gun when it went off."

"What about Owen?" Glenn asked quietly.

"He didn't have anything to do with that, Glenn," Riley said grimly. "Owen is just a dumbass predator who thought he had the right to what he did. My father would not have allowed Ernst to bring anyone else in for two very good reasons. One, he trusted no one, and he had done the work on Ernst from a young age to grow his dependence on the man, and two, he wouldn't have wanted to share the dividends."

Marcel shuddered and snuggled further into Riley's side. The two of them had been inseparable from the moment Aiden had him cut down, and Marcel ran into the room. It had been Marcel who had taken that shot, and once again Riley was left amazed by the man who held his heart. Never again would he talk shit about his reflexes. He wouldn't have had a lot of time to sight that damn detonator before taking that shot.

"What if there had been a no impact situation today?" Riley asked and almost wished he hadn't when Marcel tensed beside him.

"It's not worth thinking about," Marcel murmured and lifted Riley's hand to his lips, pressing little kisses against the gauze that encircled his wrist.

"Besides," Glenn added as he stood up from the table, "the distance was less than thirty feet. Marcel could have hit that blindfolded." Riley grinned at how nonchalantly the rest of Bravo team treated what Marcel had done that day. It was just another day for them. "Right, I am off to bed."

"Reaper." Dev's voice had taken on a more serious tone, and every man in the room turned to look at him. "There was something else that Colonel Anderson wanted me to know. Maddox has taken up with Pathfinders."

Riley had no clue what that meant, but from the way Glenn paled and seemed to sway slightly it was clear that it was not something good.

"Where?" Glenn asked his voice hoarse.

"Syria," Dev said on a sigh.

Glenn nodded. "Well, I guess he has a reason to be there. He's a big boy. He makes his own decisions. It can't be helped that those decisions are fucking dumb as shit." Glenn walked out of the room and headed to his room.

"Come on, baby," Marcel said quietly from beside Riley as he stood, and reached town do gently tug him to his feet, too. "After the shit-storm of today, I feel the need to be alone with you." Marcel turned and looked at Dev and Sam. "Thank you, my brothers, for everything you do and all that you are. We shall see you in the morning."

Sam and Dev both dipped their heads in

acknowledgment as Marcel led Riley out of the room. Both of them came to a stop when Dev called out to them.

"Cousin, the land sale cleared this afternoon. The land is now yours."

Riley grinned. "That's fantastic news. Thank you."

Dev scoffed. "Don't thank me, Riley. I'm going to insist that you build a house for each the rest of the team on this land, too. CTF is our place, our home, and I want us all to own a piece of home. It was something we never had, and now that we do, we need to make that permanent."

Riley nodded then followed his lover out of the room and up the stairs. This was home. He had a fantastic management team in place, and despite the fact one of men he'd considered one of his most senior advisors and a friend had tried to kill him today, he had faith in the people he had around him. He could work and manage the sites just as well from here, and he could travel when he needed to. He might even convince Marcel to join him on occasion. He watched Marcel's ass in front of him as they climbed the stairs, and made a commitment to himself to ensure Marcel had no reason to say no when he asked him to accompany Riley on business trips.

As soon as the door of Marcel's rooms closed, and it was just the two of them alone in the darkened room, Riley pulled Marcel into his arms and took his mouth in an all-consuming heated kiss. Marcel's emotions were just as volatile as Riley's, it appeared, as the two of them fought for dominance in that kiss. Their mouths came together hard and fast, and when Riley pushed his tongue into Marcel's mouth, the two of them dueled and Riley loved every minute of it.

With a growl, Riley pulled Marcel up against his chest, using his height advantage in his favor, and making Marcel lift up onto his toes. Once he was there, Riley wrapped his arms around Marcel's thighs and pulled him up so that his legs were wrapped around Riley's waist. Riley didn't need light to find his way to the bed, and he loved the fact that Marcel rolled his hips against him, rubbing their cocks together in a move that had his blood heating.

When he reached the bed he pushed against Marcel's legs to get him to drop to the floor, and then he began to strip. They each took care of their own clothing. Riley knew that if he touched Marcel in that moment, he'd have him on all fours on the floor and be buried to the hilt within him before they'd even had the chance to take their clothes off.

As soon as the two of them were naked, Riley locked his arms around Marcel and threw them both on the bed. Marcel laughed for a moment before slamming his mouth to Riley's in another hot kiss. The two of them were just content for those few short moments to kiss each other, enjoy the feeling of being alive and holding the man they loved safe in their arms. Then Riley began to gently pulse his hips forward, rubbing his thick erection against the hard length of his lover. Within moments the two of them were grinding against each other, and Riley felt his arousal spiraling out of control within him.

"Fuck, I have to be inside you, baby," he murmured against Marcel's skin as he licked, nibbled, and bit his way down Marcel's neck.

"Then fuck me, Riley, please," Marcel pleaded in a breathless voice.

Riley reached under the pillow for the lube he had stashed there and applied some to his hand, before kneeling up between Marcel's bent legs. Marcel flattened his back and spread his thighs and Riley groaned the sight of his puckered ass, presented to him so nicely.

"Look at that," Riley whispered in awe then lifted his gaze to Marcel's as he began to use his lubricated fingers to prepare him. "Look at you. Look at how fucking hot you look all ready and willing for me to fuck you into this mattress."

Marcel squirmed as Riley added a second finger to his exploration, then cried out when he found the small gland within his ass that Riley knew from experience had spikes of pleasure arcing through him. Riley kept up a syncopated rhythm while he added a third and then a fourth finger, driving both of them to the edge of madness at how good it felt.

With another snarl of need, Riley pulled out his fingers and knelt up, pulling Marcel's legs over his thighs and then rubbing his own cock with the lubrication on his hands, before lining the head up with Marcel's ass and sliding home.

"*Mere de Dieu*!" Marcel cried out as his back arched up of the mattress. Riley began to pump into him at a steady pace, building the pleasure within them both at a frightening speed.

"Take yourself in your hand, baby," Riley said through gritted teeth, fighting the intense reaction being buried balls deep in the man he loved brought him. "I want to see you come before I fill your ass."

With hands that shook, Marcel gripped his cock in both hands and began to pump them up and down. Riley matched his rhythm so that it would feel like he was fucking and being fucked at the same time. Moments later, Riley felt the tingling at the base of his spine that signaled he was close to losing himself to the power of the orgasm bearing down on him.

Gritting his teeth even harder, sure that he was going to actually crack one of his teeth, he began to move harder and faster, pounding into Marcel as the pleasure built. Marcel suddenly cried out Riley's name as his hips jerked, and streams of white cum shot from the end of his cock. It was a sight that drove Riley to the end of his control, and he flew over the edge into pleasure at the first sensation of Marcel's ass clamping down around his cock.

He groaned Marcel's name as he jerked his hips three times, his body surrendering itself into Marcel's just as he surrendered his heart and soul to him months ago. When his body finally ceased its erratic movements, he slumped forward, falling on Marcel's chest and dragging air into his lungs, desperately trying to get his brain to fire once more. He felt Marcel's arms wrap around him, and he gripped him tighter.

"Mmm, that was fucking hot," Marcel whispered in a voice that was hoarse no doubt from screaming Riley's name just moments before.

"Yes, it was, my love," Riley groaned as he pulled back, letting his semi erect cock slide from Marcel's tight ass. "Let me get the shower started and we can get cleaned up."

"But you do plan to get us dirty again before the night is through, right?" Marcel said with an exaggerated waggle of the eyebrows that had Riley laughing.

"Oh hell, yes," Riley promised as he walked on unsteady legs to the bathroom, and flicked the shower on. He turned at the sound of an appreciative whistle coming from the door.

"I do like watching you walk around naked." Marcel sighed as he walked toward Riley and the two of them walked into the tiled shower, Marcel moaning as the hot water hit his skin and heat soaked into their bodies.

"Once we have our own place, I promise to walk around naked as much as possible." Riley grabbed a cloth and began to lovingly clean his man.

"That would be wonderful."

Riley groaned as Marcel used the shampoo and began to wash his hair. "I was thinking about your comment earlier, about what would have happened if my shot had been no impact."

Riley opened his eyes. "I didn't ask because I thought you would miss. I asked because of the analogy behind the expression."

"What do you mean?"

"When I first approached you about how I felt about you, you shot me down cold." Riley grinned at the guilty look on Marcel's face. "I don't blame you, my love. I had given you no reason to trust me then. But when I was strung up on that beam like a piñata, I thought about what you told me about that expression, and what it meant to you and the team. My shot that day in your office was wide, and despite it being fired with the best of intentions, there was no impact, and it felt like I had laid my cards out on the table and you didn't like what you saw."

Marcel went to speak, and Riley placed his hand over Marcel's mouth, grinning wider at the way his eyes narrowed and then gleamed with promised retribution.

"Just let me finish, my love. Then, when you gave me that second chance, I was determined to make every shot count. I was gonna put every damn shot in the bullseye, and I realized that was what was going to get me, you and every single person I cared about out of that fucked up situation. I was making every shot count, and hell, that's what you and Bravo team do. All I had to do was wait for you to come get me."

Marcel's eyes widened in shock, and he dragged Riley's hands away from his mouth. "After Ernst left the room, waving that damn switch around, you looked so defeated it broke my heart. Then you seemed to take strength from something, and your head come up and you stood tall. Then you threw your head back and roared my name. That's what you were thinking about?"

Riley nodded, surprised that Marcel had seen him in that moment, but loving the fact that he had. "Yeah, I knew you would come get me, and you would get me out. I had no idea how you were going to do that, but I had faith that you would. And it was you."

"What was me?"

"It was you that I found strength in," Riley said, then pressed a gentle kiss to Marcel's soft lips. "It is you I will always find strength in."

Marcel smiled softly. "Then I will forever be thankful for that initial moment of no impact. And that is something I never would have thought I would say."

Riley laughed as he leaned in and took Marcel's mouth with his own, maybe for the thousandth time but it felt like the first, and said a silent prayer and gave thanks for that exact same thing.

The End

www.maiadylan.com

MAIA DYLAN

EVERNIGHT PUBLISHING ®

www.evernightpublishing.com